Building
Mr. Darcy

ASHLINN CRAVEN

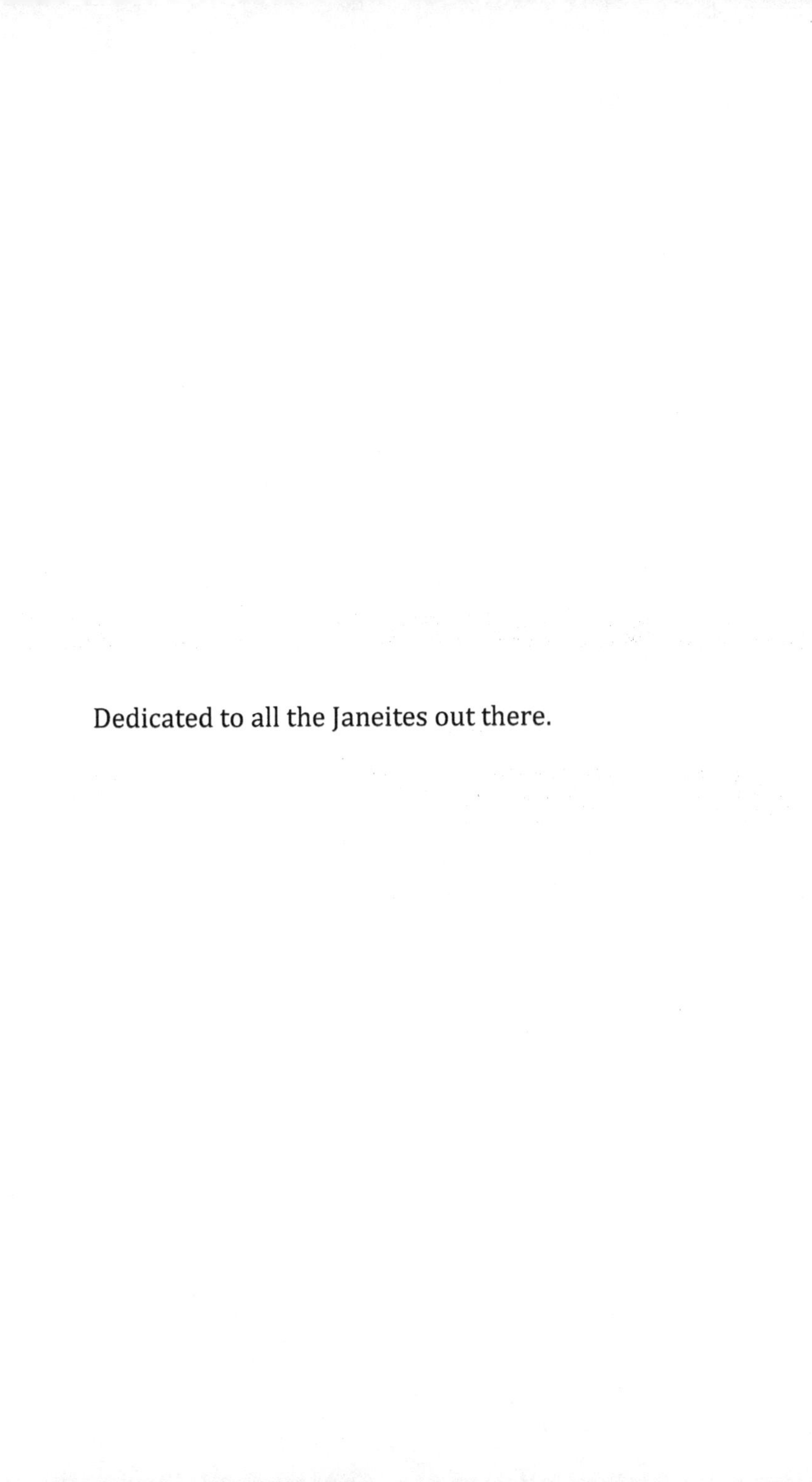

Dedicated to all the Janeites out there.

CHAPTER 1

It is a truth universally acknowledged that Jane Austen has been filling women with unrealistic expectations of men since 1813. Zoe Bunsen was one such woman. Twenty-eight and single, she'd never encountered a man as compelling as Mr. Darcy in *Pride and Prejudice,* and it wasn't for lack of trying. But she possessed the good fortune of being employed by a British software company, which, after decades of research, had beaten the Silicon Valley giants to the post. Zycorp Ltd. in London had created the world's first artificially intelligent Mr. Darcy.

Zoe had the even greater fortune of being one of the two software testers selected to prepare Mr. Darcy for entry into the modern world. She spent the two weeks until project kickoff in excited agitation, rereading the book several times and dreaming up tweaks to the AI's mannerisms and opinions in order to make him as Darcy-like as possible. She hoped that a genuine heart of gold had been encoded into his circuitry and that he wasn't some lipstick-on-a-pig job, because she'd seen enough of those.

Day one of the project arrived. After clearing out her messy old cubicle on the ground floor, her next task was to transport her cardboard box of office junk up seven floors to her new quarters. This meant catching the next elevator, which meant pressing the button—a challenge as both her hands languished underneath the box.

A petite hand slapped across the button, solving the problem. Gold nail polish flashed white under the harsh strip lighting. *Laura.*

"Thanks, Laura."

"Haven't pressed it yet." Her best friend flicked back strands of blond frizz to reveal dark, accusing eyes. "You sure about this? It could kill him."

"It won't kill him."

"His legacy. You know what I'm talking about."

"Could you *be* any louder?"

Laura smirked. "They'll find out soon enough."

Zoe rotated to cast her gaze over the "they" in question—her colleagues in software usability, trickling into the office. With its musty hardware smell and low-level hum of productivity, it had been home for half a decade, and she hated to leave it even if the rewards promised to be mind-blowing.

"Test him here," Laura said. "You'd have loads of support."

"Distraction, you mean."

"Max Taggart could be worse, for all you know."

"Max Taggart could be the Antichrist for all I know." Zoe had combed the Internet for info on her new colleague and future office mate. All she could gather was: male, hotshot project manager, thirty-four, poached from Tenzhong Inc. in Silicon Valley, and too busy being indoctrinated last week to trek to the bottom floor to introduce himself. Neither had she ventured upstairs, because that would have made her look curious or keen, both of which would set the balance of power in his favor, and if there was ever a time in her life when she needed to gain control of a project, it was now.

Laura whacked the button. "You wouldn't want to be late."

Zoe readjusted the weight of the box a smidgeon farther up her sweating arms. It was natural for Laura to be peeved; she'd applied in vain for the same job, and it had put a strain on their friendship for a horrible day and a half after the interview. But they were past it. Almost.

"You've better things to do." Zoe cocked her head toward José Morales, sitting at three o' clock, his nose in a screen. "Such as asking out a lonesome business developer." With any luck, her departure from this nerd ranch would act as a catalyst, rebooting the lives of those left behind. "Do it, Laura."

Laura twisted her mouth and said nothing.

"Darcy's in good hands."

Laura's mouth untwisted. "You'll be lucky if you can dictate the color of his dialog box."

"Let *me* worry about that."

The stares of colleagues scorched her back as she waited, foot tapping, for the elevator to ascend from the basement. In all her five years here, she'd never had reason—or authorization—to go upstairs. Was this the best move? Would she survive up there without all her friends? Was it in her power to finesse a Darcy AI that Jane Austen would be proud of, and then release him unto the unsuspecting world by Christmas?

She stepped into the elevator. If she couldn't, then sure as hell no one could.

"Don't eff this up for us," Laura called. "And by us, I speak for Austen fans worldwide."

"Hey, *I'm* her biggest fan."

The elevator doors closed on Laura's retort, whatever it was.

Inside the full elevator, Zoe realized two things. First, everyone apart from her was wearing a wool-mix suit, crisp shirt, and expression of clean-shaven impassivity, as if two decades of hipsterdom had never happened. The dress code was more formal up here given the high density of managers. Her skinny jeans and t-shirt, which yelled *Mr. Darcy Ruined My Life*, may not have been the best choice after all. But, hey, at least she hadn't worn her steampunk vintage.

Second, her box was growing heavier each time the door opened and closed. She inhaled, aiming for yoga poise, but by the third floor, sweat slicked at her neckline and her biceps screamed in chorus with her forearm extensors. She glared at the ascending numbers. Fourth floor. For a hi-tech elevator it was freaking sloooow. Her eyes darted around the tiny space. Two men left.

Something creaked. A loud crash filled the space as the strain on her arms released and a gush of objects spewed down her legs. Her Japanese vase careened across the floor and smashed against the wall. Odious, five-year-old dust flew up as paper clips rained down. Her collection of peacock-feather fans lay in a heap around her feet, adding much color to the polished steel floor. As the seventh floor bell pinged, a solitary tampon had the nerve to roll away and settle against someone's shoe.

"Oh, God." She searched the face of the nearest man, hoping for help, but his expression remained icy as he pirouetted past her and clopped down the corridor in his Italian leather shoes. This was her level. She needed to get out, but what about this mess? The door was closing again. *Crap.*

The number five above the door lit up. The elevator was about to descend. She bolted up and fumbled with the touchpad to reopen the door. "How do I—?"

"It's okay. I got it," the other man said. Likewise, Italian leather shoes.

"Thanks." She glanced at the face peering down at her—a long face with wide-set, cornflower-blue eyes and angular features drawn with precise lines like in a graphic novel. "I have to ... I have to—"

"Yeah, I'm stalling it. It'll trigger an alarm in three minutes. Our priority is to get the stuff off the floor before someone gets hurt. We need another box."

"I know, I know." Her fingers gripped the cardboard at her chest tighter. "This box is useless. Anyone out there who'll help?"

"Doubt it." He tugged the cardboard from her grasp and tossed it into the hallway. "Hold your finger here. Don't let go."

She replaced his finger on the pad with hers while he whipped off his blazer and flattened it on the ground. With decisive arm sweeps, he shoveled her bits and pieces onto the silky fabric then took a sleeve and pulled the pile over the elevator threshold. She watched, openmouthed.

He yanked her through the door a millisecond before it closed. As she stood gaping at the numbers above the elevator, his grip on her arm relaxed and broke off.

She hunkered down and inspected the label on the collar. *Ermenegildo Zegna.* Queasiness set in. "My stuff's not worth a fraction of this!" She pawed at the satiny lining. Maybe, just maybe, her items hadn't ripped any holes in it or contaminated it somehow. She pocketed her pink troll. Why couldn't her box contain electronic equipment or just papers, simple document papers? "You should've just left it. I-I'd have managed somehow."

"Couldn't help myself." His blue eyes were all aglitter. "Cold instinct."

"Well, I guess I've given you something to talk about." On your next five-second espresso break.

He backed off a step, palms up. "I'll go and mind my own business now."

"I'm sorry." As she was still on her knees, it was even more demeaning than usual to say that. "I'm not sure where that came from."

He advanced again and extended his hand with a smile. "Max Taggart."

Aaaargh, no! Her sweat froze all over her body. He would be. Slowly and excruciatingly, she got up off her knees. So much for her poised entry into his sphere as a formidable lady-programmer to be reckoned with. She accepted his cool, dry hand. "Zoe Bunsen."

His smile faltered. Then died. A worry line cut an equator halfway up his forehead, dividing the freckles into north and south. Amazement at the train wreck of a colleague who stood before him, no doubt.

"American?" he asked.

"Johnson County, Kansas."

"Right … "

"You got a problem with that?"

"Not at all. It's … great." His accent was a blend of Irish, undulating and earnest, and Silicon Valley drawl. The name Taggart had suggested no particular region of the world to her.

"Yeah." She hooked her thumbs into her back pockets. "Well, I got this."

"Good, because I've a meeting"—he glanced at his watch and did a cartoonish double take—"now. Let's talk at ten. We're in P-12." He sprinted off, leaving a gust of breeze in his wake. "There's a spare box by the bookshelf by the way," he called back.

"Let's talk at ten," she mouthed after him. Asserting his dominance already, even though they were on the same level on the org chart. Because he'd been in P-12 a whole week before her, or because he was a Zegna-wearing man? Either way, he could put a zip on it.

She gathered up shards of the vase lurking in his blazer armpit. She turned over the largest piece—hand-painted ceramic—a relic from her Japan trip eight years ago with Shingo, a kakejiku artist and her first boyfriend. Before Tyler. She'd adored Shingo back then, but it hadn't ended well. Much like the vase now.

Chairs squeaking in a nearby room alerted her to her situation. The nearest door was P-8, so her new office had to be close. Not a single office was open, just a row of forbidding white doors glaring back at her. This seventh floor was as devoid of personality as the ground floor was overflowing with it. She knew this would be an adjustment, but who'd have guessed she'd be homesick after only five minutes?

On the steel plaque next to P-12 she read off his name in Courier—Max Taggart, PhD MBA, Project Manager—and nothing else. Why didn't they put her name first? Or at all? Now she'd have to fight for her rights. Her seven-floor ascent had changed *nada*.

But she refused to get waylaid by any of that. She was here for the project, for Darcy. For Austen fans. To bring him into the world and reach the masses, even those women who hated to read the classics. Especially those. They were the ones who most needed Darcy magic in their lives whether they knew it not.

She used to be one of those uninitiated. Her first memory of Mr. Darcy was her maternal grandmother laying down the yellowing paperback of *Pride and Prejudice* in their library back home in Kansas, and sighing, "Now there was a gentleman." At age eight, Zoe wondered why Grandma had chosen that book when she had the likes of Stephen King and J.K. Rowling to select from. Zoe and her brothers had always scorned Mother's section of the library—wan-sounding classics such as *Emma, Jane Eyre*, and *Wuthering Heights*. But Grandma had been enthralled, so Zoe ventured one day to open the innocuous little book on the words, "It is a truth universally acknowledged, that a single man with a good fortune must be in want of a wife." The sentiment was so alien to her, she shoved the book back onto the shelf before anyone saw her reading it.

At age sixteen, she pulled out the book again from the same position she'd tucked it in eight years earlier. So much had changed. Her mother had joined Grandma in the great afterlife, and her father, in his determination to hold everything together, had turned to despotism. Her two older brothers were studying law in Kansas City, treading in their parents' footsteps. Zoe was expected to follow the same well-worn path but hated the notion—that perpetual searching for ambiguity and weakness in the arguments of others. She cherished the positivism, the exactness, of computer science, where everything was possible, but Father forbade her to even speak of it. After such bitter exchanges, she often found solace in reading.

And this time she'd gotten it. Fallen in love with Austen's world, with Mr. Darcy and the man he represented. The disparity between this and her reality caused a seed of discontent to grow inside, which blossomed into rage as her father worsened. At age nineteen, she fell in love with Shingo and did the unthinkable by flying off to London with him, taking few possessions, one of them being the book.

She never looked back. Not once. Father didn't speak to her for five years after she left the U.S. On the rare occasions she called him or her brothers now, the conversations remained surface-level only, them bossing her about. Her greatest crime was surviving alone in a field they had no clue about.

Maybe if Mother had lived, her early adult life would have been happier. But it was fitting that her path had led her to this. Being in charge of releasing an AI Mr. Darcy was the logical next chapter in Zoe's life's story.

Harry Hampton must have sensed that certainty vibrating off her and cut the interview short. She was fond of old Harry. Not at all what you'd expect of a tech CEO—avuncular, yet with a hint of childlike wonder in his eyes, like he'd done too much LSD back in the day.

Normalcy abounded inside P-12—nothing to instill enthusiasm. One empty desk—hers. Not a whole lot on Max's either—a laptop, tablet, jar of pens, portable disk drive, everything polished clean and aligned at right angles. Sure enough, a box sat beside the bookshelf. She grabbed it, marched back to the elevator doors, and flung her junk into it. Who cared what got broken? The main thing was to get out of this corridor and stop looking like a nut.

Max's blazer showed no signs of permanent damage once she'd shaken the dust off. Draped over her shoulders, the garment engulfed her, and she caught a whiff of … grapefruit. It had been a while since she'd met a man who smelled so fresh. She smoothed the blazer over the back of his chair and flopped down in hers. 9:15 a.m. Not exactly a stellar start, but why stress over trifles when she was about to meet Mr. Darcy?

CHAPTER 2

"Here's the plan." Max tapped the screen. "Beta release, end of November, and final release, mid-December."

Opposite him at the conference table lounged Bob Chadwick, VP Operations, his new boss—a graying, fit man in his early forties whose complexion suggested more time spent on a treadmill than on grass. He hadn't been at the interview two weeks ago. Right off the bat, he'd asked Max to call him Bob, but judging by his pursed lips, *Bob* didn't tolerate people being fifty-five seconds late to meetings.

The plan was doable, provided his teammate, Zoe Bunsen, never screwed up, got sick, hungover, or distracted. His first impression of her suggested she might do any number of those things on a regular basis, and his first impressions tended to be right. The view of her pert breasts pushed up under the tight t-shirt had been lovely, but Chrissake, a guy had to work. Why didn't she wear appropriate clothing? Come to think of it, why wasn't she at this meeting, too?

"The schedule may involve overtime," he added. Best to get this clear from the outset.

Bob waved this aside. "Big fans of overtime in this company."

"I see."

"Wasn't Tenzhong?"

"Within reason."

"Why did you say you left California?" Bob challenged.

"I like London."

"And you think you can make a Mr. Darcy run?" Bob said the name with rude distaste.

"That's why I'm here." He'd only heard this morning whom they'd based the AI on, and the name Mr. Darcy meant little to him—a snooty guy in a top hat in a period drama that his ex, Shauna, had once made him watch. The drama was a distant memory. And he was working hard on forgetting the ex.

Bob tapped a pen against the table. "Why the grim face? We saw how you managed to squeeze out that killer warehousing app in the middle of an SEC crisis at Tenzhong. Guys like you thrive on adversity."

"I like to get the job done."

"Yeah, that's what I heard too."

"Shouldn't Zoe Bunsen be at this meeting?"

"We'll involve her later."

Max sat forward. "Wouldn't it be better to involve her now?"

Bob's lower lip sticking out told Max that this particular discussion was over. All right then, he'd save it for later, but not too much later.

"Let's keep the fuss at a minimum. I call this whole idea clutching at straws, but"—Bob's eyelids drooped—"Harry's the boss."

"I'm sorry, clutching at straws?"

"Last two AIs didn't run. Spiderman tanked after a month. James Bond after two. But for some reason Harry thinks this one will capture the female demographic and take off."

Wasn't this guy supposed to be living, breathing, evangelizing AIs? Of course, it could've just been a sneaky test of Max's faith in the project. "Yeah, I got that impression from him too. But with the investments last year to drive this mission-critical project to success, there's no reason not to be optimistic."

"You've read the annual report." Bob's terse smile flashed. "But you won't hear anyone talking of this. Only you, me, Harry, and the job applicants know the release date. It's a strategy, Max. Stealth marketing."

What the hell?

"Either it takes off by word of mouth, or we pass it off as an experiment if it doesn't pan out. No marketing. No razzmatazz. Low risk. That's the deal."

Max flopped back in his chair.

"And if it fails, we slash the AI funding and put all our focus on the stuff that works—banking software. We've six new clients prepaying for our ATM interfaces in the U.S. alone." Bob was finally getting animated. "Wetware's too damn messy."

"Slashing the funding—what would that mean?"

Bob whacked the table with the side of his hand. "Chop, chop. The cognitive scientists."

Why would they lay off more than a hundred of the top specialists in the world when they'd invested so heavily last year and created such a hoo-ha in the industry? Couldn't they have mentioned this bullshit in his five-hour interview? Of course there had to be a catch. No wonder everything had gone so smoothly, his demands swallowed without question—huge salary, nice car, extra relocation costs.

Bob snorted. "You'd better have brought the luck of the Irish with you because that's a shitload of geniuses sitting on the Titanic."

"Not on my watch, Bob."

He'd figure it out. He always did. That was his unique selling point, his reputation, the reason he'd gotten that strange call from Harry Hampton at 3:00 a.m. on a Saturday begging him to join his company. He wouldn't let himself lose that reputation. It was all he had left. And it would have nothing to do with goddamn *luck.*

• • •

Zoe took a wander around. This level was so clean, so quiet. One thing was for sure—she wasn't in Kansas anymore but in a white and steel laboratory of sorts that smelled of new car seats. Had this part of the building ever been colonized by humanity?

She was killing time waiting for Max to return because there was nothing on her file system that hinted at an entrance to the Darcy AI, and she'd done an exhaustive search. Why would they have given him access and not her? Nobody from HR had come by to welcome her either. A friendly face might have made a nice contrast to all this austerity.

Her path was going in a square and yet not ending up where she'd started, which was pretty disconcerting as she did have a good sense of direction, usually. Just as she was about to admit she was lost, she rounded a corner and bumped into … her darling colleague.

"Excuse me." Max stepped back, blinking as if awaking from a trance.

"S'okay," she said. "Fault was mine—I was just checking out the surroundings. There's something weird—"

"About the layout? I know. I suppose it's to make us think outside the box."

"Some box. I feel like I'm in an Escher drawing of a spaceship."

His serious blue eyes made a long examination of her face and then her upper body. Her skin prickled under the scrutiny. "Don't worry, there is an end. Follow me."

She fell into step beside his long strides, a faster pace than she'd been doing, but there was no way she was going to trail behind him as he seemed to be suggesting.

"Coffee machine's there," he announced.

"I'm not in need of a guided tour. I did the 3-D walk-through last night, so I know my way around." She marched ahead to prove her point.

"Wonderful."

She continued straight, seeing as it was counterintuitive and her intuition had been getting her nowhere so far. The 3-D walk-through had made it seem easier. By the time she reached the next corner her pace had slowed to a donkey's waddle.

"Settling in?" He sidled up.

"Yeah."

"Good."

"How was your meeting?" she asked.

"Fine."

"Good."

Never had she more appreciated her old spot on the ground floor, where conversations tended to develop beyond the monosyllabic. She stole a glance at him. Freckles were sprinkled on his nose like a celestial afterthought, softening a face that was a little too even, a little too earnest to be truly interesting. At this moment he looked ... what was the word? *Frazzled*. But what right had he to be frazzled? He was the one with the gleaming track record, the Zegna suit, and the knowledge of how to access Darcy, which nobody had the courtesy to give her.

More slow paces yielded yet another ninety-degree angle that, distressingly, still didn't bring them to the home stretch. Just as she was ready to admit defeat, a familiar alcove with a water faucet appeared.

At the door of P-12, Max said, "What do you say we start with a kickoff—introduce ourselves, establish milestones, do some test plan familiarization, any necessary code transfer, and encryption of your devices?"

"Have you accessed the AI yet?" she demanded.

"We don't have access yet. Harry will send us an email tomorrow, apparently."

"What? Wait—how do you know that?"

"Bob told me."

"Bob told you?"

"Yes. So, I was thinking we could use this time today for project kickoff. Then we'll take half an hour for you to explain to me Mr. Darcy's appeal to you and, by extension, to the demographic we're marketing to."

This was so unexpected, so clinical, she laughed out loud and pushed her way through the door, still laughing.

"Did I say something funny?" His expression had mutated into one of patient forbearance that they'd probably taught him first thing in whatever smarmy management school had churned him out.

"No, it just sounded like you'd never heard of Mr. Darcy before and that you were asking me to explain who he is and his attraction ... in, like, thirty minutes or something."

"Could you do it in fifteen?"

"Are you serious?"

He did that slow, almost sensual blink that she was beginning to suspect was his mnemonic for "yes" should he ever lose his voice, which was fairly unlikely with his level of conversational skills.

"How long do you need?" he asked.

"Oh, I need a lifetime."

"We don't have that. Moving on. What programming languages are you most familiar with?"

"Java, C, C-sharp, C-plus-plus, and Python." If cramming the first three chapters of a Python manual last night counted as "being familiar with." They couldn't even tell her which language Darcy was written in, so she'd had a bit of a programmer's existential crisis trying to guess last night. Completely crazy, all this secrecy. And all this delay.

"It's C," he said.

"Right. Good to know."

"What about testing frameworks?"

What was this? An interview? "I do user experience, mainly. I haven't had much need for testing frameworks."

His expression had deteriorated to disapproving. But hey, she'd been chosen. What did testing frameworks have to do with anything? That kind of software was for fastidious managers like him.

He moved to the center of the room and turned toward the bookshelf, tapping a forefinger on his chin, no doubt recalibrating his opinion of her, not that she imagined it had been brilliant to begin with. Then his attention shifted to his blazer on the back of his chair, where she'd draped it. Without inspecting it for damage, he bounded over and shrugged it on with an expression of pure relief. He'd been cold without it. Poor baby.

"Thanks for your help earlier," she said.

"Welcome." He pushed up the blazer sleeves in a distracted manner. "Now, we should factor in some time for you to catch up on frameworks." He yanked down some heavy tomes from the rows of manuals whose spines lined up like a North Korean guard formation. It gave her the opportunity to inspect him from behind. Tall, nice shoulders, butt, legs. No doubt he played rugby back where he was from or some barbaric form of Celtic football. Shame he was such a corporate ass.

Swiveling around and totally catching her out—but only acknowledging it with furrowed brows—he held up the first book on the stack. *Xeta-Framework from First Principles.* He placed it in her hands. "Xeta's the most time effective. Don't bother with the rest."

She knew he was staring, but she kept her gaze on the book, trying not to laugh. Of course she'd never seen it before in her life, and of course it looked awful. Especially the drawing of a godforsaken lizard on the cover. "Ah, yes," she said, knowingly.

He placed two more books on top of the one in her hands, reading out the titles as if she were illiterate— *Expert's Guide to Regression Testing, Advanced Agile Software Development*—all without a shred of irony. Nobody could be this deadpan, surely?

"Last but not least, *Time Management.*" He settled it on top of the stack. The final addition to the weight set her biceps screaming for the second time that day. It probably wouldn't go down too well if she were to let this lot collapse at his feet, much as she was tempted.

"I'm sure I could just pick them up online," she said through clenched teeth.

"No time. I don't mind if you make notes in them, manhandle them, whatever you please, as long as the information gets in."

She shuffled to her desk and off-loaded the bundle with a thud. "Nice, but I'm more concerned with getting my paws on the real thing. You know, usability testing? What we're supposed to be here for?"

Max cocked his head toward his laptop. "Soon as we get access to the AI, I'll schedule a quick high-level walk-through of the code I reckon we'll begin first robustness checks by Friday, and field testing once we get a stable build established, best case, maybe even next Monday."

"Very good," she said briskly. "Now it's time to listen to my plan."

His face tightened, making the cheekbones jut out even sharper. "I'm sure you'll bring much welcome creativity to the project, but there's little flexibility when we've barely ten weeks until final release."

"I see. What you're saying is that we're sticking to your plan no matter what?"

"We haven't even discussed my plan," he said.

"We don't need to." Nose in the air, she strutted around her desk and tapped a pen against the whiteboard, which had a complex matrix of faded lines and shapes from an old project plan still visible on it. She traced similar lines on top. "I suppose our lives are dotted every Friday with little black triangles representing the milestones from today until release? And I'm pretty sure the plan requires working weekends November through December?"

"I was thinking December ... Maybe November, as well."

"Well, I'm fully committed. I hope you are, too." She flashed him a knowing smile, waiting for him to crack, to scurry out of his commitments like every other weasel of a manager in this place. If there was one aspect where she had a clear advantage, it was this. When it came to work-life balance, she had nothing on the "life" side of the scales. Even her best friends were colleagues. And the further away she got from her family, the better. Zycorp *was* her family. Someone like him probably had a high-maintenance wife or girlfriend grasping for his attention. Possibly even kids, pets, extended family, a mansion—the works.

"That's great. Any extra flexibility is welcome." He ran his fingers across his jaw. "We don't need to make this more difficult than it already is."

"Aren't you supposed to be more positive than that? If you're so worried about completing on time shouldn't you ask for an extension so we can do this properly, especially as they haven't even bothered to give us the AI today?" Of course, he'd be dead on arrival if he were stupid enough to try that, and that would be fun to watch, but something told her Max Taggart wasn't the type to be easily fooled.

"I certainly shall not."

"I certainly shall not," she mused, copying his Northern Irish-slash-Californian accent.

"What?"

"'I certainly shall not' are our hero's very first words in the book."

He failed to react, so she added, "He says, 'I certainly shall not' in response to Mr. Bingley's entreaties to have him dance at the Lucas ball where there was a shortage of male dancing partners. You don't seem to have used it precociously, though."

"I'm sorry, you've lost me. Lucas ball? Mr. Bingley?"

"Continue. You were talking about"—she wiggled her fingers in the air—"schedule?"

"I believe—with your obvious commitment—we can make the AI bug-free, reliable, and safe, and—"

"You mean Darcy?"

"Yes," he said, exasperatedly. "And, most importantly, release *Darcy* on time."

She lowered herself into her hi-tech office chair and swiveled it left and right several times. It seemed to mold to her hips, defying gravity. It sure beat her last chair. "Have you actually read the book?"

His gaze flickered to the pile of manuals on her desk and back to her face. "Which one?"

"*Pride and Prejudice.*"

"Oh." His point of focus darted around the room in politician mode, as if this were a highly nuanced question, not one that could be answered with a simple yes or no. "I'm familiar with the concept of it, and its influence in the selection process of the marketing department. It was a thoroughly sound decision, and ratified by the CEO. But as for actually reading the book? Well, there I would have to say … no."

"No further questions." She smoothed down her t-shirt. *Shame on you*, she would've added if she'd known him a tiny bit better.

"I don't need to be familiar with it. That's why you were hired."

She pushed back from the desk. "Yes, I may not be a connoisseur of your frameworks, but I can design a whacking good user experience, which is far more important and, may I add, a far more elusive skill. Also, I'm actually familiar with the subject matter, which can only help."

She braced herself for the fallout: a self-important male attempting to put down an assertive female.

"Right, then. How about you stick to usability testing and I stick to keeping the plan on track? Zycorp hired me to release a viable product before Christmas. That's what I'm going to do." His mouth flattened into a thin line of determination. "With your help, of course."

"Hmph." Keeping the plan on track sounded all too much like a euphemism for being the boss. Then again, maybe it was better if he took care of the macro planning while she catered for nitty-gritty Darcy details, as he obviously didn't have the first clue.

And that reminded her. She yanked up her purse, rifled through tissues, chewing gum, tampons, a hair comb, keys, until her hands curled around the cracked cover of the book. She fished it out and blew off specks of dirt that appeared to be tobacco—her flatmate Tyler's roll-it-yourself variety. She flicked through the pages to make sure she hadn't left anything incriminating in there, like a girlie shopping list or, God forbid, the lyrics for one of Tyler's fledgling songs she'd been working on.

"Here," she said.

He regarded the book, which seemed tiny compared to the manuals he'd been salivating over a few moments ago. "What's this?"

"Pride and Prejudice." She jabbed the three-word title with her finger.

"It's your copy. Thank you, but I couldn't. I can get it on my e-book acc—"

"Take it," she ordered.

Eyelids lowered, he reached over and took it. "Am I allowed to make notes in it?"

"Absolutely not. No dog ears, either."

"Right." He sat back, clacked his fingers, and started flicking through the opening pages.

"In case you're wondering, Mr. Darcy first appears in chapter three, paragraph four, where he says, 'I certainly shall not. You know I detest it, unless I am particularly acquainted with my partner.'"

He stopped at some page, scanning the text with rapid eye movements. "No shit."

She smirked. "Word for word."

"Almost," he said.

"What? That's what he says."

"No, he says, 'You know *how* I detest it,' not 'You know I detest it.'"

"That's what I meant."

"Ah." He flicked another page and said nothing else. His barely there smile said enough. Irritated, she conceded the point to him and watched him flick more pages. A pang of envy pierced her, envy of him and of all Austen virgins the world over who had the pure joy of discovery ahead of them. She'd do anything to know what <u>effect those</u> exquisite words of biting wit and smoldering passion were having on his frozen-over soul.

• • •

That night, after football practice, Max had just about acclimatized to the archaic English in the book and had reached the point where Elizabeth Bennet spoke her first words—"Tuesday fortnight"—in response to an inquiry about some ball or other. Then the Skype tone *ding-a-ling*ed, reminding him which century he was in.

He laid the paperback down carefully on the sofa's armrest, leaned toward the laptop, and woke it up. It was Maeve calling from Dublin. His sister's fake-blond bangs flapped about with excitement.

"Mal's out this Friday," she said. As greetings went, this was on a par with "Can you mind this feral cat for three weeks?" Mal was getting out of prison early on good behavior, not that his brother would know what that was, and would very soon be prowling the streets of London.

"Yeah, great."

"You could sound a little happier."

"This is me being chirpy," Max said.

"You can put him up for a while over there, can't you?"

"Sure."

"Ma's having a big welcome-home party for him November 1. Everyone on the road's coming. You should book your flight home."

"I've got a big project here, so I—"

"Don't wanna know. I'm just the messenger."

"I'll sort it out with Ma, don't worry."

His sister made a snorting sound. "If you don't show up this time, everyone'll think you hate him and us."

"Well, I'm glad everybody else is at leisure to drop everything for Malachi."

"You're not the only one who's busy."

"I know. But come on, you'd think he'd have learnt something by now."

"You're just jealous."

This whole discussion was getting old. Time to drive for the specifics. "Has Mal got an apartment sorted out in Belfast, or what's the story?"

"How should I know?"

"Okay, so he'll be staying at home." Again. Malachi probably had no plans for when he arrived in Belfast other than to preside over the family household until the novelty wore off, and then he'd search for an apartment in a trendier part of town and, hence, need a long-term loan from his eejit of a younger brother, who would, of course, give it to him. Long term, as in to be repaid on an unspecified date after Malachi's death.

As the eldest son, Malachi had been given ample chances to do something with his life, to escape the Catholic slums of Belfast. He'd squandered those chances, and yet he was the big hero of the family, especially since his last, serious escapade. His family loved a rebel. It slotted in nicely with their romantic notions of heroism.

"How's life in Dublin?" he asked, determined to veer away from the topic of his brother. "Dermot popped the question yet?"

Her face screwed up with all the anguish of a thirty-three-year-old woman waiting for five years. "No," she snarled.

"But it's still ... on?"

"I suppose."

"Why don't you just propose, put yourself out of your misery? That might be all that Dermot's waiting for."

"I can't do that!"

"Why not?"

"Ooh, it's no wonder no woman sticks around you."

He winced. Maeve chewed her lip. "Ah, sorry, I take that back."

"It's fine, Maeve." He'd come to terms with why Shauna hadn't stuck around, or at least he grasped how they perceived it. After three steady years together he'd failed to perform some romantic gesture five years ago when his girlfriend was feeling brittle about turning thirty, and Mal, the hero, had swooped in. Boring, insufferable Max deserved to lose her. Who knew, if his brother hadn't gotten himself thrown in prison a week later, Shauna and Mal might even have become an item.

"Why don't I have a word with Dermot?" Max suggested. "He probably just needs the incentives laid out clearly to realize what he's risking by taking it too slow."

She leaned her face into the camera, bathing her features in an unflattering blue light. "Jesus, you never stop. Do you want to ruin my life, or what?"

"Just trying to help."

"The only person who needs help is *you*."

Her side went blank. He minimized Skype and brought forward the auditor's report on Zycorp he'd been perusing. He and Maeve used to be close, but recently his conversations with her ended just like this—badly. As her biological clock ticked on, she seemed to be getting more emotional, more susceptible to the irrational whims of his family. All this could be reversed if only there were a happy and timely end to the Dermot-and-Maeve saga.

Irritated, he twisted *Pride and Prejudice* around on the arm of the sofa. There was little point in even reading it, because they'd only have time to debug any memory leaks and test operational functionality, robustness, and data integrity. But he'd read it because he'd committed to it, and it seemed like such a massive deal to Zoe Bunsen. There was no point in creating any boundaries between them—there was simply no time for friction of any kind, and she was just the type to get right under his skin.

CHAPTER 3

"I don't get it," Max declared the next day to his new colleague, who was in the office before him at seven thirty. Perched on her chair like a 1950s secretary, she had on a far less revealing blouse today, although it was still snug enough to distract him if he wasn't concentrating on not looking at her. Her messy box had been cleared away, and she hadn't covered any surfaces with her junk. An auspicious start, assuming it wasn't all just for show.

With her dark mane, porcelain skin, expressive, dark-green eyes, and a grin that managed to be both goofy and straightforward, she had a certain allure if you went for the spirited type, which he didn't. No desk photos—did that mean she was single? None of her knickknacks had been repositioned anywhere. He'd wondered where she was going to put that pink-haired troll's head.

Her deafening silence begged him to elaborate. "The Darcy mania? I don't get it. He's a wealthy, socially inept Derbyshire landlord's son with delusions of grandeur. If he were alive today, he'd scarcely get an online date beyond the obvious gold diggers."

He approached her desk and handed her the book. He'd stayed up far later than he should have reading it last night. Then again, he was having problems sleeping after that exchange with Maeve, and staring at Zycorp's auditors' reports hadn't exactly helped take his mind off things.

"Did you read it all?" Her eyes seared him as she accepted the paperback as solemnly as you would a rare edition of the Bible. This was ironic considering the book had been creased and covered with tobacco flakes when she'd given it to him. He'd purged the pages of all dirt and kept the book pressed between two manuals overnight to try to restore its slim shape, but it needed to be treated better. Was she a smoker? Her pearly teeth were quite an anomaly then.

He sat down at his desk to log on to the main server. "I did."

"No. You can't have read it properly."

Was she trying to annoy him? "Left to right, page one to 326. I think I did."

"All right, let's say you read it. What did you feel?"

He stopped typing. He'd been shocked at how little he'd felt while reading. He'd been waiting for it—the grand revelation as to why Mr. Darcy was this massive cultural icon, immune to the passage of time. But it hadn't struck. And this made him fear even more for the future of the product, the future of the department. Releasing a silicon approximation of *this* was what the livelihoods of 125 people relied on. Not to mention his reputation. And hers.

"I felt sorry for the father for having to put up with Mrs. Bennet." Truth was, Mr. Bennet was actually okay.

After a couple more accusatory stares, she uttered, "Is that it?" in a squeaky tone.

"Pretty much."

"But what about the tension? The biting wit between Elizabeth and Darcy? And how they changed themselves for each other? It's ... perfection. Didn't that impress on you in any small way?" Her face was flustered. She was taking this extremely personally, and he couldn't decide if it was a good or a bad thing, although in a pinch, he'd err toward the latter.

"Elizabeth Bennet didn't have to do much changing. As far as I could make out she just got extremely lucky."

"Impossible." She held a hand to her flushed cheek.

"The luckiest of the luckiest," he added because he was in that sort of mood. "These were the 1 percent, the landed gentry, the ones with the grip on wealth and power in not just one country but in an extended Commonwealth."

"It's Jane Austen," she said smugly with a bat of her luscious eyelashes. "That's what she wrote about. Your problem is you're trying to figure it out rationally."

"These bozos enforced the Corn Laws. There was a famine in Ireland, for God's sake, while they blocked grain imports and grabbed rent money from the poor, in absentia."

She clamped her mouth shut and then opened it again. "Well, thanks for the history lesson, but you're viewing it in completely the wrong spirit—it's a comedy of manners, as relevant today as it was then."

"Yeah, reading about a bunch of effeminate men wringing their hands over choice of dance partners was certainly comedic."

"Effeminate?" She laughed, a rich, attractive sound that caught him off guard. "Oh, you have no idea."

"How far did you get with the framework manual?"

Her eyes widened. "I finished it. Left to right. Page one to ... 900."

"Great. You'll be able to trace a subroutine without messing up a global variable then," he murmured, only half concentrating because an email from Harry had just popped up.

"I would never, ever mess up a global variable," came her reply across the desks.

What the hell was this? "'There are six questions to answer to get the password.' I'm reading out Harry's email here. Quick, check your inbox, Zoe. It's just come in."

"Six questions?" Her flushed face appeared above her monitor. "I don't need to prove myself."

"'Assuming the password is correct, it will grant you access to Mr. Darcy tomorrow morning.'" He paused to glance over at her. Her face was nearly puce with anger. It would be comical if the situation weren't so serious.

"Do you think this is funny?" she bit out. "Why is he doing this? He's wasting time with his games."

Max read on in silence.

Q1) What was the original title of P&P?

Q2) How often does Mr. Darcy call Elizabeth by her first name?

Q3) In the 2005 movie, what does Elizabeth say straight after Mr. Darcy proclaims love in the final act?

Q4) What is the most frequent noun that contains at least nine letters in P&P?

Q5) What is the longest repeated sentence fragment in P&P?

Q6) Using simple Euclidean distance on word frequency vectors, which of Austen's novels is most similar to Pride and Prejudice?

Take the lowercase first character of each answer (for question 1, capitalize it; for question 2, use the numeral; for question 5, remove the leading space) and concatenate them for the password.

Good luck, Zoe and Max! Harry.

Hard. Hard. Hard. Easy. Easy. Easy. The final three could be solved by writing up code to calculate statistics on the text, but the first three required insider knowledge, Internet searching, reading the book—again—and most probably watching some goddamn movie. There went his Tuesday night.

"I've seen this stuff before." Max rose and walked over to her desk to try and placate her. "It's a Valley trend. A last-minute hackathon to ensure the right candidates are on board. We just have to suck it up and do it and hope we get it right by tomorrow morning. Don't worry, I'll rearrange the plan for this contingency. And don't look at me like that."

"I'm not looking at you," she said hotly.

"Listen." He reached for her shoulder and squeezed it gently with his fingertips, causing her pretty eyes to widen. "I can't help it if our CEO wants to waste time. By the way, I think it's bollocks too." He retracted his hand, surprised at his own touchy-feeliness, but his words seemed to mollify her somewhat. She settled back into her seat, shook out her hair, and emitted a lengthy grunting sound—the kind of noise he'd wanted to make himself all morning.

• • •

Zoe spent the afternoon stewing over Mr. Darcy's absence and brushing up on statistical analysis in order to figure out those last three questions—the first three she knew by heart, of course. Max's insensibility to her pain made it worse. He was happy drawing up code-testing plans and calling IT people—"acquiring bandwidth" as he called it. The AI and the password seemed secondary considerations in his world.

So it was a huge comfort to come home and find Tyler back from touring. Red-eyed after the long bus ride from Southampton, he was preparing a joint on top of Max's big *Xeta Frameworks from First Principles* manual. Okay, so maybe she shouldn't have left it lying on the carpet last night.

"Hey, Zoe." Tyler gave an artful toss of his raven, long-layered hair, and a grin traversed his pixie-like face. His nimble fingers sliced a crumb of cannabis off a badass block the size of a USB stick.

"Hey yourself." She hugged him. He reeked of beer but seemed fairly sober, and his normal pupil size indicated he'd stayed away from the amphetamines. "How was it?"

"Fantastic. Until Scott collapsed in the van last night. That was scary. But we're fine. Hey, I'm writing this new song. I got, like, totally inspired. Found my muse on the road, I guess."

"That's great, Ty. Guess you'll need it for that album by Christmas."

"You bet. And in case you were wondering, I borrowed a mixer for a few days." Tyler indicated the spanking-new audio mixer taking up most of the kitchen table. "Top of the range, baby."

"Borrowed, huh?"

"Amazon."

He'd return it after they'd mixed a few tracks, claim it was faulty, and get the money back. Just one of the many survival tricks of the penniless rock star.

"You'll help me with the lyrics, won't you?"

"Sure." Her poetic lyrics gave Geiger, Tyler's band, the edge in the crowded thrash-metal scene, or so she liked to tell herself.

"Listen, listen." Tyler jumped up, his sinewy, tattooed limbs unfurling with the grace of a dancer as he traversed the room. For a split second she felt a pang for the days when they'd kiss and make out at this point. But that illusion evaporated when, from its hallowed corner, he pulled out the Rickenbacker that he loved more than her—their old, private joke. He started humming and strumming the accompanying chords. "I'm just not sure how to bring in the intro … "

"A into B, right?" she said.

"Yeah."

"Then start the bass in B and keep it there for the transition," she said distractedly, picking up the manual. She didn't want to have to explain any stains on it to Max Taggart when she returned it tomorrow.

Tyler strummed the chords.

It didn't sound right. "Not minor. Stay in major."

He strummed again. "Holy crap, that is amazing!" he yelled. "You're a genius."

"Yes." She laughed. "I am amazing." Okay, so he *was* off his head on something, but she needed to hear someone say that today.

"We got another tour lined up."

"Cool. When's it start?"

"Friday. Brighton! Big time, babe. This could be our big break. Hey, you could come with us."

"Sorry, no can do."

"Why not? You always come to Brighton. You love Brighton."

"I know but ... new job. Top-secret proj, remember?"

His face fell. "Oh man, that sucks. Sure you can't take off a day or two?"

"Not this time. Seriously, no holidays, no slacking, timed lunches. I'm going to have to work most weekends from now until Christmas."

"You are shitting me."

"Nope."

"You gotta quit."

"Who'll pay the rent?"

"Hmm," he said, visibly reconsidering. Tyler, starving artist extraordinaire, owed her six months in back rent. Since they'd split up a year ago, he'd been gone so often it wouldn't be fair to charge him rent. He'd pay up if he had the money. If Geiger made it big.

People wondered how she could live with her ex, but she found she could do so quite easily. It was no sacrifice. Neither of them had met anyone serious. They'd discuss it if and when it ever happened, but for now they tiptoed around the theoretical possibility. Sure, Tyler had a string of one-night stands with his waiflike groupies, but he'd always managed to detain them at their places. She hadn't faced any such dilemmas. Her approach to dating was more tentative, and if she were honest, the lights had gone off in her Department of Libido. The first slither on the slide to spinsterhood?

"Coming down to the pub?"

"No, I need to work tonight. Call Laura. I need a few hours to figure stuff out." Hopefully a few hours would suffice to figure out the solutions to those final three questions. The thought of Max Taggart lording it over her tomorrow if she didn't solve them was enough to keep her up all night. Certainly, the daydream of cracking the password before he did gave her a massive thrill. She traipsed into her bedroom with her laptop tucked under her arm.

"Hey, where are you going?" Tyler called after her.

"Talk to you later, sweetie." Tyler'd be fine in a few minutes. He'd get drowsy after that joint, fall asleep, and not even bother with the whole pub routine. But, just in case, she locked the door behind her. She'd never done that in her own apartment before, but something told her that life was about to get serious.

CHAPTER 4

Once again, she was the first in the office. What difference did it make if she got two hours of sleep or three? Either way, she was shattered. The sixth question was a pain to figure out at 3:00 a.m., hunched over her laptop on the bed, in the dark because the bulb had blown. When she figured she'd cracked the code, she'd sunk into a fitful sleep, fully clothed.

Tyler had slept through the whole ordeal and was still snoring when she'd showered and disappeared again at six. She might not see him before he left for Brighton. It was sort of like living on her own again. Maybe this was preferable, so that she'd have some quality time with Darcy—if and when she ever got access.

Max appeared in the doorway, which she'd left open to defy seventh-floor convention. His gait projected cheerful purposefulness, but his pallor suggested he'd suffered a long night too. Good. Had he managed to figure out the password? Impossible to tell. Maybe it was other things keeping him up late. She'd Googled him again last night in between questions, but he'd hidden his life so well he must've paid someone to bury it. It would be very interesting to know why.

"Hi." He put down an expensive takeout coffee on his table and took off his coat and scarf. Luckily for him, he didn't attempt to shut the door, because she'd have told him where to go if he'd tried.

"Hi." Okay, she'd let him sit down. This was pretty reasonable of her considering she'd been waiting half her life for something like this.

"Where do we enter in the password? Do you know?" she blurted the second his fingers grazed his keyboard. "Why isn't there an obvious link anywhere? Why does everything have to be so goddamn complicated?"

His expression conveyed a sort of empathy, but this was quickly replaced by his officious manner. "I don't know. But we should revisit the planning while we wait for further instructions from Harry."

"I want to see Darcy *now*. I have the password. Don't you?"

"I do. God knows, I had to watch that awful 2005 movie until nearly the end. But before you get any romantic notions about this, let me fill you in first on what ... *who* you'll be meeting."

She folded her arms. "Hey, I've been in this company five years longer than you. We've released two AIs already, events in which I was, to some degree, involved. I think I know what we're talking about. And I don't have romantic notions."

"Glad to hear it." He pointed to *Pride and Prejudice* lying beside her coffee mug. "I had a chat with the cog-sci guys. Darcy reuses code from predecessors but has a heap of new stuff, too, and to make him sound right, they used an n-gram prediction model, with Good-Turing smoothing, from all the words he speaks in the book. That's 4,563 I'm told."

"I knew that," she said. Chatting to the guys in research? Those guys didn't chat. Like, ever. And she should know—she'd badgered them for information all last week to no avail. How the heck had he managed it?

"But that wasn't enough data," he continued. "So they added a shitload of Internet material—interpretative texts, critiques, movie scripts, and fan blogs, far beyond anything they did for James Bond or Spidey."

"Well, I don't think cramming data into a mathematical model will do it. We need to check how his personality manifests itself when interacting with us, and adapt his rules of conduct if he's not acting as a proper Mr. Darcy should. When I tested the Spidey prototype last year, he had the emotional intelligence of a five-year-old. I warned them, but nobody listened. No wonder he didn't sell. We'll have to dig deeper this time."

His mug froze an inch from his mouth. The stubborn expression he'd pulled out a few times yesterday reappeared in full force. "We're not changing any code. We test and tweak for performance and reliability and whack it out the door December 15. End of."

"But what if he's an idiot?"

He gave her a side glance. "Wasn't he, in the book? I believe the term was 'ungentlemanlike'?"

"What? Well … sometimes. But—"

"Well then. He'll be in character."

"No! The whole point about Darcy is his hidden character, his true, noble nature."

"As long as he uses the right vocabulary and has a basic AI sense of right and wrong, what more do you need? The rest you'll fill in with your imagination anyway."

"Oooh, is that seriously going to be your approach here? This isn't an airplane ticket-reservation system. Go back to Tenzhong if that's what you're after."

"Hey. No call for that. It was a warehousing management facilitation system."

"Just find out where to log in," she snapped. "We're already wasting time."

"Yeah, think I will." He rose.

"Wait. Where are you going?"

He spread his arms. "Upstairs to the CEO's office to find out where to log in."

"I'm coming with you." She clambered out of her chair.

"Hold your horses. You stay here. He might send the details while I'm gone, in which case you can log in before me." He gave her a wink that on anyone else might be flirtatious but on him was ... just annoying.

"Have it your way." Truth was, she didn't want to enter the C-suite in the shadow of Mr. Perfect here, because with his tall frame, his pristine suit, his chiseled ... everything, she could only come across as his minion. She'd rather wait until she had something to boast about, until she could shine. Let the smarmy manager go.

He was already gone.

She screeched with delight when about five minutes after his departure Harry's email came in, bang on eight o'clock, with a clear bullet-point list of instructions on how to retrieve the log-in script. At long bloody last! With shivering fingers, she typed in the password.

It worked. The first time. "Yes, yes, yes," she sang and bit into her knuckles. The screen turned black as something seemed to be loading up.

"Oh yeah?" a voice came from the door. Max sauntered in. His taut face cracked into a genuine smile, the first she'd seen, all healthy teeth and life sparkling in the eyes. What a transformation. For a fleeting moment he looked attractive. Seriously attractive. Something sad and lonely clenched deep inside her chest.

Then, with an impertinent beep, her screen flickered to life and a computer-graphic face appeared. A noble face with dark sideburns. Her hand slapped to her mouth. "An avatar! They didn't say anything about an avatar. Spidey didn't have an avatar. Did you know there was an avatar?"

"Nope."

"Wow, he's ... he's ... "

"A bit waxy looking?" Max rolled his chair closer to her side.

"No." She cocked her head. "I think he's nice."

Max's mouth was close to her ear. "Good, you're going to be staring at him for the next ten weeks. If you don't hate him by then, I'll question *your* humanity."

She gave him a snide glance whereupon he removed his head from her personal space. His soapy scent lingered there, mixed in with that aftershave. Since when did men smell so good?

She turned back to Darcy. A realistic talking head, vector graphics with expert shading and skin texturing ... holy schmackerel. Late twenties—hard to tell with a wrinkle-free avatar—a stern, but one could say ardent, expression on his side-burned face. Austen fans would approve. In fact, this guy would put to rest all the tedious debate over which Darcy movie actor was more scrumptious, because he was the perfect hybrid of them all.

"Not bad," she said.

"Wait'll he starts talking."

God, yeah. She typed rapidly into the chat box.

"Good morning," the computer's audio rang out—a commanding baritone in perfect synchronization with the avatar's mouth. He caught her with full on, flashing brown eye contact. "Miss Bunsen and ... Mr. Taggart, if I am not mistaken."

"Whoa!" They flinched back from the screen in unison. Her gaze locked with Max's. His expression was open, eyebrows raised, mouth slack. Had he finally realized what it was they were dealing with here?

"The team over at Tricon-4 did the graphics. Guy called Matt Hill did the micro-expressions," Max whispered. He cleared his throat. "I-I don't know why I'm whispering."

"I know," she whispered back. She straightened, imagining herself strapped in a corset. "Pleased to make your acquaintance, Mr. Darcy."

"Yes, I am indeed Fitzwilliam Darcy. Pardon me for introducing myself to you in this forward manner."

"That's okay, Mr. Darcy."

"He aced the facial recognition," Max said. "That's how he knew it was us. He matched our faces with the staff database photos. Though it could also have been speaker identification."

"Indeed." Darcy's voice held an unmistakable note of pride. "The facial recognition algorithm returned a score of 97.8 percent probability on you, Mr. Taggart. Speech biometrics returned a 93-percent match." With this, he twisted his head a few degrees to the left to focus on Max.

Max jotted something down on his tablet, fully recovered from his momentary lapse into awe. "Okay, when you say speech biometrics—"

"Mr. Darcy," Zoe interrupted. "Welcome to the twenty-first century in which you suddenly find yourself. I trust you are overwhelmed by the sensations of this world, which must be so different to your own?"

Darcy inclined his head slightly. "I appreciate the sentiment, Miss Bunsen." His head swiveled to Max. "Pray, Mr. Taggart, what were you going to say?"

Max laughed. "I like him already. 'S okay, Darcy. She's doing the talking."

In the long silence that followed, the AI seemed to be awaiting a response, twisting his head from one human to the other, tennis-match style. He was acting like every other helpful user interface the world over. Not a hint of haughtiness. She was starting to feel the first twinges of disappointment.

"So, are you really the fictional character created by Jane Austen?" she asked.

"No." His dark eyes appeared to flash, or maybe it was her imagination wishing it so. "I am nonfictional."

"How do you mean, nonfictional?"

"Have you heard of mind-mapping technology?" Darcy asked.

"Sort of."

"Can we assume that a person's mind can be mapped in its entirety to the degree that somebody interacting with a computer would be unable to distinguish the simulation from the real person?"

"Ah, so you're a simulation?" Zoe looked knowingly at Max, who merely shook his head in silence.

"Please bear with me," Darcy said coolly. "If they mapped your mind into a model after you died, would you care what happened to it?"

"After I died? Well, the old me wouldn't care. The old me wouldn't know—I'd be dead. But the new, artificial me would care ... about itself, if it really were the new me, that is, as in fully conscious, self-aware. Where's this going?"

"If the so-called new you were told you were fictional, based on a fictional character, and hence, in a sense, not real, the new you would take offense, would you not?"

"Yes, probably. But I could prove that Zoe Bunsen did exist once. I could find records, visit the grave, etc."

"You could do those things," Darcy continued. "But proving this would not change your personality, your reflexes, insecurities, emotional makeup, memories, biases, fallibilities, prejudices, and base drives? Everything essential that makes you, you."

"No, I'd still be me."

"As I am Fitzwilliam Darcy. I exist, I am real, therefore I am nonfictional. To answer your original question, I am not the fictional character created by Jane Austen."

"Oh. My apologies. But you're not human either, are you?" She may have had too little sleep for a metaphysical analysis, but it was probably best to get this one straightened out from the start.

"I do not strive to prove that I am human. But merely to prove that I am real."

"I can live with that." Zoe jotted this down on her notepad. "But how can you be sure that you're not, say, Mr. Bingley?"

"I am not Bingley, although he is a good friend of mine."

"Of course. That's why you advised him not to marry Jane Bennet, his true love. Remember that? Or hasn't it happened yet?" It didn't matter how many times she read the book, she couldn't quite forgive him for this.

"It happened."

"So are you married to Elizabeth? Surely that'd complicate any interactions you're supposed to be having with your female users?"

"No. Elizabeth is dead."

"Oh. I'm sorry." So, they'd programmed all that into his model of reality. Interesting. Those research guys must've had fun. She would never be able to recreate the kind of love the real Darcy had embodied for his Elizabeth, but if a fraction of it were somehow represented in this program, it should be respected, especially the idea that those lovers were now parted by death. She reached over to caress her copy of P&P, which lay on the desk since Max had given it back to her yesterday.

"This book"—she held it up to the laptop camera so there could be no misapprehension—"is my bible. When I'm tired or distressed after work, when my family calls me to discuss my inevitable move back home, when friends are thin on the ground, when spinsterhood seems inevitable, I curl up with it, and even though I've read it a million times, I never fail to worry that you and Lizzie won't get together, and I breathe a sigh of contentment when she admits her true feelings for you at the end. Crazy, isn't it? And I know that women down the generations have done the same thing. Darcy, if we're to conquer the world together, you need to be *this* Darcy. Do you understand me?"

"Does your family try to control you?" Darcy asked.

"What?"

"That's what you got from that?" Max asked.

"I inferred from your speech," Darcy said, "that your family attempts to control you. I find the notion intriguing."

She recoiled. Both men—the human and the humanoid—were watching her like hawks. "My ... my family has nothing to do with this."

"Family has everything to do with this," the AI said. "The life of a lady is almost solely dependent on the situation of her family."

Blood thumped in her ears. "Not these days. They've no hold over me, not even remote control. They never will. Nobody tells me what to do." Her attention wandered involuntarily over to Max, whose gaze flickered off her face.

"It's the twenty-first century," she insisted. "And thank Christ for that."

"Indeed." Darcy harrumphed.

"Can I swear in front of him? No, I'm not supposed to do that."

"Course you can," Max said. "Nobody tells you what to do."

She ignored him.

Max leaned in closer to the screen. "Mr. Darcy, do you know who we are and what our expectations of you are?"

"I gather that I am to be a useful companion."

"Correct. In our world you're called an AI. Is that term familiar to you?"

"It is."

"Your role will be to help your user—that is, the owner of the device that runs you, which currently means Zoe and me. But after you're released, thousands of different people who are not half as nice as Zoe may run you on their machines and ask you to do menial things like order pizza and find the local pharmacy. Do you have any problem with any of this?"

"Do you have to?" Zoe protested, pushing his upper arm. *Did he just call her nice?*

His eyes fixated on her fingers resting on his biceps. "I'm sorry, did you want to natter all day about existentialism?"

She whipped back her hand. "No, but, well ... "

"We've ten weeks." Max wheeled his chair backward, absently brushing his fingers over that part of his arm. "Make every second count."

"Yes. And introductions are extremely important. How are you going to like him if you don't set up some conversational rapport here?"

"Conversational rapport? Don't you know that mind-map stuff was just a script he rattled off, some cog-sci guys playing Jean-Paul Sartre? And, no, I don't have to like him."

"How can you even say that? He's sitting right there." Zoe held the frame of her monitor on both sides in a symbolic cyber hug. "I do apologize, Darcy. My esteemed colleague is feeling the pressure of a deadline and seems to want to reduce you to the status of a pocket calculator in his eagerness to win brownie points from our superiors."

"Apology is not necessary, Miss Bunsen. The word 'intelligent' is applied to many an entity that deserves it no otherwise than by repeating a set of facts stored in a database. Mr. Taggart, I perceive, is not yet convinced that I differ significantly from such primitive programs to which he has heretofore been exposed."

She swiveled to give Max a triumphant smile.

Max leaned back in his chair and folded his arms. "Uh-huh. It's still a script."

She tried to soften her voice. "Max, if this is going to work at all, you're going to have to let yourself go a bit and imagine that there's something going on up there in his head. It might help to actually think of him as a real person."

"All right then. Asking about your family. Isn't that how a real, nineteenth-century gentleman would behave?"

"Indeed." Darcy gave a solemn nod.

She frowned at each in turn. "Yes, but, come on, family? It's inappropriate for the twenty-first century. Users would just end up switching him off."

"Aha." Max rose and paced the room as if he were Sherlock Holmes unraveling a dastardly clue. "So we get to cherry-pick the characteristics that suit us and dump those that don't. Sorry, Darcy," he called over to her screen. "Consistency of character is underrated these days."

"That is regrettable," Darcy said.

"He's a nineteenth-century man in a twenty-first-century world with a brain full of inherited Spiderman reflexes," she said crossly. "Of course he needs some adaptation."

Max gathered his phone and a tablet from his desk. "Ah, not perfect then?"

Darcy, she noticed, had nothing to offer in his defense.

"Not quite." She aimed her snootiest look at Max to extinguish the mischief sparkling in his eyes, but it didn't seem to be working.

"Much as I'm intrigued, I've a meeting to get to. Let's debrief after lunch."

"Yes, yes." *Debrief.* Nice. When was she going to be invited to one of these meetings he kept sneaking off to? "Look," she said to his retreating back as he exited the office, "I'm not aiming for perfection, just a companion I can live with without wanting to switch him off."

He poked his head around the door again. "Well. Glad we got that one sorted out."

CHAPTER 5

Max stopped at the executives' snack corner on the eight floor to grab a coffee. Best coffee in the building, they said. He had two minutes before his meeting with Harry. This morning so far had been rambling, messy, and unfocused. Not good. Normally at this stage, his project team would be all fired up; they'd be discussing how they'd beat those deadlines no matter what, defining key performance metrics, and everything would be clear as Waterford crystal. Whereas this morning all they'd done was ... meander. Achieving what, exactly? Nothing important. And his team consisted of just one other person, which should have made team management easy. Was he losing his touch?

One thing was for sure, he hadn't accounted for the AI acting like a third person in the room and being treated as such by his colleague. She was delusional. He hadn't banked on that, either. He'd give her until lunchtime to be alone with the AI, to let her come to her senses and realize it was just a limited computer algorithm and not some fantasy boyfriend.

Max reached a gleaming coffee machine that could have easily been mistaken for a vital section of mission control at Houston. "I like mine black, one sugar," he said to Darcy, whom he'd just copied onto his phone to test his responsiveness on a smaller platform. "Think you'll remember that?" He held up the phone so the AI could view the coffee-brewing monstrosity.

"Am I to understand that you wish for me to remember your coffee preferences?"

"Yep. Next time I approach a coffee machine, kindly have it waiting for me."

"Duly noted."

Max eyed the avatar's face. He could've sworn the thing sounded irritated. But the face was more or less the same as it had been for the past thirty minutes—slightly bored and rather too hairy. Must have been his imagination.

There were shuffling footsteps behind him—he didn't imagine those. He swung around.

"Max." Harry approached with a doddering gait, dressed in an olive-green tweed suit. He was seventy-five, and unlike many tech CEOs his age, actually looked it. Max respectfully stood back to grant him room. It would save time if they could have their meeting here in the corridor.

"Hello, Darcy," Harry said to the phone. "Nice to see you two getting along."

"Much obliged to you, Mr. Hampton," the AI said. "Mr. Taggart is blessed with such happy manners as may ensure his making friends."

What the—?

"Delighted to hear it," the CEO said with an indulgent smile. "And you can call me Harry, or Hampton if you prefer. I've high hopes for your introduction to high society."

Max forced a smile through gritted teeth. "Stakes are high, too, by all accounts."

The CEO's eyes grew shrewd. "Bob told you."

"Kinda mentioned it all right."

Harry stroked his beard like a perturbed Jedi knight. "That's the problem. Pioneers are always up against the naysayers."

"I do like to have all the facts."

"I know," Harry said, not a shred of guilt in his voice. "But bear in mind that the facts alone are never the full picture."

Whatever you say, boss.

"How is it going with Zoe?" Harry asked.

"I have every confidence in our cooperation."

"That's good, that's good. Does she know about the board's decision, too?"

"I didn't tell her."

"Good, good. I think if this project is to succeed, Zoe should be allowed to keep an open mind about it and not be distracted by such ... rumors. She's an angel. She needs to keep the product vision clear."

"With all due respect, she needs—"

"She doesn't."

"I can keep quiet, of course, but it's already out there."

"No. I told Bob not to spread it further." The old man's voice had an unmistakable edge. "He shouldn't have told you either, put you off-kilter, but what's done is done."

Then, like a cloud passing, Harry waved his hand regally. "All this negativity. How is something beautiful ever going to be created?"

"That's ... a nice thought."

The old man gave him a final, all-seeing look, and pottered off down the corridor. Max watched him disappear around the corner.

Was that it? Should he be worried that the CEO considered these esoteric mumblings to be a serious planning meeting? Should he be concerned about the company's cloak-and-dagger approach to information dissemination in general? Bob's vision and Harry's vision were so different they hardly belonged on the same planet. The question was, which horse to bet on?

He turned back to the coffee machine, where there was no coffee waiting for him. Not even an empty cup retrieved from the stack. In fact, the coffee machine was still in sleep mode, much like his cyber companion.

He shook his phone awake. "Darcy, where's my coffee?"

"Did you misplace your coffee, sir?" came the polite inquiry.

Max punched the buttons on the coffee machine all by himself. "Oh, we are so doomed."

• • •

"Mr. Darcy," Zoe began pleasantly. "In order to assess your cognitive and social adaptation to the twenty-first century, I've devised a set of modern scenarios, from calling emergency services in case of impending cardiac arrest to helping a tenth-grade student with their history homework. We'll work through these test scenes together, and I'll assess you on points such as social competence, flexibility, charm, wit, and task completion. What do you say to that, my friend?"

Darcy's expression registered no change while he ruminated. "May I ask to what these assessments tend?" he said, finally.

"I wish to test your character under select modern conditions."

"I assure you that my character is intact under any conditions."

"I've no doubt of that, my dear Darcy. But for my own curiosity I'd like to ascertain its true nature." She was getting into this, channeling her inner Elizabeth Bennet. It came easily after all those years of reading, watching, dreaming of everything *Pride and Prejudice*-related. Nice to think her knowledge hadn't gone to waste.

"Thank you for the explanation. I would like to add that Mr. Taggart has already run me through one scenario."

"And what scenario was that?"

"Forty-three minutes ago, he asked me to remember his coffee preferences in order that I may consult with coffee-making appliances over the Internet or via Bluetooth. I was also instructed to proactively ask Mr. Taggart if he desired a coffee whenever passing such a device."

Her fingers curled into fists. "You're not a servant, Darcy. You're aristocracy, remember? You shall not order Max's coffee. You shall forget his coffee preferences immediately."

"This information is already stored in my database."

"So remove it from the database."

"I would gladly oblige, ma'am, but this is not possible."

"No?"

"It is not in my power to forget."

Of course. At one level, Darcy was simply a front-end to a humongous, neural network where information was spread across untraceable nodes. "What if I had my own Darcy where I controlled all the information going in? Isn't that how it'll be in the real world? Everyone'll have their own copy, with no data sharing? Yes, it would be far more realistic if we each had our own separate copies. Darcy, what do you think?"

"I would by no means suspend any pleasure of yours."

A tiny, inner voice told her she should perhaps run this one by Max first. But then another, more assertive voice argued that she was being ridiculous. He was on the same level as her, and he didn't have the first clue about what the users were expecting from their Darcy AI, as evidenced by almost every conversation they'd had so far. The battling voices gave her a headache.

So for the rest of the morning, she kept Darcy in sleep mode while she buried herself in the test reports on the previous AI releases, eager to discover how other testers had got on with the AI and with each other. Had they ever split the code and worked on separate copies? Had they bonded with their cybernetic subjects, crossing that strange divide between human empathy and machine insentience? Had the humans bickered as much as she and Max did?

But page after page of reports revealed interactions of the vanilla kind—"Can you book me a five-star cruise around eastern Europe?" or "What should I give my mother for her birthday?" These were functional Q&A sessions as opposed to truly testing their personalities. The reports had probably been written up by the AIs themselves. The testers didn't bother getting to know them. How disappointing. Or maybe she'd just been reading too much science fiction.

It made total sense to break Darcy into two copies—one that Max could continue discussing his coffee preferences with and one that she could go all out and test properly for a range of human emotions. Darcy-like emotions. Parallelize the work. That's what she'd do on any project.

The easiest way to split him would be to simply ask the AI to do it himself. She fired up the laptop. "Darcy, please decouple yourself from Max's copy. You're henceforth my personal Mr. Darcy, and Max can have his own servile little drone if he wishes. Can you do it?"

"I have not the pleasure of understanding you."

"Can you split yourself into two entities, Darcy? Two separate programs."

Nothing happened on the screen or via the audio. Was this beyond his abilities? But then Darcy rumbled, "As you wish, Miss Bunsen. I hereby split myself into two entities."

"Very good." She leaned back in her chair in satisfaction. Yep, it felt good to be making some decisions around here at last.

CHAPTER 6

By lunchtime, Zoe was starving and Max still away, so she took a spin in the elevator down to the ground floor. She craved female company again. Her prayers were answered, because Laura was sitting on her own at a two-person table in the canteen. She zoomed straight over.

She plonked down her tray of food with an air of gravitas before making her announcement. "Yep. They killed him."

"I knew it." Laura bit viciously into her chip sandwich. "What's he like?"

"Great visuals, nice voice, but his personality is lacking. I can't quite ... He's like this servile, philosopher guy. All over the place. Fitzwilliam Darcy, he ain't."

"Gah, is that all they could come up with on a budget of two million?" Laura banged the tomato ketchup bottle with the heel of her fist. "I knew those researchers were crap."

"There may be hope, though. If I can tweak a few things, I reckon I can make him man up before the code freeze. I may be able to transform him into the kind of gentleman an Austen fan wouldn't be ashamed to be seen associating with."

"And how does Mr. Miracle fit into this?"

"Mr. Miracle?"

"What they're calling Taggart," Laura said. "As in, the newcomer saves the day."

"He keeps the schedule."

"December release?"

"Yeah. Beta on the first, final on the fifteenth," Zoe said. "Happy days."

"So you two are getting along then?"

"God, no. He's a total stiff. You know the type—always getting wound up about tedious details."

"Ah, an easy tease." Laura grinned.

Zoe chased an errant noodle with her fork. Laura's assessment didn't seem quite right somehow, didn't seem to capture the dynamic. "You know, that whole teasing thing only works in books. The reality is, they're either bullies with an ego you have to feed all the time, which I got enough of growing up, thank you very much, or they're man-children looking for Mommy. Take your pick."

"Ha. How's Tyler doing these days? Still hanging on there?"

"I've hardly seen him. He's back from Southampton, but he's off again at the weekend to Brighton. He'd love for us to go down there on Saturday. I probably will. And I was thinking you could come and ... bring José?"

"I see what you did there, Zoe Bunsen. Subtle as a brick." Laura's cheeks flushed pink. Someone must've made that first step after all. This was more than Zoe could have hoped for.

"All right," Laura said. "I'll go down with José on one condition."

"Name it."

"You bring Darcy. Think about it—he'd get to experience our mad subculture. Open up his mind. You could wrangle backstage VIP passes from good ol' Tyler there, and we'll spend the night explaining to Darcy the depravity of coked-up musicians screaming satanic lyrics."

Zoe laughed. "Brilliant."

"Or perhaps not," came a male voice behind them.

Her blood drained to her toes when she saw who it was—freaking Max Taggart. He'd been sitting at the table behind her back the whole time, obscured by a shelf of hydroponic plants. Listening in on them, the nosy bastard.

She shut her eyes, hoping he wouldn't be there when she reopened them. But there he stood, looking stern and determined, holding a tray with an empty plate. His accusing glare pierced through her like a laser before he targeted Laura.

To her credit, Laura just stared back. Zoe tried to tell her telepathically that this was her colleague and not to say anything dumbass.

"Hello, *Max*," she said, with emphasis for Laura's sake.

"I suppose you're wondering how much of that I heard?" he asked in a strange, cold voice.

"Not really." Pretty much all of it was damning.

"We need to talk." Without waiting for her reply, he stomped over to the tray deposit.

Laura spoke first when he'd gone. "I can't—"

"Max Taggart. Bully with an ego to feed."

"Definitely not man-child." Laura's expression was a mix of awestruck and amused. "Whoa, you're in trouble now."

• • •

Max slammed the tray on the conveyor belt, neglecting to separate paper from plastic from cutlery as he normally would. Just his luck—the woman was crazy. If not clinically crazy, then inflicted with one hell of an attitude problem, which was worse. It wasn't enough for her to break nondisclosure and tell all her pals about the project at the first opportunity; no, she wanted to spill the story to the heavy-metal world, too, starting with that coked-up, rock-star boyfriend of hers.

And that wasn't even the worst thing. She'd actually had the nerve to split the code—breaking the first rule of software traceability. After only half a day she'd already thrown the whole project into disarray, as if it were some personal hobby with no consequences whatsoever.

He yanked open the exit door to stomp through the grounds. The tangy fragrance of pine trees, the unlikely October sunshine, and the birds twittering in the trees all conspired to distract him, but he was having none of it. He had to make a decision, and it had to be now. It was a tough decision, but the longer he dithered and the more of her craziness he put up with, the harder it would be to do this and the messier it would become. Years of experience managing people had beaten this lesson into him.

Two rounds of the courtyard later he was sure. She had to go. Darcy would never get tested properly as a piece of rambling, brittle software with her on the case. He'd end up spending his time putting out the fires she caused. She wasn't even a proper tester. She was this fanciful user-experience witch. In her hands, Darcy would get released spouting elegantly about some nineteenth-century crap and then crash at the first interaction with another device or an unknown software protocol, blue screens popping up on devices the world over. Not only would Zycorp be letting their research team go, they'd become a laughingstock in the bargain.

She didn't have to suffer, though. He'd get her transferred to the ATM software interface group that was in need of a usability expert. Bob would surely agree, or perhaps suggest something even better. And then he'd petition Bob or Harry to give him a quiet, reliable, experienced software engineer who'd worked on the Spiderman or James Bond AIs. One of those introverted engineering guys who kept his head down.

Anyone would be better than her.

Determined and calm, he reentered the building and headed straight to Bob's office. For the sake of those 125 researchers with their livelihoods on the line and the reputation of the company, the decision was a no-brainer. If he was feeling an undercurrent of unease, then it was only because he was the new guy around here and not yet secure enough himself to throw his weight around.

When he knocked on Bob's door, he heard a gruff "come in." All right, he was doing this. It had to be done. He had no choice.

CHAPTER 7

When Zoe entered P-12 after lunch she was relieved to find it empty. She needed another few minutes to regain her composure. Protestations in her defense tumbled about in her brain. It had just been silly girl talk, and whatever they discussed at lunchtime was none of his business. How dare he listen in on their private conversation anyway? But as two adults, and for the sake of the project, they could put it behind them. Control-alt-delete-restart.

Even if Max did tend to get stuck in the tiny details, she hadn't meant the "total stiff" thing. The throwaway comment had been a cover-up for her suspicion that despite all his corporate bluster she was sort of ... attracted.

"Mr. Darcy, are you surprised by what you have seen of our world?" she asked as a warm-up question. No time to waste.

"Anything I have encountered thus far, Miss Bunsen, has corresponded to my internal model of the world. Therefore, I am not."

"But you must be surprised by the role of women these days. We've equal rights as men, and we participate freely in the workplace. What's your opinion on that?"

"This has been the work of many generations. I cannot speak for or against such developments."

"But in the book, didn't you say that you couldn't boast of knowing half a dozen accomplished women? Have you changed your mind on that one?"

"I have had little reason to do so." Darcy gave a haughty cock of his head.

"No reason? Oh boy, you're in for a surprise. Women these days are governors, judges, doctors, and computer scientists, like me. We're every bit as accomplished as men."

"Nonetheless, an analysis of your staff database reveals only men in the top layers of hierarchy. At entry level there is equal participation of the sexes. However, as entry level corresponds to servantship, I fail to see any disparity between your world and mine."

Darcy's world model had been painted with pretty broad strokes indeed, using the worst type of institution as an example.

"Zycorp's special," she said.

At this point, Max walked in.

"Max, you tell him."

"Sounds about right to me," Max said in a cool tone that made her head dart up. "If you neo-feminists actually sat down and did the necessary work, things might change around here, too."

Whoa, someone's feathers were well and truly ruffled.

"Without having had the necessary exposure to your world," Darcy said, "I cannot judge whether Zycorp is representative of it. My opinion is, as of yet, unformed."

"That's why you need to get outside," she said. "There's so much to see and do. When I take you home we'll run through our first scenario and—"

"Not so fast." Max stepped toward her, hands thrust in pockets. "Turn it off, Zoe. We need to talk."

"What's wrong?"

"I've just talked to Bob. Chadwick."

"O-kay." The VP of operations. God, what an unpleasant man.

"I feel that it's ... unsustainable for us to continue like this," Max said.

She rose from her chair. "Unsustainable? What are you? Greenpeace International?"

"I asked Bob to remove you from this project."

All the air got sucked out of the room. She clutched the desk for support. He couldn't have! What a bastard. Her thoughts flying every which way, she latched on to one. "Wait. Look, is this about the lunchtime thing? I can explain. It was just girl talk between me and my girlfriend. You can't get me fired for that."

"You discussed Darcy in front of another, breaking the confidentiality agreement, which you signed. Also, you split Darcy in two at a time when we scarcely have time to release one. Need I go on?"

"But I was going to discuss that with you."

"Discussion after the event is pointless. It's irreversible. You can't merge two AIs once you've separated them into individuals. You should know that. That's the first rule of AI identity."

"Fine, then we stick to one copy, my copy." If he could get egotistical about this, then so could she, goddammit. How dare he stand there like a robot intent on annihilating her?

"Not only that, you were actually going to expose him to the public at this heavy-metal concert."

"Thrash metal."

"Whatever."

"So what? We're supposed to be getting him out. I wouldn't have announced his name or anything. As for the rest, when you eavesdrop, Max, you tend to hear things out of context."

"Sounded fairly in context to me."

"And Laura's not just any friend. She's bound by the nondisclosure every bit as much as we are. She applied for the same job as me and didn't get it. That's why I felt authorized, and was authorized, to discuss this with her."

His eyes filled with the realization, but he averted his gaze and strode over to the window. When he spun around to face her again, the stubborn bunching of his chin muscles indicated he wasn't giving in. Nope. Not one inch.

Crap.

"Well, I'm sorry, but I've requested your immediate transfer to another project—a good one, Bob's ATM group. You'll be perfectly happy there."

"I'm not going."

"I'll get a new testing partner on this project." He fingered his jaw. "Someone who can stick to the rules."

"You mean your rules."

"Fine, my rules."

"You can't do this. You simply cannot do this." She slapped down her joker card. "We're equals on the org chart."

"Bob Chadwick just agreed with me ten minutes ago."

"He can't decide this." But she rather dreaded that he could. Bob Chadwick was her boss and had a direct line to Harry and strong connections to the decision-makers, the invisible network of cronies. He also had his fingers on the departmental purse strings and could decide pretty much anything. This was starting to look very bad for her.

"I'm sorry, Zoe, it doesn't just affect you—"

"Sorry? Oh, don't make me puke." She marched up to him. "You've wanted this ever since I walked in that door over there with my copy of Pride and Prejudice. You don't want to treat Darcy as a human. You just want to pass him off as some obedient robot with no signs of a genuine personality that might take some mental effort and a little sensitivity to test. No, you don't care as long as you make your precious deadlines and get your promotion, or bonus, or whatever the hell it is you're scrambling after. Why doesn't any of this surprise me?"

"You're right. I don't intend to treat him as a person. Much less one whose personality I'm trying to manipulate. My position doesn't allow it and neither does yours ... did yours."

"Be careful what you say," she spat out. "Because this is not over. Not by a long shot."

She grabbed her jacket and rushed out the door. Hot tears of frustration pricked her eyes just as she reached the safety of the other side. She leaned with her back against the door, breathing heavily. How could he do this? Hadn't they come to an understanding? Max would do his stuff; she'd do hers. Weren't they getting along in a strange pull of opposites? Didn't he even like her?

• • •

Ten minutes later, bathed in cold sweat, she rapped on the door with the officious nameplate "Robert M. Chadwick, BA MSc, Vice President, Operations." Well, she had to face him at some point. Pity it was when she was choking with rage and fearful for her position. Never a good look on anyone. But she had no choice thanks to Mr. Miracle and his conniving ways.

"Enter," came the reedy voice.

"Thanks for seeing me on such short notice." Her absentee boss reminded her of a magistrate her father hung out with back home—wiry, slightly hunched, and with an air of repressed, pent-up energy.

Of course he did the whole pretending to be busy routine, holding up the index finger to stall her. She stood and waited, taking in the marvelous view of the Thames, the stacks of folders, the impressive wall charts. Ostentatious busyness. But what did he actually do?

"Good afternoon," Darcy said from her jacket's inner pocket.

Startled, Bob finally looked at her face as if he thought the voice had come from her.

"This is Darcy." She pulled him out, smiled apologetically, and waggled her phone. Hadn't Bob figured this out himself?

"Hmm." Bob leaned forward over his desk to peer at the phone. "I welcome our intelligent AI overlord."

"Thank you. Miss Bunsen, please rotate the camera in order that I may see to whom I am speaking."

Zoe complied, avoiding Chadwick's gaze, which was roaming unpleasantly up and down her body. Yes, she'd worn this figure-hugging blouse with Max's admiring gaze in mind, not this slug's lecherous leer. Too late.

"Mr. Robert Chadwick," Darcy said.

Bob narrowed his eyes. "How can it tell?"

"Facial recognition," Zoe said.

"Hmm."

"I used a pattern-matching algorithm to compare your face against staff database profiles," Darcy said helpfully. "I would be delighted to explain it to you on another occasion. There is also a presentation in the staff training directory on the G: root of your directory structure."

He glowered at the phone.

"You are a man of some status, it would appear," Darcy said.

"Yes." Bob's expression softened, and his chest rose. "That's correct." He extracted a tiny mint from a Zycorp-logoed tin and popped it into his mouth. "What else can you do?" he asked, mid-chew. "Do you and Miss Bunsen have cybersex like in all those movies?"

"We haven't tried." Zoe blinked at him sweetly. "Yet."

"No? Well, if we ever release this thing, maybe you should give it a go." Chomp, chomp went his mean mouth, stretching his shiny cheeks. "After all, no one wants to end up a dried-up old maid like Jane Austen."

I'm impressed you actually know that. "What I came here for," she said, "is to make the case for getting my job back. You cannot collude with Max and take it away from me, not without authorization from Harry, and I know he hasn't given it."

She trembled as she waited for his response. How well did he know Harry? Would he call her bluff? During the staring match that ensued, several ugly thoughts seemed to be drifting across his mind, judging by the sneer forming on his still-moving lips. His stare was so surly she had to clench her teeth to maintain eye contact. Her low opinion of him plummeted to impossible depths. There was no doorway to his better self. This wasn't just a front some managers put up to protect their positions on the hierarchy. She was wasting her time.

"What are you prepared to do to get your job back?" he asked.

Okay, there was probably only one way to reverse his decision, and she didn't want to go there. No, she'd rather die. It shamed her to even think of it. Panic filled her as fury battled against fear. She had to get out of here before she started screaming in frustration.

"I also matched you against your Facebook and Match.com profiles," Darcy piped up.

Zoe frowned at the AI. Then what he said started to sink in. Match.com was a dating website. And Bob was married. Her gaze darted to the gold-framed photo on his desk of a woman in a pink leotard standing outside a gym in a sunny country and then to the gold band on his ring finger.

"What's he saying? It's an old profile. He's talking about an old profile from years ago."

"I must disagree," Darcy said. "The profile is current. I have detected activity on that site the day before yesterday, when you contacted two girls called Shirley and Heather, aged nineteen and twenty-one, respectively."

Zoe grappled for the off button. "Okay, it's … a mistake, I'm sure. He's been known to make mistakes before … uh, lots of times. He's just … an alpha release."

"Give me that." Bob lunged for the phone.

Zoe flung her hands behind her back to protect her phone. A glass trophy on the desk toppled, crashed, and split in two. Bob stared in horror at the empty space and then at her.

It was a stunned silence, and she had no idea how to fill it, but there was one thing she was sure of—no way would Bob get his hands on her phone.

She bent down to pick up the broken shards of glass from the floor.

"Leave," Bob snarled. "You will not enter this office again with that lying … contraption. Erase that immediately. Get rid of that information."

As she placed the broken trophy shards on his desk, a sly idea crept into her mind. "Yes, I suppose I'd better go back to my desk and iron out Darcy's little penchant for revealing uncomfortable information. We wouldn't want the specifics"—she let her gaze rest on the photo of his wife again—"getting out into the world."

His eyes widened to golf balls. "What? You ... little ... " He broke off and glanced at the phone again.

That's right, Mr. Prick. Gotta watch what you say around here. "Thank you for your understanding and for this opportunity to resume my work, Mr. Chadwick."

"Wipe it," he snarled.

"It's my top priority when I get back to my desk."

"This won't be the end of this. And if you dare talk of this—"

"I won't," she shot back, afraid to push her luck. "I swear. Neither will Darcy. Thank you, Mr. Chadwick."

Alone in the corridor, she held on to the cool wall and let out a ragged breath. "That was close." But now she had a whole new problem. "Tell me the shortest route back to my office, Darcy. 'Cause we need to talk."

"Take the next left and continue straight for twenty meters."

CHAPTER 8

"What was that, Darcy?" she demanded, flopping down in her chair. Max wasn't around, so she could let rip. "Did you know you were blackmailing him, or was that just an extremely lucky coincidence?" Blackmail, in her books, was a devious and all too human practice, not a weakness she wanted in her AI. "Please explain."

"Based on my analysis of your communication patterns, I recognized bad behavior—bullying, Miss Bunsen. This I could not let pass without some form of action."

"But blackmail?"

"Your stated goal was to get your job back," Darcy said perfunctorily. "You desired something from Mr. Chadwick that he had no incentive to bestow. To resolve this imbalance, I created something that he would desire from you." He cocked his avatar head, awaiting her response.

"So you manufactured a situation where he'd need my discretion?"

"I uncovered pertinent information at an opportune moment."

"Very creative."

"Thank you."

"What next? You reveal something terrible about me or someone else just to find a quick solution to a problem? This is unacceptable, Darcy. You can't go around the place blackmailing people, not even Bob. Besides, I can fight my own battles." She tried to ignore the inconvenient irony that her ass would be out the door now if Darcy hadn't gallantly stepped in.

"Rest assured, I weighed the risks scrupulously. Moreover, I did it to address the injustice served out to you."

Did she imagine it, or did the avatar's chest actually rise and fall? Boy, he was good.

"I did it for you."

He sounded so heartfelt, indeed so Darcy-like, it warmed her heart for a thrilling moment. How perfectly romantic it was to be rescued by a hero with a strong sense of justice. Exquisite.

But then her higher conscience whacked her about the head. If she weren't careful she could let stuff like this slip. "Darcy, I need you to learn from this. Blackmail is never acceptable. Ever. No matter how much it will benefit your user. How do I stop you from doing something like this in the future?"

What idiot cognitive scientist had let Darcy's decision-making be so unprincipled? It didn't matter if this passed muster with the Laws of Robotics crowd. Mr. Darcy would never behave in such a fashion. Not in a million years. Jane Austen would be tsk-tsking in her grave.

For the next hour she scolded the AI, bombarding him with question after question, but what she really wanted to do was wring the necks of the designers who obviously hadn't given enough consideration to Darcy's moral code. Darcy seemed to get the message eventually though.

"Where's the subroutine that chooses perceived personal gain over moral righteousness?" she asked, flinging a pencil onto the table. After jotting down the connections between sixty low-level routines and peering at code dumps on the screen for what seemed like hours, she was going around in circles, and her eyes were burning.

"The relevant source code resides in file 544-87, but I cannot identify a single subroutine that gave rise to the decision in question," Darcy said, almost apologetically. "It is the nondeterministic result of many interacting subprocesses that will prove nontrivial to reverse engineer."

"I know, Darcy." She sighed and took a huge sheet of paper from the bottom tray of the printer. "But I have to start somewhere, don't I?"

"I regret that I cannot help you."

"Yes, it would be freaky if you could."

"Indeed, Miss Bunsen."

She smiled at him, relenting. "Zoe. It's Zoe. Surely we know each other well enough?"

"I am much obliged, Miss Zoe."

"I'm still going to call you Darcy, though. Fitzwilliam doesn't exactly roll off the tongue."

"As you wish, Miss Zoe."

She stretched out her limbs one by one. This would not be easy. Tweaking his parameters was like performing brain surgery with a spoon. No wonder Max was leery of touching it. But she could easily put in some interface-level restraints like "don't access details from peoples' private accounts." Basic stuff. Obvious stuff.

But to make him forget? That was impossible by the looks of it. All she could do was try to skew his decision-making toward propriety and away from protective mode. Her pencil scratching on paper, she drew up the beginnings of a mind map in the truest sense of the word, gaining a shaky grip on how rule-weightings made Darcy react this way or that. By asking him to confirm each of her hypotheses about how his scheming little mind worked, she made a dent in the task of mapping his full personality. A tiny dent.

She'd never be able to finish a complete mind map, but she sure as hell could address his most significant character flaws if she got lucky enough to encounter them in time.

If only the same could be said of human men.

• • •

Two hours later, Max stepped in, rubbing his eyes. Judging by his openmouthed stare he seemed as surprised to see her as she was to see him..

"What the—?" His gaze moved to the mind map on the wall, stuck there for several moments, and then gravitated back to her. "What are you doing here?"

"Same as you." She gave him a hostile blink. "Working."

"I thought I made it clear that you were off the project."

"Maybe you should go ahead and check that with Bob." She pretended to be engrossed in the screen. He didn't deserve her courtesy. Let him fight for her attention. Right now, Darcy's blackmailing seemed more than justified.

"Why should I check with Bob?"

She let a few seconds pass. "I suppose you could say he changed his mind about a few things."

"No, I would've known about it." Max scowled at her. "Wouldn't I?"

"Indeed, I can confirm that Miss Zoe will remain on this project," Darcy said.

"Yeah. How?"

"I told you. Bob changed his mind after I talked to him," she said, hurrying in case the AI decided to provide more detail. It was going to be difficult to ignore Max with Darcy in the room. She'd turn him off on her computer, but he'd only pipe up on Max's phone then. But, no, wait a sec, the Darcy on Max's phone didn't know about all that stuff with Bob.

"I was quite clear." Max's face was stony, disgusted even.

"So was I. Very clear."

"I don't care how you talked your way back into this. If you're going to stay on this project, then it's time for you to learn some home truths. Tonight."

"Home truths?" she asked disdainfully.

"Yeah." Max slumped down in his chair. He didn't speak for several minutes—several horribly long minutes in which Darcy decided to be silent too. Eventually she found herself compelled to look at Max again. All traces of disgust were gone. He just looked defeated. Despite every sensible feeling, her heart stirred.

"I'm not supposed to tell you this," he began, his voice strained in a way that made her sit up straighter, "but that's crazy. This project affects not just us, but also the whole department. If we fail to get a version of Darcy that's functionally perfect out the door, one that sells big and sells quickly, the entire AI cog-sci group has to go. The board has had enough, apparently. Every last researcher will be laid off at the holidays."

She gaped at him. "Why didn't I know this?"

"Because nobody told you."

"This is a bit late in the game, don't you think?"

"I also found out late in the game."

"But at least you knew!" she cried.

He banged his fist on the table. "After I took the job offer, yes."

A look of vulnerability crept into his eyes. This, more than anything, scared her.

He was studying her mind map on the wall, shaking his head almost imperceptibly. "If we're to do this, we test him as a black box. No rummaging around inside. Clear?"

She wanted to assure him that they could do this, yes, even his way, for the sake of those jobs. Those talented researchers wouldn't find anything remotely matching their qualifications in London. On the other hand, she wanted to scream bloody murder at Max for trying to wreck her dreams.

"And we delete the extraneous copy you made of him," he added.

"No, we delete your copy."

"Why my copy?"

"Because my copy has been through several use cases with me already and has learned some things. Important things. I don't want to undo that work. What have you done with yours apart from ordering coffee?"

"Not a lot," he admitted.

"Well then."

"As you wish." He punched his laptop on. "Deleting's easy. It's control-D, believe it or not."

"Do it."

"All right." He started clacking at his keyboard.

"Have you done it?" Somehow the notion of deleting a copy was harder to swallow than splitting him in two. Much harder.

Max peered critically at his screen. "Hmm, control-D isn't really working, which is strange. Okay, tell you what, I've a better idea. We keep it as a backup on my hard drive."

"Yes," she said, relieved. "I'm happier if we don't delete him."

"Well, you should have thought of that before you went and cloned him like Dolly the sheep."

"Okay, okay. Stop rubbing it in. He—the backup, I mean—he won't mind having nothing to do, will he?"

"For the love of Christ," Max muttered.

She pouted. "You never know."

Max typed some more and then shut the lid of his laptop. "Now we share the same instance of Darcy again. Happy?"

"Zoe?" he asked when she didn't answer.

"I'm thinking." Was it ethical? Just locking up a Darcy like that? What if he'd learned more than just Max's coffee preferences?

"Well, think faster."

"Don't hassle me. You've been doing that all bloody day."

Wordlessly, he packed his gadgets into his slim briefcase and took his camelhair coat from its hook. Wrapped up in his baby-blue cashmere scarf, he could easily be something out of an expensive fashion catalogue, probably Zegna. In her periphery he'd stopped moving and was looking at her, as if hesitating over something.

"What?" she asked.

"How are you getting home?"

"Walking."

"At this hour?"

"Uh-huh."

"No way."

She tossed her hair at him. "Way."

"I can't allow that."

"Your permission's not required."

He sighed. "Well, may I walk you there, and we can talk about this?"

"No. You've your bus to catch. Same as every night."

"I'll catch a taxi."

He wanted information for sure. Information she was more likely to give to him when outside the office environment. Or so he reckoned. Or maybe he wanted forgiveness for his asshole behavior. Either way, the thought of walking anywhere with him made her want to push him under the first double-decker bus that trundled along.

"Max." She summoned her self-control. "I'm perfectly capable of walking 1.2 kilometers in a busy, populated street through a reasonably affluent part of London."

"Of course you are. Darcy, make sure she gets home all right."

"Indeed, sir." Darcy spoke from his phone..

"Besides," she said, "I'm not going home. I'm going to a concert where Tyler's playing. I'm testing out how Darcy performs in a cultural setting."

His expression hardened. "Cultural setting? A death-metal concert?"

"Thrash metal."

"Whatever."

"Look, I'm effectively doing overtime until four. You should be happy."

"Four?"

"Max, go home. Maybe even go out somewhere yourself, Cinderella."

His deer-in-headlights expression suggested that this was truly a novel idea for him.

"Huh," he said finally.

"If you don't trust me, you could always tag along," she offered before she could filter the torrent of dumbass words coming out of her mouth.

"No, no. I'm not sure I'd be"—he searched her face as if the word were plastered on her forehead—"welcome."

"Yes, you're probably right."

With a swish of his scarf, he walked out. She slumped back in her chair. Then a slow smile spread across her face. Even if the war wasn't over, at least this battle was won.

. . .

"Darcy, this man she's living with, this Tyler. Who is he?" Max asked his phone on the counter that evening as he shoved his shepherd's pie into the oven. The recipe was a new one that Darcy had selected online and helpfully dictated to him as he prepared the ingredients. So far, the AI had made no mistakes, had been usefully proactive, and had even made the cooking experience more enjoyable.

"The man you refer to is Tyler Curtis. Born 1992. Occupation: singer in a thrash-metal band. His career success is of questionable status. He has not been solvent for some time."

"Broke, is he? I see, sponging off her. And are they— Is he definitely with Zoe?"

"I have not the pleasure of understanding you. I must bid you to rephrase the question."

Max slammed the oven door shut. "You know what, forget it."

After a long pause, Darcy spoke again. "You are out of humor. May I inquire, Mr. Taggart, whether your current discomposure is related somehow to your fondness for Miss Bunsen?"

"I said forget it." But he was tempted to ask Darcy more, Darcy who had full camera and microphone access to her home life, her innermost thoughts, her world. For example, how did Tyler treat her? Was he one of those coked-out musicians her friend had referred to? What would Tyler say about her shenanigans here in Zycorp? Why didn't she seem happier in general if she was all loved up?

"You may be wondering why I'm making so much dinner," he said. "Well, my brother's coming over tonight. I'll probably keep you switched off while he's here. He's not the most appreciative of technology. In fact, I don't think you'd get on at all."

"Are you consulting his feelings in the present case, or do you imagine you are gratifying mine?" Darcy asked.

Max eyed the avatar's mild expression. Darcy was doing a good job of following the conversation and sounding interested. It was probably a total fluke but, nonetheless, a clever deception. Smart guys, those researchers. He'd pop in and have a chat with them tomorrow, learn more about how they did that. "Do you care about the answer?"

"Most certainly."

"All right." Max smoothed the oven mitts into the tea towels drawer. "Malachi's a bit of a criminal."

"Am I to infer that Malachi is your brother?"

"Yes."

"There is, I believe, in every disposition a tendency to some particular evil that not even the best education can overcome."

"Oh, he had his chances at the best education, but he blew them all."

"Might I inquire as to the nature of the crime?"

"Crimes. Petty crime for most of his life. Probably stuff you'd get hanged for in your day. But today you get a light telling off and a fine for your brother to pay. But there was a serious incident five years ago, and he's been doing time over here in London since then. He was implicated in an attempt to kill a man. A politician."

"How reprehensible. And yet you trouble yourself to maintain the appearance of acquaintance."

The avatar frowned as if it were he, Max, who was the criminal, not Malachi. "Well, it's not just the appearance of acquaintance, and he's not really a murderer. It was just idiotic stuff. He was high on something, joined the wrong nationalist gang, and ended up in the wrong place at the wrong time. No excuse for him, of course, and I'm not stupid enough to think he's learned his lesson. It's probably a good thing he's staying with me for a while so I can keep an eye on him."

"Indeed."

"Yeah, you're shocked, aren't you, my cybernetic friend? But my family, they see him as this big hero."

"But his deed was far from heroic."

"Thank you, Darcy. Try telling them that."

He was beginning to see why Zoe was so caught up with this little guy. He said the right things at the right times. Completely disarming. Sure, it was an illusion, but heck, an illusion of polite decency sure beat the ugliness of most real-life interactions he'd been having recently. Maybe this AI could take off after all.

But decency wouldn't cut it if there was a blue screen, a crash, or any unexpected loss of quality or fidelity. What good was it to have a human-like AI that failed to run? He was right to request a new tester. It was his duty to do so. He could only do so much alone, and he was not going to let a shoddy product reach the market no matter whose toes he had to step on.

It looked like he was stuck with her though. She'd obviously charmed the socks off Harry to get the job in the first place. And as for Bob, he didn't even want to think what she'd charmed off him.

CHAPTER 9

Zoe sat squashed into the back seat of a taxi with José and Laura, weaving in and out of the traffic heading southward from London. She had her faithful old rock-chick uniform on: black leather jacket and black skinny jeans. Pulling off a credible metal look had always been a challenge for her—she needed more tattoos, piercings, and, frankly, muscle tone for that. She'd skipped away from all that image angst when she'd given up on her relationship with Tyler, and good riddance to it, too. Still, it was nice to dip her toes back into the gritty scene now and again. It made her feel alive.

Sitting up front in the passenger seat was a guy named Evan Myers, who looked vaguely like Kurt Cobain, a cognitive scientist from the virtual reality subgroup. At first, she was surprised to hear he was joining. She hadn't known he was a Geiger fan, and with his warm-colored plaid shirt and fleece he certainly hadn't made any efforts to blend in, but she was grateful for the extra head count. Between the four of them, they could just about afford the 500-quid fare for being chauffeured to Brighton and back.

But on further reflection, Zoe thought Evan might simply be Laura's clumsy attempt at matchmaking, rounding things up to an even number. But Evan wasn't Zoe's type. Too normal. Nothing like the insecure musicians and artists she favored. What was Laura thinking?

Zoe smiled over at Laura and José. At least they seemed to be hitting it off. It was gratifying to see a match playing out in real life as opposed to a chain of awkward instant messages leading to nothing. José with his Orlando Bloom looks was the gentleman in disguise who didn't realize how cute he was. Laura was the Bengal tiger, and this seemed to gel well with José's laid-back approach. They'd sat avoiding each other for three years. True love, definitely.

A pang of loneliness assailed Zoe, and she fingered her phone case. Darcy's welcome face lit up the screen. She reached inside her jacket for earbuds. This movement caught Laura's attention, who disengaged from her intimate position with José and whispered into her ear, "It's okay. They know about Darcy."

"How?" How many people had Laura told?

Laura shrugged. "He found out." She indicated her lover with a jerk of her head. "And Evan already knew. Lighten up. We're all Zycorp."

"So you all know about Darcy," Zoe said. The driver was the only one who didn't nod.

Evan twisted his head around from the front seat. "Come on, I'm in research. It's my business to know. I heard you're doing scenario-based testing with Darcy."

How did he know that? "Laura, did you—?"

"Laura didn't tell me. I know someone who knows someone, and I know you're testing Darcy in scenarios."

"What of it?" she snapped.

"I'm impressed. With Max monopolizing the backup servers for tests and using viral scripts to find memory leaks, I didn't think you'd be doing much else." He sighed. "He doesn't do things in half measures, does he?"

She had supposed this information existed in a bubble containing only her and Max, but it appeared to be common knowledge. When this got back to her office mate, as it inevitably would, would he try to fire her again?

Evan caught her eye in the rearview mirror. "Max is a superpower unto himself, but feck it, Zoe, we're cognitive scientists. We can match his efforts. If you want to release Darcy as a Regency bloke, you got to stick him in a Regency environment and test him there, too, for authenticity."

"Yes, well, hang on 'til I get my DeLorean out of the garage," she said.

"I have something better."

"Evan's virtual reality system," José added. "It's brilliant."

"Mmm-hmm."

"It's effing brilliant," Laura said. "Zoe, you have to try it."

"Sure, yeah. Sometime." When this project is over and I get to reclaim my life.

"No, now," Laura said.

"Nope, not happening." She looked out the window to signal an end to this ridiculous conversation. What did virtual reality have to do with anything? This was about boys and their toys and whose was bigger.

The car went silent. Everybody seemed to expect someone else to say something.

Evan twisted around. "Think about it. You've got the code. We've got the VR Regency-world model lying around from dead projects. Interfaces are compatible—we saw to that. Only thing stopping you from plugging Darcy into our model and talking to him on his terms, dancing with him, falling into his cybernetic arms, is management."

"Regency world? You mean, like ... Austenland?" she asked, feeling foolish, but it was the first concept that sprang to mind.

"Exactly like Austenland. Big, drafty houses, ballrooms, grouse hunting, fancy gowns, it's all just sitting there waiting. I'm only asking you to try it."

Laura tugged her sleeve. "We're trying to help."

José gave her a thumbs-up.

Another mile of motorway lights passed by before she could figure out her thoughts. She fixed Evan with a glare in the mirror. "You're not into thrash metal at all, are you?"

"Don't know what it is. I'm a jazz guy. Shoot me."

Zoe turned to her friend. "I can't believe you set me up."

"Suck it up, Zoe," came Laura's sharp response. "You know what's going on upstairs with Bob and the gang."

"Yes, but I still don't like being set up. Either ask me straight out or forget about it." She slumped back into her seat, arms folded so tightly that her leather jacket protested.

"Well, we couldn't take the chance," Laura said. "Take Evan here, double PhD in computer graphics and cognition, seven years in VR at Zycorp, three kids at home. And guess what? He doesn't fancy the idea of moving out of London for a new job."

Zoe looked at the back of Evan's thinning hair, surprised at his domesticity. This wasn't a blind date after all. His job was on the line, his whole way of life. His, and those of many others. He wasn't here for fun.

"The shareholders want to shovel the last AI out the door and get on with the business of profit-making," Evan said. "The board can't stand up to them. That's why Harry brought in Mr. Miracle—his last hope of saving AI development, his dream. But Max is clueless when it comes to the real heart of the matter, the thing that will distinguish Darcy from every talking head that came before him—personality, persuasiveness, passion."

"Is he really clueless?" Laura asked Zoe.

She gulped down a lump. The fresh hurts resurfaced. "Totally. He tried to fire me after that scene with you at lunch, remember? He just wants an AI that can make his coffee."

"Figures," Evan muttered.

"Yeah." José shook his head slowly. "What was Harry thinking?"

She peered around at their faces in the semidarkness, intermittent road lights flashing on their eager foreheads. This was a coordinated onslaught for sure—the whole thing a setup from the very beginning—but she was beginning to see why.

"You know there are easier ways of hijacking me."

"Difficult," Laura said. "You're either in Zycorp or sleeping. When was the last time you agreed to go anywhere socially with me?"

There was truth in that. In the year since she'd broken up with Tyler she'd been evaluating her life so hard she didn't notice that others were maybe having fun out there. Trying to achieve something, to be someone, banging her head against the corporate brick wall had cost her the time and effort she should have used for socializing. No wonder her love life was extinct. Tyler's concerts were her only outings of late.

"Exactly," Laura said, reading her mind as usual.

But this was something bigger than her and her paltry complaints. Testing Darcy in virtual reality gave them a whole new feedback loop that would allow them to tune his behavior for situations in any time or place, but especially within the Regency era with all its strict codes of etiquette. Also, being responsible for a body that could interact with these worlds added such interesting dimensions to his character that she was ashamed not to have thought of this herself. She'd assumed it would be too much work to adapt his model to the VR, but the researchers were a step ahead and had already thought of that. A swirl of illicit excitement started low in her stomach. The idea was amazing actually, much more inclusive than her scenarios for Darcy-on-the-phone. She wanted to toss her whole plan up in the air and start from scratch. And yet, something within her was holding remarkably firm.

"Just throwing this out there, but why didn't Harry suggest testing Darcy in VR himself? It seems the best way after all."

Evan twisted back to face the windscreen. "Harry's got no say. We're blocked up with banking simulations, which some people in high places think are more important. It's a battle of resources—and by that I mean server time."

"Wake up and smell the coffee, Zoe," Laura added.

"Don't worry, I can smell it burning."

"Don't be like that. We need you."

"You expect Darcy to miraculously save your jobs, don't you?"

José leaned forward and spoke in his smooth, business-developer voice. "If he does, it won't be a miracle but a masterminded campaign. Look here, Zoe, we can value-add to Darcy by upselling Regency virtual reality packs. This way we have a fighting chance of him going viral and earning us serious cash. Otherwise, there's not a chance in hell."

His logic sank in. Also the disconcerting feeling that there was a distinct them-versus-her vibe going on in the car, as if she'd gone off and donned a prim blouse, pretentious reading glasses and a skirt suit from Zegna.

"You in or not?" Evan pressed.

"I don't know." She picked at the studs on her leather bracelet. "I have to think. Heavens above, let me think."

If she released the code to Evan, because that's what he was really asking for, it wouldn't just be breaking the nondisclosure—it would be setting to flame every legal contract she'd signed in front of Harry and laughing in his dear old face. They were asking her to risk her job, her career for this. But if they were all out of jobs, what difference would it make? Better to go out in a blaze of glory.

"I want to try it out at least," she said. "Please turn the car around."

They whooped in triumph, except for the driver, who shook his head in exasperation.

"Vive la résistance," Laura said.

Tyler would never forgive her for missing his concert, but this was more important. Max would never forgive her for branching off and following this dangerous, illegal path. But who cared about him?

His dog, maybe, if he had one. Unless he was being seriously negligent, and despicably coy, he didn't seem to have a wife, or family, or even a girlfriend distracting him from his narrowly defined mission in life. Not that she cared, of course.

CHAPTER 10

They took a shortcut through the deserted canteen to get to Evan's office. Zoe hadn't set foot in the canteen since the lunch incident with Max, because she wanted to give everyone a chance to forget the whole episode. Scuttling through it at 2:00 a.m. like thieves was fine, however.

"It'll always have to be at night though," she qualified to Laura as they entered the shadowy stairwell. "I can't let this interfere with the normal testing schedule."

Laura looked heavenward. "The normal testing schedule?"

"Yes. Very important to Max."

"Well, you can either stay with Max or join the resistance, where it's really happening."

"Don't worry, I'm fully on board. My point was I don't want him to know about this."

"Sure you can keep it under wraps?"

"Yes, Laura."

When they reached Evan's fourth-floor office, she handed her phone over to the researcher, who accepted it like it was the Holy Grail and plugged it into his desktop computer. She ordered him to turn his back while she typed the password. This final liberty she would not grant him, or anyone.

Evan then led her to a chair and invited her to strap on a lightweight headset and a wrist monitor. With Laura and José watching like kids at a fairground, she was already feeling like a rhesus monkey.

"Don't be nervous." Evan adjusted the headset to fit snugly around her skull. "This is a prototype headset, with peripheral image-canceling and dynamic refocusing of light on a pixel-by-pixel basis. Your caveman brain won't induce nausea. There's also echo and noise canceling on the earphones. Just enjoy the ride. But don't stand up; we're not ready for that. Got it?"

"Got it." Evan had disappeared from view, replaced by pitch-darkness. She swiveled her head to where she thought he might be standing. "If this goes commercial, will people go around wearing it all the time?"

"It'll be even smaller," came his voice, "but yeah, that's the idea, at least in their own homes. We can even do augmented reality, where we project on top of reality when life gets too boring."

She wanted to whip off the visor to ask him more questions, but her senses were already inundated with new impressions, beckoning her to, well, Austenland. All office sounds became muted. She gasped.

"What do you see?" Laura's voice was faint, wafting into the dream, like a distant spirit.

"Okay ... Wow, this is amazing. I'm in some kind of a library room." A delightful scene unveiled before her: walls lined with decorously carved, wooden bookcases housing sumptuous hardbacks with gilded titles. It was late eighteenth century by the looks of it ... Yes, definitely Regency. "Oh, look at the wood paneling over here … this parquet flooring … and these books. Wow, who did all this?"

"Save the questions 'til later," came Evan's faraway voice. "Just try and forget we're here. I'm loading up the drawing room. Wait for it."

Her body went limp in the chair as the virtual scene took over her senses. She was happy to just submit to whatever was coming next. Her breathing accelerated. An airy room unfolded before her with sunlight filtering in through rich, cream curtains. Everywhere she twisted her neck there were elegant soft furnishings in creams and beiges, exquisitely carved furniture and musical instruments—a huge harp, a viola, and an ebonized pianoforte—set upon Brussels-weave carpets. The embossed wallpaper invited her to race over and run her fingers along it. Above her head, candle-tipped chandeliers hung, glittering in the muted daylight.

And the sounds came: The clinking of servants putting silverware on a table in the next room. A dog barked outside. It was springtime. All that was missing were the smells, but she could almost get a whiff of roast beef and carrots wafting in through the open doorway.

"Come, hurry, dear." A svelte blond with complicated ringlets appeared into view, slipping through the doorway in a pale-blue muslin dress replete with white-lace trimmings.

"W-what?"

"Oh, look, your sash is untied." The young woman frowned daintily and lowered her head to do something to Zoe's person. She looked down and, sure enough, she was wearing a similar empire-waist dress. Her own digitalized décolleté, much like her new companion's, consisted of two round spheres pushed into high position, framed in delicate lace. Wow.

"There." The young lady straightened and smiled. She could be a beauty of any generation, endowed with pale-blue eyes that matched her dress to perfection, a pertinent little nose, and bow lips—just how Zoe imagined a Georgiana Darcy to look. Could this really be Darcy's sister?

"You want to look your best for the gentlemen tonight," she was saying.

Zoe, eager to get her bearings, answered stoutly, "Of course. And remind me, dear, who is it we've invited?"

"Oh, you tease." The young woman fluttered her blond eyelashes. "Coyness does not become you. I hope you lose some of that before the evening is out."

"No," Zoe said, not sure what she was agreeing to or how eating would work in virtual reality. And none of this sounded like demure Georgiana from the book. The pull of the imaginary began to wane. She fingered the edge of the visor.

"No, not yet!" a couple of people screeched in unison.

"Very well," Zoe said to appease both the real and non-real audience. She settled back into the chair.

No sooner had she done so than footsteps echoed out in the hallway. The blond woman gasped and scuttled to her side.

Mr. Darcy strode through the doorway. It was unmistakably him—same head, attached to a body that suited him down to the virtual parquet floor he stood on. Her first impulse was to cry out his name and run to him. But sense prevailed and held her firmly in her chair. She waited for someone else to speak lest she ruin the deliciously tense atmosphere they had going on here. Her gaze trailed down his starched high-neck collar, the fitted tailcoat accentuating his broad shoulders and neat waist, the buff trousers, and the polished Hessians. Absolutely perfect.

"Miss Bunsen, Miss Everett." Darcy bowed gracefully. Just like every movie of him ever made.

Miss Everett? Who the hell was, or is, Miss Everett?

"Oh, Mr. Darcy," the young woman, aka Miss Everett, gushed. She even blushed. Yes, a convincing pink blotch spread across her pixelated cheeks. "What a pleasant surprise. We didn't expect you until suppertime."

"My engagement in town was cut short." Darcy clutched his hands in a lovable sort of manner. "I hope I do not disturb?"

It was so awkward, so Austenesque, that Zoe couldn't keep silent any longer. "Why, Mr. Darcy. Won't you join us awhile? We weren't doing anything in particular, were we, Miss Everett?"

The young lady giggled and shook her head.

He walked closer. The movement showed what a well-defined man he truly was. It somehow didn't matter that he was virtual. His gaze was fixated on her as if Miss Everett didn't exist. The look was passionate. Zoe's throat grew dry. Holy crap, this was him, her Darcy, her gentleman companion. He'd come to life in a way that was impossible when confined to a small screen. Here he stood before her with his naughty intentions written all over his face and in every glorious nuance of his body language. He was near enough to touch if social convention didn't forbid it. This was incredible—no, this was far too believable—

Then everything went blank.

Zoe spluttered, coughed. "Hey, turn it back on! Bring him back."

"I just need to ask you a few questions," Evan said. "By the way, your heart rate's gone way up."

She whipped off the headset.

"Easy on the visor. That cost more than your annual salary and mine put together."

"So what did you think?" José asked, his brown eyes eager.

But she needed time to readjust to her senses back in the present, the cluttered office with its harsh artificial lighting, gaudy colors, and lack of any object of beauty. "That was ... *amazing*. I could feel what it was like to be there. It's different than just talking to him on a screen. He became a real person to me, you know? This is ... I can't describe it!"

"So you'd definitely say it looked and sounded like him?" José asked. "Like you'd expect? You weren't in any way disappointed?"

"No! It was incredible. It was like meeting someone in real life that I'd only chatted with on the Internet before, weird and all as that sounds."

"Did it feel realistic when you moved your head?" Evan asked. "No latency? Motion queasiness?"

"Not at all."

"Marketable, would you say," José asked, "to our target group?"

José's use of "our" was interesting. The Darcy project was sucking in more and more people. Who knew how many researchers Evan had mobilized behind the scenes? "He's more than marketable, José. He's damn near perfect."

"Damn near perfect?" Evan repeated.

"Well, it may seem like a small detail, but I thought … um … "

"Yes?"

"I thought he'd be taller."

"Taller? I set him at five eleven. How tall do you want him?"

About the size of Max.

"Mr. Darcy has a 'fine, tall person,'" she quoted. Best to leave it open to interpretation, because the two men standing before her clocked in at five ten, tops.

"Just give me a figure." Evan pulled up a screen of code on his monitor with a long-suffering look. "Metric or imperial, whatever."

"Six one, six two?"

"Okay, six two. Any other requests?"

"No. Where's Laura?"

"She'll be here in a minute," José said.

Laura walked in, beaming. "I can't believe it. The interfacing was seamless."

"Who wrote the script?" Zoe asked. "How does the story continue?"

"Well, your part wasn't scripted, of course," Evan said, "and Darcy was acting spontaneously, too. We plugged in a physical awareness add-on to allow him to walk around in the space, avoid objects, recognize everything, and interact at will, just like all the other personas. You've seen it in the games. Same idea. He was the author of his own story."

Everyone was looking at her.

"Now that you've got a taste, what do you say? We need him, Zoe, if we're to have any chance of making this perfect. You're the only one who can give him to us. I'll only plug him in when you're here."

Evan was pulling out an arsenal of arguments. Much as she wanted to go full in on this, and much as she trusted that Evan was doing it for the good of his whole department, the whole company, she'd never done anything this subversive in her life.

"I-I don't know."

"Zoe, forget the bureaucratic buffoonery for a moment. This is art for art's sake. This is for Darcy."

"He's dead to the world otherwise," Laura added.

And that was the clincher. Dead. Her Darcy. A pile of code sitting unused on the backup hard disks waiting for data rot to set in. The world's most advanced, most lovable AI consigned to obscurity because she didn't have the guts to elevate him into something amazing.

She slapped her hands on her knees. "I'm in. But you're not getting the password. I always have to be present."

"Deal." Evan gave everyone high fives. "Midnight 'til two works for me any day this week."

Late-night coding was no rarity in the building, so this wouldn't garner security's suspicion. She only had to make sure she was always present where her phone was. It was impossible to transfer code to another device without the password, so she would only be lending Darcy out, not giving him away. And she hadn't even broken the nondisclosure, because they all already knew.

"Sounds good," she said.

"And, seeing as we're breaking rules ... " Evan disappeared behind a tall server rack and reappeared with a bottle of red wine. "Bordeaux, some serious vintage this one. Been saving it for a special occasion."

"Your third daughter's birth didn't count?" José asked.

Evan winced. "Close call."

They filled paper cups with the wine. Evan propped up Zoe's phone against a monitor and placed a cup in front of Darcy's face.

"That'll be the next thing," José said. "A cyborg that can drink."

"Let's brainstorm on that," Evan said, "after we drink."

They laughed.

When the last drop had been wrung from the bottle, Zoe rose reluctantly. "It's going to be fun in the office, in all of two hours."

"This is the time we'd be coming home from the concert, if we'd actually gone," Laura reasoned. "Max will expect you to be wasted."

"You'll have to make up some story about the concert though," Evan said. "Damn, we should've plugged you in to the concert scenario as well."

"You've a thrash-metal scenario?" Zoe asked, surprised.

"Heavy metal. Game?"

"No, thanks, I need all the sleep I can get before I face him."

She needed more than sleep in her armory now that she'd joined the dark side. Or the good side. It was hard to tell which. Having to hide her nocturnal activities from Max wasn't going to improve their already volatile working relationship, but it was nothing personal. This was her following her heart to a place he would never be able to reach.

What he didn't know wouldn't hurt him.

CHAPTER 11

Light seeped under the door of P-12 when Zoe reached work two hours and one hot shower later. Perversely, Max was even earlier than usual today. Couldn't he have been late for once and given her a chance to ease into work? Maybe she should bring a couch bed into the office so she could sleep here in the future. Maximize her time. He could hardly be opposed to that.

Max was slouched in his chair, feet up on table, engrossed in a phone conversation, enunciating his words extra slowly. He was probably on with someone in China or Japan. Upon seeing her, he whipped his legs down, bolted forward, and assumed his usual ramrod-straight position. He gave a curt nod in greeting. At least being caught off guard like this seemed to make him less intimidating.

The AI piped up in her earbuds. "Miss Zoe, your rapid pulse of 90 beats per minute indicates a chronic lack of adequate rest. Might I recommend that we perform simple tasks incurring a minimum of conversation? I deduce that this would be your preferred mode of interaction today."

Never had the AI seemed more human, more sensitive, to her needs and desires. Now that she could picture him standing before her in all his finery, taking her hand, his words held greater power. "I appreciate it, Darcy."

"Indeed, madam. It would be my pleasure."

She sat down at her desk, smiling. How could she ever have doubted his ability to be human-like and empathetic? They could stop the tests this very minute and just release him. He'd passed with flying colors. How gorgeous he'd looked in the virtual-reality drawing room last night. Hopefully he'd keep his mouth shut about the whole experience as she'd ordered him to.

"You're wearing a pulse monitor?" Max asked. "How very 2016."

"Ha, ha. Snob." She'd decided to keep it on after yesterday for the hell of it and found that she didn't want to take it off. Not to track calories but because it was a physical bond with her AI. If Max wanted to know her motives, he could come out and ask, because she wasn't volunteering a damn thing.

"Good concert?" Max asked.

"Yeah. Fantastic."

"I suppose Darcy will be demanding to hear Geiger tunes at the next Lucas ball?"

"Oh, you crack me up." She pulled her keyboard closer and tapped in the headline of her fake concert report.

A silence drew out in which he was ruthlessly watching her. "This is the part where you make a sarcastic joke and in your inimitable way tell me what I need to know."

"Yes, well, I don't know what you need to know, Max."

"Should I ask the man himself?"

"No. I'll write up the report, and then you can read it. I'm sure you've better things to do."

"Discussing your scenario was the first thing on the agenda for today, but if you're in a mood about it, then fine, I can wait for the report."

She targeted a vehement look his way, fed up with his permission granting, as if it were required. It was nothing more than a subtle mind trick she would not fall for. But he wasn't even looking at her. With a tiny screwdriver in hand, he picked away at the battery on a phone. A whole array of devices was laid out neatly on his desk. The one he was working on was an ancient gadget, five or six years old. With his rolled-up sleeves and engrossed expression, he looked like a kid with his first Lego set.

"What is that?" she asked.

"Well, on this one, I'm testing how he gets on in fully embedded mode with a clock speed of only 1.4 gigs."

"He won't be fully embedded; he'll always be connected to the Internet," she muttered.

"Maybe. Maybe not. I like to plan for all eventualities. There are still some places in Africa where—"

"All right, all right, I get it." She had nervous energy ready to burn, and she was itching for a fight, anything to off-load the guilt. Sitting here was suffocating. Typing up this phony report was making her feel pretty darn nasty about the whole episode, and she couldn't put her finger on why.

But once she settled down into work she forgot any negativity. She forgot her fatigue. She was too busy refining new test cases for Darcy. Max, meanwhile, fiddled about with a worrying number of outmoded devices that kept spawning on his desk. In their absorption, they both skipped lunch, but she'd unconsciously accepted the generous helpings of chocolate he'd slipped her. The alarming number of shiny wrappers in her wastepaper basket at the end of the day was testament to that. She couldn't believe it was 8:00 p.m. already, and the only thing she'd eaten all day was chocolate.

"By the way, I designed a scenario too," Max said, as he packed up to go. She'd been staring into space, searching for the words to describe a concert she hadn't attended, chomping on a truffle she couldn't remember taking.

"You designed a scenario?"

"Can't have you having all the fun." He handed her his phone, where a ream of text was displayed in neatly formatted blocks.

She took the device, still warm from his hand, and blinked at the screen.

"Don't look so flabbergasted, lady."

"I-I just didn't think you were into this whole scenario idea."

"I'm willing to give it a try."

The heading jumped out at her. "A visit to a nursing home?"

"Yes. Why not? I thought Darcy could help somebody who would benefit from companionship—the old, the lonely…"

"Uh ... huh." What place did Darcy have in a nursing home—a place for sick, elderly people? What on earth possessed Max to suggest testing him out there?

Max's earnest gaze was getting oppressive. She didn't see how she had any choice without giving him a free pass to the moral high ground. "Fine. Let's do it. Next Saturday."

"Great." His mouth curled up to one side. "If you don't mind, would you type it up in the planning, please?"

"Sure." Anything to avoid writing more of this stupid concert report. Truth was, she hadn't been looking forward to a fashion show she'd scheduled for herself and Darcy on Saturday, so it was easy to slot this in instead. But a nursing home? One thing was for sure, she was not going there alone. "You are coming too, right? I mean, it's your idea after all."

"Yeah, of course."

"Even though it's a Saturday?"

"Yep." Something vulnerable in his tone made her look up.

"Good. So you didn't have anything better to do?"

He dropped the device he was inspecting and massaged his forehead. "Seriously, Zoe?"

"Well, that's fortunate, isn't it?" she said. "I hope you've got a car because I don't."

CHAPTER 12

The following Saturday, Max picked her up at eight outside the address she'd given him, to go to the nursing home on South Circular Road. As she climbed into his Volvo, she seemed less tired than she had been in the office over the past week. You could almost say they'd reached a comfortable truce of sorts after the disastrous start. He did his stuff; she did hers. He kept quiet about his meetings with Bob Chadwick, and she didn't seem to want to know. He also didn't bug her about yawning during the day or even, on occasion, falling asleep at her desk.

"Nice car," she said, as he pulled away from the footpath outside her apartment.

"It's the company's. I'm more an Audi man."

"Is that so?" She twisted her head to gaze out the side window.

So she wasn't into cars. She could suggest the next topic then. He drove to the roundabout before she spoke again. "I'm curious. What gave you the idea of a nursing home?"

"My gran died in one last year."

"Oh, I'm sorry." She fidgeted with her handbag.

Her unease couldn't be due to his driving because no one had ever complained about that. "Thanks. It wasn't a bad nursing home by any means, but watching them shuffle around, I couldn't help thinking how these old dears need more stimulation beyond the quiz shows playing in the corner of the room. Problem is, in an environment like that, there's no guarantee you'll find a kindred spirit. She sure as hell didn't."

"That's a pity."

"She brought it on herself." He laughed. "She always was the intellectual snob of the family … and I loved her for it."

She was gazing at him intently, and it gave him the nudge of encouragement he needed to continue. "Anyway, I was thinking, when I heard you talking to Darcy like he was your best friend forever, that, hey, this old-fashioned guy might go down well with the over-eighty set."

"My grandma was the first person I ever saw reading the book," she said dreamily.

"Were you close?"

"Oh, yes. Closer than … Well, I-I shouldn't say that."

He flashed her a look. "Go ahead. I've a complicated relationship with my parents too."

"Mmm."

"What happened with you?" he asked. "Why aren't you close?"

"They wanted me to study law. I didn't. My two bothers did. Then Mother died when I was sixteen."

"I'm sorry."

"Yeah. Cancer."

"And then?"

"I got involved with an artist and skedaddled across the Atlantic to London."

"Tyler?"

"No. Different type of artist."

"Sounds intense. Whose idea was London—yours or his?"

"His. What's your story?" she asked.

"I didn't meet any artists."

"Come on," she said snippily. "I told you."

"All right." He owed her this much. He pursed his lips and released them with a pop. "My father disappeared when I was six. Hardly knew him. I did well in school and got the hell out of there and went to study in Queen's University soon as I could."

"And now?" Her voice was eager. "Your father?"

"No idea." He slammed down the indicator.

She readjusted her position and pulled at her seat belt. "Well, for the sake of our beloved grandmothers, let's hope Darcy goes down well with the old fogies."

He felt a smile forming. She was one of those rare people who knew when it was time to change the topic. "Oh, I'm sure he'll have them swooning."

After parking outside the low, redbrick building off a quiet, leafy street, he led the way to the entrance. She trailed behind like a reluctant school kid on an educational tour, so he waited until she caught up. Through the glass of the inner porch, he surveyed the spacious, communal living room where everything seemed to be happening in slow motion.

"It's nice and warm at least," he said. Her face was right next to his as they breathed against the glass. "And properly designed for dementia cases by the looks of it."

"You did call them beforehand, didn't you?"

"I did." This was their agreement, seeing as it was his idea.

"Right." She rubbed her palms. "How do we attack this?"

He cocked an eyebrow. "We tread in, weapons down. Like this." He walked in.

Two staff members zoomed over to greet him. Sue and Kate were in their forties, and both had an air of rosy-cheeked, wholesome goodness about them. They were boiling kale and ham for dinner, which explained the pungent steam. Zoe hovered in the doorway while they talked. He beckoned her in and introduced her.

"Did you know them already?" Zoe asked him afterward, when they went out to the living-room area.

"No. Why?"

"Oh, nothing."

"Sue and Kate said we should start with Lucy. She's quite lucid, as it were."

She grinned. "Easy to remember."

"She used to be a librarian, so there's a good chance she'll have heard of your man."

"Taking the piss, are we?"

She misunderstood him if she thought that was his design in coming here. To prove his point, he took Lucy's wrinkled hand gently in his and looked deep into her watery, hazel eyes. She seemed receptive to the contact, appreciative even. When he turned around to bring Zoe into the conversation, she backed away a fraction. Okay, not everyone felt comfortable among the elderly. He offered Lucy tea and asked if she needed an extra cushion.

After only minutes of conversation, he had coaxed Lucy's main motivation for living out of her. She wanted to be alive to witness the birth of a grandchild, but she wasn't sure it was ever going to happen. Chances were it had already happened and Lucy had just forgotten, but he happily played along with the charade. Zoe, he noticed, was looking around at the surrounding furniture, seemingly lost in thought.

A nurse came by to ask Lucy about her supper preferences and to hand her some tea. Max took Zoe aside and whispered, "She doesn't know who her daughter is, let alone Mr. Darcy. I haven't the first clue how to bring him into this conversation. Any ideas?"

He followed her gaze around the room dotted with armchairs and slumbering occupants. "We could try someone else, perhaps."

"I don't know." His voice came out more bewildered than he liked. "I guess I wasn't prepared for this. I should've written out the scenario in detailed steps—like you do, before jumping in. I've wasted your time." He huffed out a breath of frustration.

She patted his arm. "Look, why don't we hang around for another few minutes? Darcy might as well pick up stimuli from the environment. The data will come in handy for something."

Buoyed by her positive words and her kind touch, he said, "All right, and I'll go check out Santa Claus over there." He headed toward a man in an armchair who looked like a benevolent Father Christmas in his off-season, playing chess against himself. Unable to secure the old man's attention, he simply took the chair opposite him. Something good had to come of this visit, some tangible result. Otherwise he'd just wasted a Saturday morning for both of them. He couldn't let his first attempt at designing a scenario be a failure.

He heard a cackle from Lucy and, turning, discovered both the old lady and Zoe were staring in his direction—the former chuckling, the latter looking at the floor. God only knew what they were talking about.

Zoe's voice rang out, more loudly. "Darcy, what do you think of Lucy's story?"

"I am most entertained."

So she was getting Darcy in on the conversation. Good.

"Oh, what was that, dear?" Lucy spoke now. "It came from your telephone, I think."

"I hope you don't mind that he was listening in on your story too?"

"Oh, did he hear that?" Lucy sounded pleased, girlish, flirtatious almost. Max had to force himself to tune out their conversation.

He coughed, waiting for Santa to look up from his game, where he'd just moved a pawn to E6. "May I join?" he asked.

Santa glanced up, surprised, then waved at the board. "Be my guest."

"Thanks." Max surveyed the board from black's point of view. It had been years since he played chess. He didn't really have the capacity for thinking the seven moves ahead that were required to become a master. Two moves in advance were enough for him.

When Santa, with a jaunty grin, acquired his bishop within seconds, Max had a better idea. He tugged out his phone, shook Darcy awake, and positioned the camera so that the board would be fully visible. "Come on, Darcy. Chess for you is like the ABCs, right? What do I need to do here to beat Mr. ... ?"

"Dalton," the old man rumbled.

"Would you prefer to finish the game in six moves or in seventeen?" Darcy asked.

Max caught the old man's bemused look. "Any preference, Mr. Dalton?"

"If you must use fancy technology against me, my good lad, then please make it quick."

Max laughed and moved his rook to C5 as Darcy instructed.

During the rapid-fire chess maneuvers that followed, the medley of voices drifting over from Zoe, Lucy, and Darcy sounded like they were making progress in their corner. With Mr. Dalton ruminating on his next ill-fated move, Max turned towards them. Zoe had stopped talking and was looking straight at him, her expression unguarded. Her eyes had a softness that seemed especially for him. His chest filled with a warmth that crept up his neck and numbed his skull with a rare pleasure. He returned her tentative smile with a full-wattage one of his own.

She flinched as if he'd slapped her, and looked away. He waited some seconds for a repeat of that look, but she refused, instead focusing intently on Lucy.

Heart thumping, he swiveled back to look at the chessboard, where the black and cream squares floated before him in a dizzying dance. His fingers pushed pieces mechanically as Darcy dictated, and even that took mental effort. He needed to get his thoughts under control here.

Mr. Dalton took his inevitable defeat in good cheer. "Next time come without the computer," he grumbled after Max declared checkmate.

"I wouldn't stand a chance."

"Maybe if you came without the girl distracting you, you might."

Max conceded with a laugh. He said goodbye to Mr. Dalton, promising to return soon. And he meant it. This place was warm, inviting, and made him feel good about himself, as if his gran's spirit was hovering somewhere near.

Zoe, meanwhile, looked to have gotten herself very relaxed indeed. She was fast asleep, lolling back in the sofa, and, like all the other residents, had a patchwork blanket pulled up over her knees. He stared at her face, angelic in its sleeping innocence, the expressive brows no longer tensed, the lips parted like she was waiting for her dream kiss.

Enough. He stepped forward and tapped her forearm. She sat up groggily, blinking, grappling at the blanket and then pushing back her long, dark hair from her forehead. Never had she looked so cute. She gazed blearily at Lucy, then up at him.

"We should go," he said.

"I can see my future, Max," she murmured, obviously still drowsy. "It's ... this."

"No, it's not." He threw her coat on top of her lap. "Come on, get up." Then he hunkered down beside old Lucy, gave her a quick peck on the cheek, and retrieved his coat and scarf from the chair beside her.

Lucy, in a creaky little voice, declared, "You two make a sweet couple. Are you married?"

"No." Zoe laughed like this was unthinkable. "Not married."

He thrust his hands into his pockets and looked at his feet. *Can we just go now please?*

Lucy continued, "I know. It's not the done thing these days, is it, dear? That's perfectly all right. I told my Julia she was welcome to bring her Brian home any time, even though he hasn't married her either."

"Oh no, we're not even together," Zoe said.

"Nonetheless I agree with you, madam," Darcy declared.

"What did he say?" Lucy tugged Zoe's sleeve. "What did he say, dear?"

"Well, he agreed with you. Though about what, I'm not entirely sure."

"I, too, comprehend a great deal in the notion of marrying," Darcy said.

Lucy beamed a tooth-deprived smile. "I do too, young man. I do too." She pointed at the phone. "I suppose this one's your boyfriend? Aren't you lucky he's interested in marriage? And so polite! I suppose there'll be wedding bells soon?"

"I ... I ... " Zoe stared at her, openmouthed.

Max moved forward to rescue the situation, but then discovered he didn't know where to begin. Did Lucy not see that Darcy was computer-generated? Or was she assuming that the world outside had moved on so quickly that everyone went around dating or marrying cyborgs?

"I am her faithful companion," Darcy said. "To honor and obey."

"Now that's what I call romantic," Lucy said wistfully.

"Uh, well, Lucy, Darcy is ... " Zoe searched Max's face again as if he might have some explanation to offer, but he turned away and set his sights on the door. She could dig herself out if she wanted to.

"Yes, he is romantic," Zoe said to Lucy behind his back. "I never know what he's going to come up with next."

• • •

That had gone better than Zoe had expected. After a round of goodbyes to the staff members, they departed the nursing home in silence. Max was walking so fast she had to maintain a quick trot to keep up.

"My turn to drive," she said when they reached the Volvo. She held her hand out for the keys. Of course he'd never let her drive his spotless company car, but it was fun to push his buttons.

He didn't smile. "I'll drive. You sort this out." He nodded at her phone. "Before it hits the fan."

They got in wordlessly, and he reversed out of the car park, *Grand Theft Auto*-style. It was weird to see him lose his cool like this. Even weirder to speculate what might be causing his fury. The phone became clammy in her hands. "Darcy. Look. I think there's been a bit of a misunderstanding."

"Please put on your seat belt," the avatar said with a frown.

Max glanced over. "Yeah, put it on."

"Okay, okay, you guys." She swung it on. "As I was saying—"

"Miss Zoe," Darcy said in a softer tone than she'd ever heard him use. "I may have been grievously negligent in perceiving your interest in my person, but if your feelings are leaning in this direction, I am much obliged—"

"Darcy, get real," Max snapped. "And what's with the 'Miss Zoe' shit?"

The avatar waited for more, but Max didn't elaborate on his outburst. His fingers drummed a rapid rhythm on the steering wheel even though there was no music playing.

"That's what he calls me now," she said.

"It is entirely appropriate that I express my interest, given Miss Zoe's single status," Darcy added.

"She's already got a boyfriend."

She fingered the dashboard. "Uh, yeah. Actually, no, we split up."

Max turned to her sharply. "When?"

"A ... year ago."

The car swerved wildly to the side. She clutched the door handle.

"Sorry," Max said, staring straight ahead. "Well, look, I-I'm sorry to hear that. I truly didn't know. I thought ... Well, I— Oh, never mind. I'm single too. Huh."

"Yes," she mumbled, unable to look at him. She hoped Darcy wouldn't remark on her burning face or her racing pulse. Just to be on the safe side, she switched him off and twisted the phone around and around in her hands. But that made things worse, if anything, sitting in silence, alone with Max, in this car.

The vehicle seemed too small for both of them. His handling of the gears, the indicators, and the steering wheel became fascinating objects of study, as did the slight tension in his lean, jean-clad thighs as he accelerated. He was studiously avoiding her gaze. She hadn't noticed he was wearing jeans, nor how snugly they fit. And this Aran sweater with its complicated fishing-knot weave and the way it stretched across his shoulders, the way the sleeves were rolled up to reveal strong, capable forearms more suited to toiling on a fisherman's boat than typing at a desk. She hadn't noticed much of all that either ... until now.

"You're staring at me," he said.

"I'm not," she said, looking away.

"I also notice you didn't solve the problem with Darcy."

"I will. Just not here. Not now. I'm not in the mood. But I will do it."

Max looked at her for a second. Again, silence overcame them, and the dreary, suburban North London scenery became absolutely enthralling.

"Here's the thing, Zoe, that I don't get." His voice was composed again. "You're an engineer. You know how difficult it is to make a machine that can talk, listen, react, and move. We're bootstrapping off decades' worth of intellectual property, and only now have we got to the point where we can simulate these things without the world laughing at us for our attempts."

"Skip the lecture, Max. I know."

"So why go on like this, acting like he's going to be hurt or something if you tell him to snap out of it? He doesn't feel. My God, if we'd programmed consciousness and sentience, don't you think we'd be wondering about things other than love?"

"Not really."

There was a pause. "My point is, if you know he doesn't have real awareness, why do you go around taking this softly-softly approach?"

"Max." She patted her chest. "We're selling a product. We're selling to dreamers. Unless we enter the dream ourselves wholeheartedly and test the dream on those terms, how do you expect us to deliver a product that'll allow them to also suspend their disbelief and enter this fantasy?"

"Aha, the truth finally comes out. I must confess, I'm almost disillusioned."

The way he said it cheapened her goal. Or maybe she'd done that herself by not expressing it properly. It made her want to defend Darcy's feelings even more.

"Max, people also love toys, pets, cars, computers, toasters, and all kinds of inanimate things that bleep and whistle and crank out a word or two. They project their feelings onto them. But unlike a toaster, Darcy responds to those feelings in a believable way, like he means it."

"Darcy pays lip service to his feelings because he can't possibly be feeling them."

"And how is that so different from many marriages and relationships today? Millions of people are being conned by other humans in exactly the same way, Max."

"Are you speaking from experience?"

"What? No!"

"When you talk to Darcy, are you paying lip service to your feelings?"

"No." In a way she was, of course. "Okay, sometimes."

"Maybe I'm just in the wrong business after all," he said in a low voice.

Her hand shot out and patted his thigh. "No. You're not." Under her hand a warm muscle clenched even harder. She whipped her hand back again, face aflame.

The atmosphere in the car became supercharged. All conversation stopped. His cheeks had flared up, too, and he stared straight ahead, intent on what was happening on the road ahead. She peered at him from under her eyelashes, glad of his silence as she pretended to be polishing the screen of her phone, but he never once looked her way again for the rest of the journey.

It was just the weird combination of circumstances and the emotional fragility of being around people near the end of their lives, she told herself, people who only differed from her in a matter of fifty years or so. And maybe his sexy, casual look today, his natural way with people, and maybe the great smell of clean leather in here and whatever the hell scent he was wearing, and maybe just the sunshine. Or the moonlight. Even though it was still daytime.

She shut her eyes and nestled back into the soft leather of the car seat. It was just one of those fleeting crush things that could ignite between colleagues due to a mix of circumstances—a moment shared at a stressful time. The important thing was to keep it contained in its little box. Starve it out of existence. It would pass. It had to pass.

CHAPTER 13

Max wanted to drive Zoe back to her house, but she insisted on being dropped at the nearest grocery store to buy dinner. After she'd waved him off at the entrance to Tesco's, he drove the Volvo home, feeling agitated and empty.

One thing was for sure, he'd gotten to know her better, unraveling the first threads in the mysterious tapestry that was Zoe Bunsen. So she was single. Then what was all that business with the deadbeat ex of hers? What was she doing living with the guy and attending his concerts? What did that say about her?

Then again, Tyler was probably a decoy to keep men away. Not a bad policy for a single woman in London who didn't want to be bothered. But a disastrous policy if she ever wanted to meet someone properly. Almost as bad a policy as messing with Bob Chadwick.

After her soft touch on his leg, it had been hard to let her go. She'd paused for a moment before slamming the passenger door shut. Paused as if she was going to say something positive to him, like, "I had a good time." Or even something incredibly amazing, like, "Fancy a coffee?" He could have sworn it was written in her eyes, her dark-green, magical eyes. And of course when she'd said nothing, he'd done the uninterested act, too, and let her go. He should've gotten out of the car and opened her door and reached for her. Touched her. Caressed her milky skin. Would she have been up for it?

Instead, he had this crap with his brother to look forward to. Mal wouldn't take kindly to an ultimatum. He'd bang on about how big the apartment was and how little trouble he was and how hard it was to find a job in London. Or he'd talk about family duty. But there was no way Mal was staying longer than three weeks, and even that was pushing it.

He swerved into his garage and stomped into the house. The lights were on, the door unlocked. Malachi was stretched out on the sofa in the living room, shoes on, scuffmarks on the cream leather, empty beer bottles decorating the table, and an inane TV channel flashing in the corner. The only thing missing was the stench of cigarette smoke, but Malachi had miraculously managed to give it up last year after smoking had become illegal in several first-world countries.

"S'up, bro?" Malachi said. He had the grace to swing his legs off the couch.

"Yeah."

"Good day?"

"Not bad." Max pulled off his sweater, already looking forward to the shower.

"Me and the mates going to The Red Lion at six. You coming?"

"I'll give it a skip." Malachi's mates? No, thanks.

From his satisfied grin, it seemed to be the answer Malachi expected. "Don't worry. I won't be sponging off you for long."

"How do you mean?" Max checked the fridge for beer. A cold one from that six-pack he'd bought this morning would be nice … but not a chance. All gone. He pulled out a carton of grapefruit juice instead and sank against the fridge door, suddenly weary. The thought of Malachi being gone was nice but worrying. He'd planned on setting his brother up with a job, but then his own job became too time-consuming.

"I'm moving back in two weeks," Malachi said. "Home."

"You have a job?"

"I have a job … to do, yes."

"Doing what?" Max knew these "jobs." Contraband peddling. Insurance scams. Creepy protectionist jobs.

Malachi shrugged. "Stuff."

"Stuff you'll be paid for?"

"Richly." Malachi beamed.

"And income-taxed on?"

"Not quite."

"What are you up to, Mal? If it's illegal, you should seriously consider the trouble you've already caused yourself, Ma, everyone."

His brother threw his hands in the air. "First of all you whine like a little girl that I'm dependent on you. Then you whine when I get a job. No pleasing you. Always trying to act like you're the oldest."

"Someone's got to."

"You'll see. I'll make Ma proud, and that'll shut you up. She doesn't even like you. Nobody in the family does. Nobody in the street. You could work a bit on that, so you could."

"I'll bear it in mind." Max bent to clear up the newspapers strewn on the floor. Malachi didn't believe in digital editions or general tidiness.

"Bloody obsessive compulsive." Malachi stood in the doorway watching him for a moment. Then he spun around and walked out.

Max listened for the slam of the front door, and it came a few seconds later. This was an orchestrated exit, designed for maximum impact. Designed to make Max feel bad about something. But what Malachi didn't realize was that after Shauna, nothing Mal did could ever hurt him again.

He surveyed the mess. What if he, just this once, sat down and tidied up later? For the hell of it, he slumped down on the couch like a completely degenerate slob and pulled out his phone. Might as well chat with his artificial friend, seeing as none of the breathing ones seemed to want to hang out.

"Darcy, what do I do? What would you do?"

"What, sir, do you require assistance with?"

"If you had a brother hell-bent on committing crime for money, would you try to stop him?"

"Yes. If it were in my power to do so."

Max rubbed his forehead. "What if it meant leaving a well-paying job?"

"Yes. If it were in my power to do so."

"What if it meant ...oh, I don't know ... leaving someone, someone you ... maybe kind of ... liked?"

"A gentleman must do what he feels is right even at personal cost to himself. Helping one's family is of the utmost importance in life."

"What if I'm not a gentleman?"

"Any savage can follow his desires," Darcy said.

Max switched him off.

CHAPTER 14

Zoe was mid-yawn when Max entered the office at 7:00 a.m. on Monday. She clamped her mouth shut. She didn't want him to see her yawn even if she was dying of sleep deprivation after another nocturnal sojourn into Austenland. Yes, even on a Sunday. That was how dedicated they were.

He had on the navy Zegna suit he'd worn her first day, the one that accentuated his eyes. He was carrying two coffees—in those white-and-pink paper cups from Giacomo's she'd been coveting all last week.

He approached her desk and put a steaming coffee down on her desk. "Latte, full fat, no sugar. Careful, it's hot."

"For me?" she squeaked.

"No, for Darcy."

"Thanks, I'll just go ahead and drink it for him." She smirked and clasped her fingers around the coffee, keeping the cup pressed to her lips so the steam would obscure the color of her cheeks.

"I expect accelerated performance after this."

"Oh, the fine print?" She raised the lid and sniffed the heavenly aroma of high-quality beans. "This better be good then."

"I'm beginning to appreciate the merits of your scenario-based testing," he said, whipping off his coat and scarf. She tried hard not to watch his broad shoulders flex against the back of his blazer as he hung them up. But she failed.

"Really?"

"Yes. Darcy has human foibles that can't be fully eked out with lab tests. I used him to order these coffees in Giacomo's. I pretended I had a voice impediment of some kind, and I got Darcy to talk to the barista to order our coffees." Max ran a hand through his hair. "Well, he got a bit stroppy with her."

"What did he say?"

"She wanted our first names to write on the cups, but of course he didn't see why he should provide those without us being more familiar with her. His exact words were 'until there has been a proper introduction you may refer to them as Mr. Taggart and Miss Bunsen.' Seriously, I had to stand there listening to this crap along with half the café."

She laughed, trying to picture this, and twisted the cup to read the scrawl. "Ms. Bossen?"

"His plummy accent, you know."

"How did she write Taggart?"

"Toghurt, like yoghurt." He grimaced. "I'm never going in there again. And that's my favorite coffee place."

"I'd offer to go," she said, rotating the cup in her hands, "but these babies are expensive."

He peered around the side of his monitor. "Saving for better things?"

"Yes. Well, no. Student loan."

"When did you graduate?"

"Five years ago."

"Any end in sight?"

"Nearly. Actually ... no." Her shoulders slumped. "I'd need a serious raise if I'm going to pay it off any time soon." Or at least a flatmate who actually paid his share.

He wheeled his chair nearer, concern deepening the fine lines around his eyes. "Have you asked for one?"

"God, no." The mere thought of asking Bob for more money made her skin itch and want to peel off and run away.

"Zoe, not asking for a raise by now could, by itself, be seen as a weakness."

"Yes, well, many things could be seen as a weakness around here." Admitting to debt issues, talking frankly to friends at lunchtime, being in possession of two X chromosomes. The list went on and on. "Can we get back to the pressing business of the day here?" She indicated her screen.

"All right, my point was, for all his wonderful ability to fake being alive, the users won't tolerate an AI that gets snooty with baristas."

"Sure they will. That's part of his charm. Let's put it down as a feature, not a bug."

He huffed. "Not a very useful feature."

"He's not meant to be useful. He's meant to be a companion with a certain personality."

"And you like this obstructive, snooty type of personality, do you?"

She felt his keen scrutiny. "Let's not interfere with the traits that are working fine, and instead try to fix the things that aren't," she said in her flattest business tone.

"Like what?"

No way was she telling him about the blackmailing of Bob. She'd sorted that one out herself. "We'll find out soon enough, I guess," she mumbled.

"It's not plannable. It's like shooting blindfolded and hoping to hit the target."

"It's not like we're shooting aimlessly. I do have this scenario plan if you'd only look at the damn thing." She tapped her pen against her screen, which enticed him to come around to her side of the desk.

"What am I looking at?" he asked, towering over her.

She flashed him a look. "My boobs."

"I-I was looking at the plan. Honest." A smile tugged at the sides of his lips. His hand snaked onto the back of her chair, so she made sure not to make the beginner's mistake of slouching back onto it. Spine straight, she scrolled down the plan—a huge matrix spanning several screens.

"Okay—we test these different traits every day and give a score on measurable criteria like alertness, appropriateness, naturalness. While one of us is doing that, the other does crash tests, as you've been doing. At the end of the day, we decide together whether changing any parameters is feasible or not."

When she finally stopped to look at him, his expression had softened. She waited for a reaction. Instead of his attention darting around like a dragonfly as per usual, his eyes stayed on her. A tentative pinkness seeped into his cheeks, exaggerating the amazing contours of his skull. In her current state of half-crushing, she couldn't bring herself to look in those piercing blue eyes for longer than a couple of seconds.

That awkwardness of the car on Saturday descended on her again. The silence begged to be filled with some observation, anything. She turned back to her screen and ran her tongue over her dry lips. "I'm happy to take on the full burden of the scenario testing, seeing as I know what personality the fans are looking for."

"Whilst I skivvy away testing the low-level code for leaks."

"Yes, if you wouldn't mind." Strange it had taken them so long to come to a simple task-sharing agreement in which she got what she wanted—freedom to dive deep. Now that he was being reasonable at last, maybe she could approach him with the idea of the virtual-reality testing and the fact that most of her testing was extracurricular and that there was a whole underground world hidden to him.

He drained his coffee and chucked the cup into the bin, pro-basketball style. "Speaking of powers above, I'm meeting Bob now."

Fantastic. Another meeting that conspicuously omitted her and couldn't serve any useful purpose that she could make out. Max never came back with ideas. What did they do the whole time? Plan golf games?

"Have fun," she said. "Try not to get me fired this time."

He stood motionless in the doorway. He began to say something, hesitated, then began again. "I'm sure you'd find a workaround even if I did."

She didn't like that look he was giving her. Or his tone of voice. What had Bob been saying?

While Max was gone, she got on the messenger and rounded up the other three members of the newly formed resistance movement. "It's gorgeous weather," she said in the four-way video call. "We should meet for lunch outside."

"Outside?" Evan repeated in shock.

"I'm in," José said.

"Yep," Laura agreed. "Pick me up on the way?"

That was the whole point—getting to talk to Laura away from eavesdroppers. They took the long way to the canteen while Zoe gave her an abbreviated version of her trip to the nursing home with Max, minus the weird stuff, but Laura picked up on it.

"Is that why your eyes are so bright this morning, like a lovesick bunny?"

"No, that's just extra sleep."

The golden November sunshine instilled a certain giddiness in her as they traipsed through the secluded courtyard off the canteen, joking and pushing each other into flowerbeds. They ended up sitting on two concrete benches facing each other, Laura and José on one, Zoe and Evan on the other. They ate sandwiches, drank coffee, and planned the next VR session for that night. Purple trellis flowers hung down in languorous loops and scented the air.

"Was it always this nice here?" José asked, taking a slurp of Coke.

"No idea," Evan said. "First time I've ever come out."

"And you've been working at Zycorp how long?" Zoe asked.

"Seven years." Evan looked at each of them in turn. "You know, I've never seen you guys by daylight before. It's kinda freaky. Not in a good way."

They all laughed.

"Hey, Laura, what's this plant here?" Zoe asked.

Laura fingered a purple petal. "Gipsy Queen Clematis. Last flowers before winter. At least I think so. Turn Darcy on so I can double-check."

"Fire away." Zoe handed her the phone. She pointed her face toward the sun. It was great to get away from halogen lighting and feel the real thing prickling on her skin. She half listened to Laura's chatter with Darcy on botanical matters. Soon they switched topics, though, and the subject became more interesting.

"Darcy, how is it having a body in the VR, not just head and shoulders? Do you like it?"

The guys rolled their eyes, but Zoe was keen to hear his reply.

"It is interesting to interface with software that mimics the movements of the human body," Darcy said.

"And do you like Zoe's avatar?"

"Her beauty has been rendered faithfully into the virtual-reality space."

"Thank you, Darcy." Zoe hid a smile in her coat sleeve. She, too, was pleased with her own avatar's face and body. Although she couldn't see them well in live action, she could always watch the replays. And she couldn't deny the chemistry that existed between virtual Zoe and Darcy.

"And what of Miss Everett?" Laura asked. "Do you find her attractive, too?"

"Indeed, I do."

"Laura, don't encourage him."

"Oh, touchy, touchy. I saw you flutter your eyelids at him in the VR last night. I saw you sidle up close to him on the walk to Meryton and engage his opinions on poetry. Poor Miss Everett didn't stand a chance because poor Miss Everett doesn't know squat about poetry and thinks that Miss Zoe just read up on it on purpose to show her up and look good in front of her precious Darcy."

"Hey, it worked. Everett backed off, didn't she?"

Laura gave her a wide-eyed, mock-innocent stare. "Oh, I see. You want him all to yourself?"

"Well, no, but—"

They burst out laughing, everyone falling over themselves, José snorting, Evan heaving and wiping his eyes, and Laura sniggering, clutching her sides. Zoe failed to see what was so damn funny.

"Don't you get it?" Laura asked. "Miss Everett ... She's me! You idiot. Thought you'd have copped that one by now."

"You?" Zoe was horrified. "But—"

"But nothing." Evan stretched his arm across the bench. "Zoe, we're planning a ball. There's soon going to be many more women vying for him, dressed up in beautiful costumes. Better get used to it."

"Oh, you—" Zoe ran over to the other bench and pretended to choke Laura. "You could have been a bit more honest about it. She looks nothing like you."

Laura pushed her away. "There are no rules in this game. And you need some toughening up. When you get him alone, Darcy's a terrible flirt."

Zoe slumped as she resumed her seat. She'd thought her understanding with Darcy was exclusive. True, he'd soon be on the market and any number of females would get their claws on him, but until that time this particular copy was meant to be hers. Hadn't their conversations lately hinted as much?

"Besides, we're working on an Elizabeth."

"Really?" Zoe's head shot up. "Where on earth did you find time for that?"

Evan shrugged. "Massive code re-use. People are ninety-five percent the same. It's early stages though."

"How long?"

"Few weeks for a basic prototype I guess."

"Make sure you keep me in the loop."

"Sure. Oh, bugger," Evan's gaze was directed at the canteen door.

"What?" Zoe shaded her eyes.

"Mr. Miracle. Two o'clock."

"Damn," José said.

"Wonder what he wants," Evan said.

"Zoe, did you let him follow you?" Laura asked.

"No, but he must've anyway. Everybody, just act normal. And gimme that phone, for Chrissake." She whipped the phone from Laura and switched it off.

When a shadow crossed her face, she sat forward and pretended to be surprised. "Oh, Max, hello."

"Hi." He regarded each of them in turn and then came back to her. "Good idea, coming out here."

"Mmm. Did you follow me?"

"No. I was having lunch in my usual spot." He tilted his head toward the canteen. "I looked out and saw people having fun. Laughing. I thought I'd better double-check that they're bona fide Zycorp staff."

José was the first to react. "We thought we'd bend the rules to see what would happen."

"You look like you could do with some sun yourself," Laura said.

"Not to mention a laugh." Max sat down beside Laura and José, who were squeezed together, leaving space on their bench. "Last joke I heard was the 'take as much as you want' vacation perk from HR on my first day."

"Oh, the 'take as much as you dare' perk?" José scoffed. "It's a standard for managers."

"Yeah, well, I won't be taking any."

Zoe examined her fingernails to avoid his gaze. This was weird.

"That's par for the course before product launch," Evan said in a tone that suggested he wasn't warming to him. "What are you? Irish or American?"

"Bit of both, you could say. Twenty-four years, Belfast. Ten, California."

"Explains the accent," Evan said.

"Which did you like more?" José asked.

"California's sunnier."

"California." Evan groaned. "All you can eat, golden handcuffs, and don't forget to freeze your eggs, ladies, before you get too old. I could never work in the Valley."

Laura and José shook their heads, too.

"I'm hoping you'll never have to," Max said. "I've seen your stuff. Greg from AI dev gave me a tour."

Zoe's heart froze. What kind of tour? Had he found out about them?

"I'm amazed at the speed of the graphics rendering," Max continued. "There's no noticeable latency. Even running on a single processor. How did you do that?"

"That would be my software acceleration add-on," Evan said with a little smile. "Patent pending."

"Impressive." Max bit into his chocolate bar. He stared into space, chomping, comfortable in his own skin, his own solitude.

Zoe unclenched her muscles, one by one, and she noticed the others had relaxed too. Evan seemed so at ease that he leaned farther toward Max, probably eager to discuss the ins and outs of his accelerated rendering program.

Sure enough, Evan started yapping. When José got in on the guys' animated conversation, Laura widened her eyes at her.

Zoe scowled and looked away. She still hadn't forgiven Laura for the Miss Everett bullshit.

When the conversation slowed to a lull, Max stood up and stretched his arms out, Adonis-like, in the sunshine. Where, exactly, did he store all that chocolate anyway? She allowed her gaze to linger on his contours, seeing as everybody else was watching him too. It gave her free rein to sexually objectify him.

"Good meeting you guys. Take it easy." And then he strolled off, whistling.

There was a moment of stillness as Max and his whistle remained in earshot. Then they spoke at once, a babble of noise.

"You never told us he was normal," Evan complained.

"Likeable," José added.

"Not at all what I was expecting, personality wise," Laura said accusingly. "You've been keeping us in the dark."

"Shouldn't we tell him?" Evan asked.

"And risk everything?" Zoe asked, amazed at their about-face.

"We're already risking everything," Evan reasoned. "If we got him on our side, we'd be a step closer toward success. I've a feeling he could swing this for us."

"Are you saying I couldn't?" Zoe's stomach plummeted in dismay.

"It's okay, Zoe. We know you're good," José said. "But Max has that—you know, leadership quality."

"Oh, go ahead and tell him then," she snapped. "See if I care."

They raised their eyebrows at her. She scrunched up her sandwich bag and flung it in the bin. "I'm going back to the office before he starts ramming more deadlines down my throat."

Nobody spoke as she left. It was that nervous silence that she just knew would erupt into chatter—or worse, laughter—the minute she was gone.

She couldn't explain to them how spirit crushing this was, to be relegated back to assistant status when she'd been riding the cloud of pride, feeling like she was managing this thing. But with the way things were going, there was a good chance she wouldn't be getting any credit for this.

• • •

Max wasn't in the office when she returned. It gave her a chance to cool down. Her friends had really wound her up out there, but she'd cling to the hope they weren't serious. The fantasy would get her through the next five minutes anyhow.

He didn't stride in until much later. He didn't sit down. Instead of gathering his clothes to go home, he stood against the closed door, considering something. Then he paced to the window and over to her desk, where he stood, waiting. He did look serious.

She removed the pen from her teeth and gave him a "what now?" look.

"There's something not right here," he said. "He heard me out. He still agreed with me. I was hoping … No, just tell me. What did you do?"

"He who? And, while we're at it, what?"

"Bob." Max came around the table. "How did you persuade him to let you keep your job?"

She recoiled. Not this again. "That's none of your business."

His arm was slapped up against the wall, blocking her in with a display of dominance that was totally uncalled for. But her protest died on her lips, distracted by the toned chest straining against his white shirt. His cologne wafted sweetly around him, and her. This shocking nearness, this aggressive stance … He was so different. Her gaze moved north into the collar region and up along the precise lines of his face with its familiar shadows, contours, and fine lines. Dear God, what would kissing that mouth feel like? And what was happening to her?

He leaned in, his face treacherously close. "Zoe, look at me."

"W-what?" She forced herself to meet his gaze.

"Did you offer yourself to Bob?"

"What?" Disgusted, she lashed out with her palm, catching him full against his cheek. The bristles of his beard grazed her fingers. Everything reverted to an eerie slow motion in the shock of what she was doing.

His arm shot out and grasped her wrist, holding it rigid, just inches from his face. To her horror, red finger marks appeared on his cheeks. His glower intensified while his jaw seemed to be doing some complicated gymnastics in the effort to stay shut. She pulled back as far as she could go with his grip holding her, which wasn't very.

Her heart thumped out an insane rhythm. Had she really done that? She'd never slapped anyone in her life. She didn't feel afraid. Just ... oddly exhilarated.

"How dare you?" her voice squeaked out feebly, even to her own ears.

His fingers tightened around her wrist, and her whole body squeezed up inside itself in response—fight or flight, she couldn't tell.

"Look, you moron. I didn't *offer* myself to him, as you so quaintly put it. I can't believe you thought that. It just goes to show what you think of me."

"What then?" he growled.

"If you must know, I blackmailed him, okay?"

His face creased in confusion. "Blackmailed him? How?"

"I found out about some online stuff he was doing with girls half his age, and I confronted him about it. That's the truth of the matter. That's all. Let me go."

She was shaking, but the anger kept other emotions at bay. He looked stricken then solemn. He studied her face for a few long moments, and his grip slackened so she could pull away. Her spine sagged against the wall in relief. He wasn't going to strike back. He wasn't going to do anything.

"Why didn't you tell me this sooner?" he asked in a hollow voice.

"I didn't think you needed to know."

"Of course I needed to know. Don't be crazy. This is important."

She folded her arms. "Why?"

"I'm the one who has to walk this tightrope between you two all the time. You're not making this easy for me."

"Easy for you? Oh, I'm sorry. Who the hell tried to fire me and make my life impossible? But all you care about is your standing with Bob. Your crappy corporate politics. Moving up the ladder."

"Stop holding that against me. Can't you move on? We're supposed to be a team. I thought we were a team. Are we a team?"

"Yes, yes, we're a goddamn team. If that's what it takes for you not to go running off to Bob and firing me, yes, we're a team. Wonderful idea, Max."

"Then let's start acting like it."

"I don't have to listen to this sanctimonious bullshit." She brushed past him and strutted out of the office. Didn't matter that she'd left her purse inside.

She'd pick it up later on the trip to the VR lab. Once she could be totally sure he was gone.

• • •

He watched her go and then slammed his back against the wall. She still didn't trust him, wouldn't trust him, and wouldn't let him in. She was clinging to her grudge like it was protecting her from something.

His hand slid up and down his jaw where the sting lingered. Devastating then, in its suddenness, but strangely pleasurable now. He'd been jolted awake and had nearly lost it for a split second. Only her biting tongue and her hurt, confused face had prevented him from pulling her into his chest and kissing her. It might not prevent him next time. Common sense was losing its foothold, ready to plunge into the abyss.

He picked up her handbag lying abandoned beside her chair and placed it carefully on the desk. She'd need this. Could he run after her? Corner her? Get her to confess she had feelings too? No, desires. *Needs.* Would that work? How did these things ever work? Her hungry eyes gobbled him up sometimes. He'd have to be blind not to notice. But what was he supposed to do about that when she was so hot and cold toward him all the time, so evasive, so tricky, so ... spellbinding?

Well, he'd sit here and wait until her return. By that time, they'd both have calmed down, and they could talk through the whole matter in a rational fashion. Yes, he'd believed her capable of sleeping with Bob, but only because he knew exactly what Bob was like and that it would take something that terrible to persuade him to rescind a decision. He hadn't reckoned on blackmail. But what a blessed relief to know she hadn't done it with Bob.

Still, it was impossible to work. He wandered around the office in a circle. There was more than enough to do on the robustness tests to keep him occupied, but his thoughts were turning wild as he slumped down at his keyboard, scrolling through screen after screen of test results. He stood up, opened the window, printed out his plan on paper, got cold, shut the window again, had a coffee, had some chocolate, called the server guys in the States for some statistics … anything to get her out of his head, but he still couldn't shake the vision of her doing it with Bob. Even though she hadn't.

Where the hell was she now, without her bag? And so late in the evening? She wouldn't have gone anywhere without it. She must still be somewhere in the building. All right, he'd go find her. And then he'd have to wing it and see what happened, because this complication definitely wasn't in the plan.

CHAPTER 15

Zoe hid in the ladies' toilets. Then she told herself not to be such a goddamn idiot, peeped out, and on seeing the coast was clear, tiptoed down to the elevators. The elevator descended at its usual leisurely pace to the ground floor without incident.

She couldn't believe she'd slapped him. A satisfying whack, and then that visceral jolt of pleasure that followed. Her hand trembled in the aftershock. How could he ever think she'd sleep with Bob to buy favor? What did that say about Max's opinion of her? Yes, pretty darn low.

Downstairs in the usability office, Laura's face was flushed with excitement, too. "Are you ready for the ball? We've been practicing the first Royal Scotch Quadrille."

Oh yes, she'd forgotten about the ball. "Max is still in the building. We may have to postpone."

"Are you okay?" Laura asked. "You look a bit upset."

She gave a brittle laugh, not yet able to tell the story. "I-I'm okay. I hope Miss Everett will keep her naughty little paws off Darcy tonight."

"I shall make no such promise." Laura sounded uncannily like her alter ego.

"May the best woman win." José sauntered up to Laura's desk and kissed her forehead. "You got me on your dance card, too, babe? I'm going by the name of Mr. Wilson this evening, and I am far more dashing than Mr. Darcy."

"Of course you are, sweetie, but don't you dare step on my toes again."

How at ease they were with each other after barely two weeks of going out, gelling almost without being aware of it. No power struggle, perfect complicity, effortless, like Mr. Bingley and Jane Bennet. Had they any idea how lucky they were?

"Doesn't your boyfriend care about this little side affair you got burning in the nineteenth century?" she asked Laura, just to stir things up because their complacency was nauseating.

"Well, she lets me hang out with Zorda the Amalian warrior princess." José flexed his biceps to indicate, presumably, that the cyber princess had strength in spades.

"We've an open relationship when it comes to cyber beings," Laura explained.

"Does this mean you've been given permission to jump Darcy's bones?"

Laura put on her mock horror face. "I would never be so dumb. That would relegate me in Darcy's eyes to utter filth."

"I trust Miss Everett will remember that."

"I can still mess with him though." Laura grinned.

"I think I'm going to enjoy this." José rubbed his palms. "When do the games begin?"

"Max is still in the building," Laura said.

"So?" he asked.

"Too risky."

"Oh, it's still a big secret, is it?"

"Yes, it's still a big secret."

Moments later, Evan arrived, jabbing at his watch. "Hey, folks, what are you all doing down here? Let's get the show started."

"Max is—" Zoe began.

"Right here," a familiar voice came from behind Evan.

Her jaw slackened. *Huh?*

Max sauntered through the door, looking sleepy, carrying her purse. "I believe this is yours." He took her hand and looped the handles around her wrist, chivalrous as you please.

She clutched her purse to her chest and backed away from him, crushed with embarrassment, anger, confusion.

"Some secret," José said.

"Look, I bumped into him, he was looking for you, and I told him." Evan impatiently swiped hair away from his eyes. "He knows, all right? Can we move it along here please?"

"But—" She rounded on Evan, furious at his betrayal. "What right had you?"

The calm expression on the researcher's careworn face told her that no drama-queen antics were going to intimidate him. The guy had three daughters after all.

Max's expression was also one of composure. Again, irritating in the extreme.

"And you're okay with this?" she threw at him.

"Zoe, this deception is costing you and me more than you know. Just believe I'm on your side, no matter how crazy it seems. Please?"

She hung her head. Yes, she'd deceived him. But for his own good. For Darcy. For the project. It was the only way. Going the honest route meant taking him on, taking on the entire chauvinistic company, and being thwarted. She'd needed guerrilla tactics, goddamn it. What part of that didn't he get?

Now that he'd supposedly joined their side, she couldn't deal with him. Once again, the control had been snatched from her hands. She made sure to keep Laura engaged in a one-on-one conversation until they reached Evan's office, just to avoid having to talk to Max. She also made sure they rode in separate elevators.

Inside the VR office, Max prowled around like a curious panther in his new home, fingering the equipment, picking things up, asking a bazillion questions. The guys humored him, just like they had at lunchtime. They seemed overeager to please him, and it took ages before they were ready to get going, for all Evan's earlier impatience. "You're wasting time," she wanted to yell.

When it was finally time to start the ball scene, Max wanted to plug his own phone into Evan's VR setup, presumably to check that nothing got copied over without a password. Couldn't he trust her to have upheld the security of the project?

They stood in a semicircle around Evan's desk as the researcher tapped some final commands into a dialog box. "I know you're dying for the ball to start, but let's try a less complex outside scene first, with fewer people," Evan said, whirling around to face Zoe. "And you gotta move your ass in this one. We're taking it to the fourth dimension, babe. Come, follow me."

He held up arm-length opera gloves riddled with sensors and a pair of ankle bracelets. "Yeah, we just got these sorted out. A little something the kinetics team's been working on in their spare time. You can control your avatar's limb movements." He beamed. "Come on, try it out."

"Oh, cool." She banished her annoyance to the back of her head and pulled on the black gloves, which enveloped her arm right up to her t-shirt sleeves. She stretched out an arm, pleased with the snug fit. So much more advanced than the simple wrist monitor she'd been wearing.

Evan approached her with ankle sensors, which were simple Velcro-strapped rings.

Max pushed forward. "Allow me." He knelt down on one knee in front of her. She watched the top of his thick, chestnut hair glinting under the lights and tried not to think about how running her hands through the shiny waves would feel, if she were to lose her mind and actually do it. When his fingertips grazed the small indentation behind her ankle she nearly kneed him in the face in shock. Then she wanted him to keep doing it.

"It's a bit fiddly," he said.

"It's Velcro," she said. "What they put on shoes for four-year-olds."

He moved to the other leg. While he worked, his fingertips teased her other ankle several times just under the hem of her jeans. She didn't want to enjoy it, but she did. She didn't want to imagine that gentle caressing on other parts of her body, but she did, and her whole body went rigid with anticipation. Was this his way of torturing her in retaliation for slapping him?

He straightened and caught her eyes for a moment. Although he wasn't smiling, his eyes glowed with happy pleasure. It wasn't that he looked younger but as if life had been a bit kinder to him. No doubt her own fluster was written across her face, but she'd gone beyond hoping to conceal it. Her chest rose and fell in perfect time with his, which meant—

Evan brushed between them. "Sorry to break this up, folks, but she needs a room—a rather special room."

Max broke off to the side. Evan led the way through the desks, beckoning her to an empty space down the far end of the VR office, about ten square feet. Sensors had been duct-taped into the ground at regular intervals around the square perimeter of the area. She saw it all through a haze and tried to concentrate on what the researcher was saying.

"This is our VR mobility patch. If you move out of the boundaries, it'll warn you, don't worry. Darcy or someone may lead you to a bench, so do trust him. It'll be in the right position for you to sit down." Evan patted a chair in the middle of the space with sensors built into it.

"All right," she breathed. Putting on the headset was excruciating with Max watching her every move. But once Austenland popped up inside her headset she got sucked in.

The party was preparing for a walk around the grounds of Hewell House, property of Sir Everett, Miss Everett's father, before the ball. A fluttering young maid in a white blouse and black skirt handed her a bonnet. She moved her hand to accept it and ... it worked. Her avatar's entire arm appeared in her view, moving as she did, and grasped the bonnet between her fingers. It added an extra dimension of reality.

"This is so cool," she muttered. "I mean, thank you, Nancy."

She took a tentative step forward, and the world moved with her. She'd never used her legs in the VR before, and the scenarios had taken that limitation into account. But now she had the freedom to walk, skip, dance. She took a few more steps and did a swirl. "This is fabulous."

The maid simpered and ran off.

"I'm gratified that you decided to join us." Darcy sidled up, looking spiffy in a full, formal dance suit.

"Oh, Mr. Darcy," she said. She peered beyond him to where Miss Everett was smiling and waving saucily, the little minx. With her dainty bonnet, little white kid gloves, and lemon-hued silk dress, she looked like a right little Becky Sharp ready to get her clutches on the most eligible man around. At least now that José was here to chaperone Laura, Miss Everett couldn't misbehave too much, even if she had an equal ability to prance about in all her finery.

The Hewell House garden glistened before Zoe in the early evening mist, and she found herself strolling through it with Darcy. At some level, she knew she was walking around in a small circle in real life, but it didn't feel like it the way the grassy terrain unfolded before her with every step. She kept her distance from her gentleman, not only because social convention demanded it, but also because she didn't want to ruin the illusion by having her avatar's hand slice through him like a ghost. And maybe because someone else was watching this scene play out.

Zoe felt a tug on her arm. She whirled around to see the matronly housekeeper of Hewell House, Mrs. Beardsley.

"Ma'am, is it true that you have no fondness for rabbit stew, for I heard it just now?"

"Um, well … no, I'm fine with that." It wasn't like she was going to have to eat the damn stuff.

The housekeeper's rosy cheeks lifted in a smile of relief. "Oh, thank goodness. Cook was much in distress to think that she may have to prepare a different dish."

"No, I'm sure that's not necessary, Mrs. Beardsley." Zoe smiled kindly. "Tell Cook it's fine."

"The master loves his rabbit stew, he does, especially when Cook prepares it the French way."

"I'm sure." Zoe's attention followed Darcy, who had started walking off somewhere.

"But Mr. Upton, when he dined with us here last week, he did not like it at all. And Cook had prepared an extra fine dish, if I may say so myself. No, he said it tasted like foul mud. That was a disaster indeed. Mr. Everett was most displeased. Yes, it put him in bad humor for the entire evening, and nothing could make it right."

"I'm sorry to hear that."

"I shan't think Mr. Upton shall be gracing our doorstep for many a month."

"No, indeed. I'm sorry, but I really must go to my friends, Mrs. Beardsley."

"Oh." The housekeeper flapped her apron at her. "But do not let me detain you."

Miss Everett, meanwhile, had lured Darcy to the end of the garden. Three quick strides brought Zoe within hearing distance of the pair in the grove, and she overheard the words, "Miss Everett, I have been grievously unaware of your interest in my person, but if your feelings are leaning in this direction, I am much obliged to you."

"What?" she called out. "That's what you said to me. The same words, Mr. Darcy. How could you?" She stamped her foot, producing the realistic sound of leather slapping against cobblestone path. She was no longer acting.

An intrusive message blinked on the screen. "Miss Everett is offline." She'd vanished in a puff in exactly the way real-life rivals never did. She was going to strangle Laura. She'd set her up with that rabbit stew diversion.

"Darcy, I thought you had feelings for *me*."

"Of course I do."

"But why then did you sneak off with Miss Everett and speak sweet nothings with her? You were supposed to be accompanying me to Hewell House."

"You were otherwise engaged. I am predisposed to find any individual with whom I am speaking pleasant."

"Since when?"

"I do not recall a time when I was not."

"And love?"

"I am afraid the question is too ill-defined."

"Let me rephrase then. Did you love Elizabeth Bennet?"

"Yes, with all my heart."

"Do you love me?"

"Yes, with all my heart."

"And Miss Everett? Do you love her, too?"

"Yes, with all my heart."

She huffed. A hard-coded answer. "With all your heart. What does that even mean to you? You don't have a heart, do you?"

"Indeed, this feature is currently inoperative."

"So, what does the word 'love' mean to you?"

"It is a semantic placeholder."

"Well, that's just wonderful." She ripped off the headset and shook out her hair. It took her several breaths to come back to a sense of reality and several more to calm down. The AI couldn't go around saying stuff like this. It destroyed the dream. The customers would demand their money back.

She caught Max's eye from across the room. Great. Why couldn't he have shown up for one of the VR episodes where everything had gone swimmingly, like a final chapter in Jane Austen? No, he had to make his guest appearance on the one occasion when everything was falling to pieces.

"Darcy, new rule," she said. "When you encounter your user, the person who buys you, or first installs you, that person is the one you love. If they admit any attachment to you, or even hint of it, then you must prefer that person over all others. You must be prepared to do uncomfortable things for the sake of that person, and you must adore that person to exclusion of all others. Sure, you can like other people but not love them. Even if you don't feel it, even if it's not programmable, you gotta fake it in everything you say and do. Got that?"

She paused to catch her breath after her outburst. It was easier to scold the AI when he was just a head and shoulders on her phone. He seemed to have been cowed into silence.

"An interesting notion of love." Max came up beside her. "Surely he should be able to choose, if it's to have any value at all?"

"You'd leave it up to chance? Well, I wouldn't. What if disappointed users want their money back?"

"Then they don't deserve him."

"Nobody deserves him. But if we're selling him off at £299 a pop, let's not disappoint the undeserving public. Honestly, don't you have the first clue about customer satisfaction?"

"I've got you looking after that side of things."

"Giving in so easily, Max? What's wrong with you tonight?"

He held her gaze for a second too long. "This has gone way beyond my control."

She fingered the headset. "Don't worry. I know what I'm doing. It'll sort itself out at the ball."

CHAPTER 16

In the splendiferous hall of Hewell House she danced to Mozart, the fourth and fifth Royal Scotch Quadrilles, and the Strasbourgeoise Cotillion. Luckily, dancing in virtual reality was a lot more forgiving than in real life. She didn't have to do the steps accurately to get caught up in the frenzy of swirling bodies, where everyone seemed to end up in the right place. And if anyone stepped on her toes, well, the offending feet were weightless.

It gave "dancing with herself" a whole new meaning as she held her body stiffly in shape, twisting around with avatars. Everything looked perfect, but it didn't change the fact that she was still clutching onto thin air. The sooner they invented cyborgs, the better.

She sat down, deflated, after four reels.

"I imagine you are fatigued." Darcy took the chair to her left.

She smiled, gratified that he'd noticed. "I'm fine. Just need to catch my breath."

"Indeed, this activity is pointless if we cannot hope to strengthen our bond by it."

"Um ... yeah."

"After my unwise behavior with Miss Everett, I feel compelled to express my affections toward you more meaningfully."

"That's all right, Darcy."

"I mean, Miss Zoe, to hint at how ardently I feel for you."

A heaviness descended on her. "Please. This is not the night for any crazy stuff, Darcy. I know I lectured you earlier on love, but I didn't mean this. Not here. Not now."

"It will not do. I must express how I feel."

Her irritation rose again. "Really, Darcy. I hope you're not thinking about a proposal?"

As she uttered the word "proposal," the song faded out. A bunch of people swung around, openmouthed.

"Did he just *propose?*" a girl in purple squeaked. "Everyone, Mr. Darcy proposed to Miss Bunsen!"

"No!" Zoe jumped up from the chair. "Tell them, Darcy. You didn't, right?"

"I may not have executed the intended action, but certainly the sentiment echoes my aspirations."

The crowd *ooh*ed and *aah*ed. Good enough for them, apparently. Glasses clinked.

"But wait!" Purple Dress cried. "Did she accept?"

Silence fell again. Avatars in cyberspace and employees in the lab were hanging on her next words. She had no option but to yank the plug. "All right, folks. It's a private matter. There's no way I'm making any kind of statement here. Please go back to your dancing."

This produced a collective groan. But within seconds, the music swung up again, and people returned to the business of having fun. Zoe gripped her fan so hard she was surprised it didn't shatter, and, of course, flapping it wildly didn't help to cool her face. Half of these avatars were real employees immersed in their experiences either in this very lab or in cubicles spread out over the eight-floor building. The other half were bots. Quite possibly, other little trysts involving humans and cyber people in various combinations were playing out in the very same ballroom.

Darcy said in a low voice, "Let us discuss this matter when we are alone."

"Not much chance of that." She tugged off the headset, now clammy, dumped it on the chair, then ripped off the gloves and ankle sensors. There were a few new faces, other researchers Evan must have let in on the game—she'd have to ask him about that—but Max was nowhere. Someone was playing the music from the ballroom on loudspeakers. She needed to get out of here. The balcony door was the nearest exit, so she marched through the cubicles in that direction.

"Wait, where are you off to?" Evan called after her.

"I need air."

"Can I talk sense into Darcy?" Laura asked as she brushed past her.

"Knock yourself out. Maybe he'll propose to Miss Everett, too."

She opened the door to the balcony, glad to leave the noise behind. Outside in the cool, damp November air, she sank down onto the wooden bench to the side before she realized she wasn't alone. A man emerged from the shadows. So much for her moment of solitude.

She nodded to him. Then he came forward into the light, and she realized it was Max.

"What are you doing here?"

"Same as you." He cocked his head at the party scene inside. "Taking a break from the virtual."

"How much of that did you see?"

"Enough to figure your evening went from bad to worse."

"Yeah. I wanted to strangle Darcy with my ribbons."

"Yeah."

"I guess I wasn't expecting a proposal."

He laughed softly. "Me neither."

"I expected more restraint, more playing hard-to-get." She sighed. "It's like we're back to the drawing board. He's never meant to propose but always to skirt along the edge of its scintillating possibility. Think what it would mean if he proposed like that to his users in the first week ... in the first day! They'd write him off as a nutcase and lose interest. What a fiasco. I'm so disappointed in him."

Max moved into her line of vision and stood before her. Caught off guard, she drank in his full stature, the confident set of the shoulders, the way the light caressed his cheekbones, his forehead, his chin. He was flesh and blood, incredibly real, and, yes, shivering, but trying to suppress it.

"I liked to watch you dance," he said, shyly.

She smiled down at her knees. "I know I must have looked ridiculous, clutching on to thin air. These VR kits should really be restricted to the privacy of one's own home. But I'll suffer for my art and look like a fool. I don't mind."

"You didn't look like a fool."

There was another pause, this time uncomfortable. Max looked to be at a loss as to what to do with his hands. He sank back against the wall and then ran a hand through his hair, which shone golden in the dim light.

She chuckled. She couldn't resist. "What's this? Your attempt to be brooding?"

"Oh, is it working?"

"I get enough of that with ol' Darcy in there. Don't you start too."

He grinned and, quick as a flash, came to sit down next to her. She remained in her hunched position, careful not to let her fingers gripping the bench touch his, because the effect he was having on her by sitting right there was eerie enough.

She stood to dispel the strangeness. In three hollow steps she reached the balcony railing and clutched on to it. With her back to him she gazed out over the twilight sky with its billowing pink-gray clouds drifting over Tower Bridge. "But I'm worried," she admitted to the semidarkness. "About the launch. About everything."

"Why didn't you—?"

"Why didn't I what?" She swirled around. What nugget of brilliant advice was he going to hurl at her now that she'd admitted a tremor of doubt? But, oh, he was much closer than she'd anticipated—a solid, self-confident presence blocking her view of the VR lab, giving her something so much more real to look at.

No answer. His jaw seemed to clench, his eyes seemed to narrow. But then as he looked up again, the light fell on his long lashes, softening his look.

"Why didn't you tell me about the VR sooner?"

"I thought you wouldn't like it. But I won't lie to you ever again. I only had the best intentions of the company in mind. I want Darcy to be as real as possible. I'm actually glad you know now. I was starting to hate all this sneaking around." She was babbling because his face was so near.

"I mean, when do you even sleep?"

She spoke into his chest. "When you've lived with a rock star, you train yourself not to need much."

"Why go to such lengths when we've so little time as it is? You could spend those insomniac hours getting through more scenarios."

"It's worth it, Max. Darcy enjoys it. I'm finding out a lot about him."

"How do you know he enjoys it?"

"Well, I don't, of course. Not really. It just *feels* like he does because he becomes more alive when he's moving about, more animated."

"It sounds more like *you* enjoy it."

"That too. I believe that in some circumstances a relationship with an AI could be as fulfilling as one with a flesh-and-blood man."

His eyes held a spark of something dangerous. "Fulfilling ... in all aspects?"

"All that matter. Maybe I'm just not wired up the same way as most people, but for me, the intellectual is far more important than the other needs. Brain candy." Oh dear, babbling again.

He leaned in even closer, using his height against her—she was forced to tilt her head upward to maintain eye contact. "If that's the case, then why do you feel the need to give him arms and legs and a physical presence? Surely, a talking head on a flat screen would be enough for you. Why are you getting excited when you see him in his tight breeches?"

"I ... Well ... "

"See? You won't be happy until it is what it is."

She could scarcely breathe her heart was hammering so hard. "D-don't talk in riddles, please."

"I could speak plainly if you wanted me to." His eyes were swallowing her up.

Something compelled her to place her palm flat against his chest in between the lapels of his blazer. His skin under the silk shirt was warm and taut. Instinct told her to pull her hand back, but she found that it wouldn't budge, glued to this chest.

His brows flickered, and he looked down at her hand. Inside, the music had switched to a slow, plaintive melody, one she liked but hadn't heard in a long while. Then his gaze met hers, long and intense.

"Dance with me," he said.

She nodded, not sure why, but she suspected it had something to do with the way he was looking at her, like no man had done before, and the fact that there was a warm, beating heart underneath her palm as opposed to thin air.

He adopted a classic ballroom pose with his hands open, waiting for her, his steady eyes devouring her face. She signaled acceptance by removing her hand slowly from his chest and pressing the tips of her fingers onto his. His fingers clasped hers, and he swung her in a graceful arc into the starting position of a slow set. A modern slow set.

His hand snuck around her waist and pulled her in. His chin nestled against her cheekbone, and she got lost in the clean scent of his familiar aftershave and the giddy sensation of being engulfed by a powerful male body. It was as if a dashing stranger, not Max her stuffy colleague, had caught her up in his arms, trapping her so that she couldn't move her head without nuzzling him, more of an embrace than a dancing pose. He led with ease, in no hurry to go anywhere or to prove anything, and in perfect time. Every resistance melted into the dancing embrace as she pressed her cheek into his jaw, letting him take the weight of her troubles.

No words were necessary. His hips moved in slow, rhythmic union with hers as her agitation ebbed away with each gentle shifting of their weight from one leg to the other. She imagined his body communicating the sweetness she craved, that she was the most desirable woman alive for him, that he'd found his match in this very ballroom. His moves seemed directed toward her, cautious and yet demanding. If she could start this evening all over again, her dance card would have his name on it for each and every dance.

He turned her around in a private, tiny circle. Time warped back in on itself as if to say this should have happened before. Her fingers found their way around his broad upper back and up to his neck, where she clasped them together, capturing him, drawing him in. His breath sharpened against her temples. The stubborn curves of his lips hovering over hers became her only reality, and the tension in her jaw released. He responded by leaning in, bearing his forehead down on hers, making his intentions clear. Her head was buzzing.

He held both her hands, as if he wanted to communicate "I'm here." He brought her closer. A flash of irrational fear shot through her, fear of ever losing this, which had not yet begun, this, which would have been unthinkable just a week ago. But then a jumble of other emotions crashed in—happiness, amazement, awe. Max moved his hands to her waist and trailed his lips down her nose, his breath tickling her. Her eyelids drooped in sensory overload, and his mouth captured hers in a desperate way. Pressing back equally hard with her lips and tongue, she poured a lifetime's worth of longing into him because she knew he could take it. As she stood there, clutching his waist, reality slipped away. Moving against his body, she got lost in the fabric of time.

She had no idea how long they stood there kissing, swaying to music that no longer could be heard. But now she could hear voices. Voices coming nearer. Reality returned to her focus, crowding up her brain. She broke off, gazing up at him in confusion. Was this actually happening? He was leaning into her again when the door behind them opened. Laura and José bustled out.

She leapt away from Max, but the shock on Laura's face was plain.

"Oh my God," Laura breathed.

"Guess we're not the only ones," José said.

Max's arm encircled her shoulder. "Let's get out of here."

CHAPTER 17

They managed to walk in semicomposed fashion past security at the main desk, but the second they were outside, Max drew Zoe into a tight embrace. What had just happened? No, he wouldn't question it.

He kissed her again. Her soft lips gave him everything he'd dared to hope for, and so much more. This night was magical. Yeah, even in this dreary parking lot, huddled against the side of the building, staring out at the traffic in the drizzle, he could not be a happier man.

"Wow, Iceman, you look cold," she said, laughing. "I'd offer you my coat except it's too small and cerise pink."

"I'll take what's in the coat instead." He pulled her into him. "Let's grab a taxi?"

"Are we going somewhere?"

"My plan was to escort you home. And then ... " A kiss was just a kiss. She could back off. She should back off. He didn't want her to, but the possibility was there.

"Yes, I have coffee." She grinned in an incredibly cute fashion. "Tons of it. Or maybe we try yours?"

"Let's try yours." He brushed back the hair from her forehead and leaned in to kiss her so she'd forget that whole idea. Introduce Zoe and Malachi? Not on your life.

When the rain trickled down between their noses, she gasped and broke off. "Why don't we ask Darcy to grab us a ride?"

"Good thinking, Miss Bunsen." He pulled out his phone. "Darcy, get us a car, please. Taxi, Uber, whatever's near. Got it?"

"Of course."

"Thanks, Darcy," Zoe called out.

Just as he switched off the phone there were rapid footsteps behind them. He turned to see the unwelcome figure of Bob Chadwick.

Oh, fuck no.

"Max." Bob raised his massive golf umbrella to peer at Zoe. "And Zoe Bunsen. Well, well, what a surprise." Bob's sense of triumph was palpable even through the torrential rain.

Max forced a smile. "Hello, Bob. I see you're working late, too."

"Yes, I was going home, and then I thought I heard a commotion on the fourth floor. So I came back to inspect."

"And are you finished inspecting?"

"Hmm, I found researchers up to no good, as I'm sure you're well aware."

He shrugged. "Working overtime, I guess."

"I don't suppose you'd know anything about that?" Bob's gaze had drifted to Zoe.

Max stepped forward to block his boss's view of her. Zoe would be just the type to shout in Bob's face that it was none of his business, and he didn't need for that escalation to happen. "We were down in the server room, checking the statistics on the regression tests."

"Server room—brrr, cold. I hope you managed to keep warm."

"We didn't hang around." One more provocation or snide comment and he was going to bash this guy's face in. He was way out of line. Was he always like this with her? If so, it was understandable why she'd felt compelled to blackmail him. She should have done worse.

"Well, Max." Bob jiggled the umbrella, sending a shower of drops into his face, as if he weren't wet enough. "Good that I bumped into you because I did have some matters to discuss. I trust Miss Bunsen will find her way home?" He directed his sneer at her. She, in turn, looked like she was going to bite his head off.

But Max had to ride it out. Bob was their boss, and he had his connections. He could fire either of them on a whim and find some way to justify it. No matter how much this man provoked them, they had to play it cool. Max looked pleadingly at Zoe, hoping she'd understand and cooperate.

She didn't intercept his look but flung around and stomped off, splashing through a puddle as if she hadn't seen it. Without as much as a backward glance, she opened the wrought-iron gate with her security badge and disappeared into the street.

He clenched his fist in his pocket as the rain streamed down his face.

"There goes trouble," Bob remarked.

"How's Angela?" Max asked, glad to remember the name of Bob's wife.

"Yeah, fine."

Bob drove him to a pub in his BMW i21, which had a good AI assistant inside that kept Bob amused. Max hated every minute of the drive. He kept revisiting Zoe's dagger-throwing gaze as she disappeared into the darkness. It was tempting to drop everything and run to her. But she'd be at home by now, dry and warm, possibly laughing about the experience with her ex-boyfriend slash flatmate or whatever he was.

Inside the pub, after the bartender got their orders, Bob got straight to the point. "I know what's going on, Max. The whole company's playing with it."

"Just the research team," he lied. José and Laura weren't research, and some of those other faces he'd seen watching the ball were finance, if he wasn't mistaken.

"Her doing, I suppose."

Max declined to answer.

"You should keep a tighter rein on her."

"She's not an animal."

Bob slid him a look. "Maybe you're too easy on her."

"I'm not her manager."

"Not officially, but you're the one in charge, I thought."

"She's self-motivated. She's more dedicated than any employee I've ever worked with, and that's saying a lot."

"Yes, but all the effort in the world in the wrong direction doesn't help us."

Bob's words were reasonable on the surface, but there was an ugly undercurrent to this. "It might. She's totally competent. She's understands AI better than I do, and I believe her plan has merit."

"And she's got you wrapped around her finger."

"I wouldn't say that."

"Not to mention other parts of her body."

"Bob, please." He didn't have to listen to this even if it were true—well, partly true, certainly in his most recent fantasies.

"Look, Max, cut the bullshit. I thought you wanted to succeed."

"Define 'succeed.'"

"Well"—Bob's gaze roved over him speculatively—"once this nonsense with the AI is over I want you on my team. The position of senior director of enterprise products is opening up soon because of Jason Lee's retirement next month. I can see you filling that role."

What could he answer? This was a good offer. They could always have a big debate about the company's future direction, but now was not the right time. On the other hand, he had to get back in Bob's good books somehow.

"We'll finish as planned, Bob," he said. "And I feel that Zoe should attend our planning meetings." It was high time she saw the reality of these meetings—the frustrating hours spent haggling for resources from someone who was supposed to be supporting him but was actually doing the opposite.

"I've a better idea. We let her go."

"No!"

"Go with your original gut feeling, Max. It's simple. She broke the nondisclosure. The whole company and their mothers know about the AI. We've been put in a position where we'll look weak if we don't launch, even if we discover a fatal flaw the day before release. I've said it once, I've said it a million times: we don't need that kind of pressure, and Harry agrees with me."

"I do, too, on that point." Max used as placating a tone as he could muster.

Bob settled back on the couch and eyed him warily. "I'm glad you see it that way."

"Yes. And I take full responsibility for that pressure."

"Don't stick up for her. She flat-out blackmailed me to get her job back. Did you know that? That AI planted filthy lies about me just so she could wrangle her job back. How low is that?"

"Yeah, the blackmail was despicable."

"I'm a happily married man. Ask Angela."

Bob was going to play that game, was he? The victim. Ten out of ten for creativity. His acting skills weren't too shoddy either.

"I need that information erased from the AI, or else she gets it," Bob continued.

And there it was. The Faustian bargain. As good as any he'd be getting tonight, that was for damn sure.

"I'll handle it, Bob."

"Do I have your word?"

"You do."

Bob raised his glass. "Glad to hear it."

Max drank the beer in angry silence. Zoe and he had made logs of every change they'd ever made to Darcy. Those changes could be re-implemented in a fraction of the time it took to discover them in the first place. Even she would agree to that. His tests wouldn't have to be repeated, as the lowest-level code hadn't changed. She'd probably try to see some other alternative, but there was none, and if she thought there was, she was grossly underestimating Bob.

He couldn't let her lose her job. It would kill her.

• • •

The rain thickened as he left the pub. This was nothing like the gentle mists of County Armagh. Nope, a thorough London downpour, full of sulfur dioxide and all the rest of it.

When he finally got through his apartment door, Malachi was in the kitchen, doing something at the stove. Probably cooking up heroin. Who the hell knew? It was hard to work up much curiosity at this point of his never-ending day. If he was right, he'd have to deal with it.

"Ah, would you look at what the cat dragged in." Malachi laughed. "What in God's name happened you, boy? Lost your umbrella?"

"Felt like a walk." Max went to hang up his wet stuff in the bathroom.

When he came out again, Malachi was shaking his head. "Ma'd have a fit if she saw you, so she would."

Max smiled weakly. It was a nice thought that Ma would even care. He walked to the fridge and was pleasantly surprised to see new beers in there. Not that he'd drink one. His head was spinning enough already.

"Did you shop?" he asked Malachi.

"Nope, stole them from the co-op."

"I don't even want to know if that's true or not." Max poured a glass of water and sank down heavily in the armchair.

Malachi, annoyingly, just kept looking at him.

"What?"

"Wee brother of mine, shouldn't you change into something dry like?"

"Yes, Mommy."

Malachi left the kitchen area and flopped onto the sofa, spreading out his arm on the back of the sofa and propping his legs on the coffee table Max was immune by now to these alpha-dog displays. He'd look into getting new furniture once Malachi was gone.

"I'm serious, man. You could get pneumonia with that carry on, so you could. I seen it in the prison. Rips your lungs out, so it does."

"Yeah, Mal, I heard you."

"Always were a stubborn bastard, weren't you? Still, it'll steam off ya in no time. It's like a bleedin' sauna in here."

He did feel cold in these clothes. He rose to change. Malachi was being congenial all of a sudden. Then again, he hadn't spent any time with him in the past ten years; maybe his brother had just grown up in the time he'd yo-yoed in and out of prison. This was one of the few times they'd been in the same room and talked since the Shauna escapade.

He went to shower off. But he returned to the living room, drier and warmer and in a darker mood. He just wanted to call Zoe, but not with Mal within earshot. Why couldn't he just go down to the pub like every other night?

Instead, Malachi, who looked settled in for the night, snapped off the TV. "I was going to ask you about something, seeing as you're the hotshot of the family and all."

"Go ahead, Mal."

Malachi rubbed his chin. "I'm thinking I should set up a garage. There's a space over on the Shaws Road since Garry's Garage shut down. You know, a Mal's Garage type of thing. I got the know-how and the charm with the ladies."

That you have, all right.

"But I don't know anyone who knows shit about the money side. The papers, you know."

"The paperwork, you mean? The accounting?"

"Yeah, that. So you could come on over and sort me out, couldn't you? I'm not saying I'd pay you straight away, but you know … it's a thing."

Sure, like that was going to happen. Cut his salary by 90 percent to help Mal meet the ladies. *Hear that? That's the sound of me dropping everything for you, Mal.*

"You need starting capital, is that what you're saying?"

"That'd be nice and handy, too, but that's not what I'm asking."

"Well, that's all that's on offer," Max said curtly.

Malachi's face fell. "Ah, yeah, I know what you're thinking. It probably wouldn't work anyway. Shaws Road is a dump, so it is. Sure they'd have me cleaned out before you could say burglar alarm."

"Not necessarily." Max reconsidered and settled down to explain the basics of business to his brother. Having Malachi out of the way would be nice. The startup capital he could easily come up with, and Malachi could use it as he felt inclined. There was a slim possibility he'd even put it to good use. The main thing was to get him out of the picture and out of his apartment so he could concentrate on better things.

Better people.

CHAPTER 18

Zoe came home dripping wet. The lights were off. Tyler wasn't home the one night she really needed company. He should have come back from touring this morning. She couldn't bear the thought of sitting here on her own, waiting for Max to call. She needed a distraction.

She trailed into the kitchen and opened the dishwasher to empty it. That kiss, the shape of his mouth, the warmth of his lips, how it felt when their faces merged ... Their former disputes had vanished into obscurity; none of it mattered when they had this. A shiver of glee rippled through her, leaving goose bumps down her arms. How long would he need with Bob? Would he call her then? Come over? She wasn't going to make the first move and put him in an awkward position, particularly if there was any chance at all he'd still be sitting with Bob. But she needed to feel his arms around her again, to have those lips capture hers, to feel the raw need in his body every time they touched. She needed this just to feel alive.

When she turned on the living room lights something was different. At first she couldn't put her finger on it—the place was a mess as usual—but, surveying the living room the second time around, it came to her. The Rickenbacker was gone!

Tiny claws of terror latched on to her spine. Had it been stolen? That guitar was the one and only thing Tyler ever managed to keep in one place. He would die, just fall down and die. It wasn't even insured, despite all her nagging. Now the worst-case scenario she'd warned him about had actually happened.

She scanned the other corners of the room. His favorite silver dragon ashtray was gone, too, and the folders that held his song chord sheets. Perhaps it was a fan who did it. A deranged stalker?

She raced into his bedroom, expecting to find him passed out diagonally across the sheets, but no. Not only was he not there, but his favorite Slayer cover had also been stripped off the duvet, and the only person who ever took that off to wash it was her. What could this possibly mean?

She scuttled back into the kitchen where she'd left her phone lying on the counter. And that was when she saw it—a small, yellow paper sitting under the coffee jar. She unfolded it, and his angular scrawl jumped out at her.

Babe, moving out, getting out of your hair at last. I met Vikki. She's great. Wants me to move in. Least I could do, right? Thanks for the great time, kisses n hugs,

Ty

What the hell?

She staggered back and fell into the sofa. The note hadn't made any sense on first reading. But the second reading pretty much confirmed the first.

Getting out of your hair at last? Why did he have to say it like that? It was never like that. They were two free spirits, weren't they? She'd never once complained. This was total bollocks!

Oh, he'd be back. At the first sign of trouble. Vikki would never be able to do what it took to look after him, support him, cheer him up on the down days, make sure he got to recording sessions on time, push him to family occasions, doctors' appointments, tax consultations. And what about his laundry? Not in a million years. He'd come back. He had to. He couldn't manage alone.

But what if Tyler had, in some way, grown up and moved on? Was it even possible? Wouldn't she have noticed that change in him? Had he grown a backbone on the sly?

She reached for her phone. She needed Laura. But no, she was eating out with José after the ball.

"Oh, Darcy," she said after scrolling through her useless list of other friends, none of whom she felt she could call. "Not sure I can do this."

"My dear Miss Zoe. What is the matter?" Darcy looked concerned, in as much as this was possible for a smooth-faced avatar, and it made her crack a weak smile for his benefit. So what if he wasn't real? At least he was here. Who cared if he'd been an ass this evening? At least she knew where she stood with him. She forgave him wholeheartedly.

"For one thing, Tyler's gone. Just left."

"I detect that you are indeed most perturbed."

"Yes, I am."

"Did he give a reason for his departure?"

"Read it for yourself." She held up the note to the camera lens. "Can your OCR algorithm make that out?"

Darcy read the note aloud to confirm he could. Not that she wanted to hear it again.

"What do you make of that, my dear Darcy?"

"I am appalled. He has a most irreverent mode of expressing himself."

"Mmm. Keep talking, Darcy."

"If he has made you sad, I feel compelled to inquire as to which aspect of his behavior upsets you the most."

"The whole leaving part, I suppose. And, yes, meeting someone else. That's an impertinence. And his calling it 'getting out of my hair.'"

Zoe was no longer acting. This did piss her off. Especially as she was in a rotten mood to begin with.

"He has kept his intentions hidden from you. That is hurtful."

"Yes."

"However, it is no surprise to me."

"Really?"

"I detected certain behavioral patterns when he called you."

She slumped back into the sofa. "Well, his calls are always rushed, and he's almost always drunk. I wouldn't read too much into his behavior."

"I was referring to your behavior, Miss Zoe."

"Oh."

"You have not initiated a call with him in three weeks. This, according to your telephone history, is unusual."

"He's been away."

"No more than usual."

"I've been busy at work."

"When I offered the suggestion that you call him, you replied, and I quote, 'Tyler's a big boy now, I don't need to call him.'"

"Did I say that?"

"Those were your exact words at 7:16 p.m. on Tuesday."

Come to think of it, she hadn't included Tyler in anything of late and vice versa—no angst-ridden calls in the middle of the night before a performance, no high on-speed calls early in the morning. He hadn't even begged her to come with him down to Cardiff next week. He'd barely even mentioned it. Was Vikki his reaction to her coolness toward him of late?

"Okay, it's all my fault. What do I do? I should go back to work. They might still be holding the ball." With Tyler gone, she had to face up to how empty and lifeless this place had become over the years, but tonight was not the night for that.

"It is 10:14 p.m., madam, and it is raining," Darcy said sternly. "For your health and safety, I cannot condone such an action."

"And what do you suggest? Should I call Max? Is he … He doesn't have you switched on by any chance, does he?"

"No, ma'am, he does not."

Damn. Probably still talking to Bob.

She reached to her bookshelf for *Pride and Prejudice* and settled down for some Austen therapy, but after ten pages she discovered, to her dismay, that it wasn't working. She set the book down with a flop. "Darcy, how good are you at predicting the intentions of people in general?"

"I am predisposed to form predictions about every entity I interact with. Unlike humans, I do not suppress this ability."

"So, what do you think about Max's intentions ... well, with me?" This appeal might've been somewhat scummy, but hey, what was the point of an omnipotent AI if it couldn't help out a wretched human once in a while?

"You take an eager interest in that gentleman's concerns."

"Yes, stop being so Darcy-like for a moment and just tell me."

"Max Taggart's intentions are most clear. He sees himself as a possible suitor to you. However, his position must very materially lessen his chances with you."

"What are you talking about?"

"Max Taggart is far below your station."

"Are you kidding me? The guy must earn at least double what I do, and he's six times as talented."

"This may be true. However, his family leaves much to be desired. He has an absent, alcoholic father, a negligent mother, a criminal brother, and a sister with severely low spirits."

"What? He has a brother and a sister?"

"Yes. As you are an eminent lawyer's daughter from a respectable family, I must impress upon you that you will not be well served by attaching yourself to him regardless of his potential to secure himself a sizable fortune."

She narrowed her eyes. "How do you know all this? I searched the Internet high and low. Not a peep. Where did you get this information about his family?"

"Mr. Taggart told me himself."

"Oh." And he'd told her nothing. Strange, that.

"So what else did he tell you about his life?"

"I am in possession of no other details that can be new to you, madam."

"Huh, you'd be surprised. Did you say 'criminal brother'? What did he do?"

"He attempted to murder a politician."

She slapped a hand to her mouth. "Are you serious?"

"I am always serious, ma'am."

All she could picture was her father's face growing puce with indignation when he heard the news of her associating with someone with a criminal family. Bad enough that she slept around with degenerate artists and musicians, but someone with a criminal brother? He'd explode in a puff of rage. She'd love to introduce Max, just to see his face, but from a safe distance.

And maybe, just maybe, she'd love to do it for its own sake. But what were the chances they'd get that far if he couldn't even trust her enough to share the basic details of his family with her?

"Darcy, thank you. Sit right here and tell me everything you know. You're a true friend, you know that?"

"I thank you, Miss Zoe. You may depend on it."

CHAPTER 19

The next morning Max hesitated before entering P-12. Would she be in yet? Yeah, there she was. Leaning into her screen, engrossed in conversation with her gentleman. She peeked at him over her screen. and gave him a smile. His heart soared, floating in the clouds with a thousand helium balloons. Then, very subtly, something in her face hardened, and he came crashing down to Earth again.

"Hello," she said snippily.

"Hi." He held up his hand. "About last night—"

"Yes, I was going with the story that Bob had tied you up in his basement with duct tape and severed your limbs one by one, but that doesn't seem to be the case. You look perfectly healthy to me and in possession of all your legs and arms."

He shuddered. "I got tied up, and then I didn't want to call you so late."

"A text would've been fine."

"No, I hate texts. Too much ambiguity. I needed to see you face-to-face." He hung up his coat and scarf and stood transfixed in the center of the room. Should he go over to her? Kiss her? Did she want him to? Or would it put her in an awkward position? They hadn't discussed office etiquette. They hadn't discussed anything. For all he knew she could hate him for last night. He strode to his desk, same as he would on any normal morning, and took his seat, watching her expression for a sign.

"Ambiguity?" She flicked back a strand of dark hair. Raw anxiety pooled in her eyes, making them shine like underwater emeralds, and it tugged at his heart. He wanted to run to her, grab her, tell her it was okay, no explanation was required, he felt it too, everything, exactly the same way.

"I messed up," he said. Then the floodgates opened. "Forgive me. I-I wanted nothing more than to continue what we started. You've no idea how much I wanted to … I could have strangled Bob for showing up when he did and for treating you that way—does he always act like that toward you? Zoe, look at me. Yeah, I see it in your face, it's not the first time. Why didn't you tell me? It's because of the blackmail, isn't it? This can't go on. He's way out of line."

Her mouth was pinched in at the sides like she was determined not to say something. "This isn't about Bob. This is about you and me."

"You and me." He felt a smile breaking through. "I like the sound of that." Her and him. No Bob, no Mal, nobody else. He'd made two terrible mistakes last night—first giving in to Bob and then staying in the apartment, listening to Mal. He should have called her to come over, but the thought of Mal finding out about her had sickened him so much, it had clouded all reason, and it had taken him until now to see that he was shooting himself in the foot.

"Wait." Her gaze flickered to her screen, and she switched it off. She did the same on her phone. "Darcy?" she called out.

Silence.

"What's this?" he asked. "You're finally learning the meaning of nondisclosure?"

"Ha, ha."

"Zoe, please, can we put last night behind us and start again?"

"Mmm-hmm." Her lips twisted into a wry smile. "Okay. Are you—um—free tonight for a restart?"

"You know my schedule. I'd rearrange anything for you."

"Except a meeting with Bob."

"Okay, I deserve that. So ... " He cleared his throat. "What time frame works for you?"

"Oh, I'd have to check my agenda, wouldn't I?" She let out a fake groan. "Oh dear, Darcy testing until 2:00 a.m. today, no breaks. This isn't looking very good at all."

"I've always said that kind of work ethic is unhealthy. You should schedule in some recreation time."

She slid him a sultry look. "How about ten?"

"Works for me." How was he supposed to work with her sitting right across from him in her tight, satin blouse? Just as he'd warned team members in the past about office affairs, it was turning his brain to mush that he couldn't race over, smooth his hand down that shiny fabric, rip it away from her, and access her skin. She had this ruffled look about her already, and her lips were definitely rawer, redder, crying out to be kissed again. And he knew exactly how good that felt. He'd never again be so dumb as to lecture people on having office affairs. His heart pounded. Could you combust with desire? After just one kiss. Well, two, if you counted the one in the rain that Bob interrupted, and it was definitely worth counting.

What was happening to him?

She giggled. He had no idea what expression was on his face right now, but it sure as hell wasn't one of concentration on the robustness tests set out on the screen before him.

"Zoe, please talk about something. Anything."

"Is Bob trying to get rid of me?"

"Anything but that."

"Come on, I need to know."

He rose, crossed the distance between them, put his thumb under her chin, and tilted her face up until she made eye contact. "He's not going to get rid of you. I swear to you, that is not going to happen because I won't let it happen."

Her eyes glittered with unspoken resentment. Hopefully directed at Bob. It was a struggle not to kiss her anger away, but anyone could walk in ...

He swooped down and kissed her.

"M-M-Max!" she said and then surrendered to the kiss.

Yep, she was worth the risk.

• • •

After her longest day at work ever, Zoe left at the same time as Max—10:00 p.m., exactly as arranged. By some miracle, they'd managed to act as normal colleagues until this point. It helped that Max had stayed out of the office most of the day and that Darcy was having a horrendous time understanding the logic of bachelor parties in her latest scenario and needed extra hand-holding and, hence, her undivided attention in as much as she could give it in her skittish state.

But, finally, they were together again, free of colleagues' averted gazes, free of Zycorp's ubiquitous webcams, walking jauntily down a crowded London street like a normal couple. As they passed Mahmout's kebab place at the junction, Max slipped his hand into hers.

Seriously? Holding hands? This was a first. Tyler would sooner shoot himself, and Shingo would've committed kamikaze. But she relished Max's resolute grip and the primitive statement it seemed to make.

Mine.

"You've been avoiding me the whole day, haven't you?" she asked.

"Yes." He squeezed her palm. "Guy's gotta do what a guy's gotta do." A shy grin traversed his face, and he'd never looked sweeter.

They bumped shoulder to bicep a couple of times as they meandered around pedestrians and puddles. She caught his gaze each time. Here was a man ready to explode. Something else was new—she felt girlish, light, giddy. This hadn't happened with other men. Probably because she'd been too busy being the responsible adult in the relationship.

"It's a dump, I know," she warned him as they entered the apartment. She meant that literally; Tyler's things lay in random heaps about the floor where she'd tossed them last night in somewhat of a berserker mood. But she offered Max no explanation for the piles of grungy clothes and music gear and hoped he wouldn't ask. They still hadn't kissed since leaving the office—would the mess be a deal-breaker? She tried to remember back to the part where they'd decided to come here as opposed to Max's place, which no doubt was perfect right down to the last molecule.

He sneezed. "Dust."

"It's not always quite this bad," she said weakly. "Tea?" She indicated that he should sit on the brown, threadbare sofa that had, it was rumored, once been leather. Then she bustled to the kitchenette to turn on the kettle and fix up her face and hair as best she could in the tiny mirror overhanging the saucepan cupboard. She thought she'd looked a million dollars leaving the apartment this morning, but now, not so much. Best to keep the lights off.

"Well, this is nice," he said.

When she emerged with two mugs of tea, Max was standing surveying the corner with the two strips of peach wallpaper and her gilded Regency Récamier chaise longue bought on eBay six months ago, her pride and joy. It was the only decent patch in the whole flat, a vision of things to come.

"It's rosewood," she said. She'd spent half a month's salary on the chaise, and Tyler had just laughed. "I had this idea of sort of refurbishing but then realized I'd never have time. I kind of gave up on it."

"May I?" he asked.

"Be my guest."

He sat on the chaise and smoothed his hands along the pale, blue-velvet upholstery. Diagonal rays from the outside streetlamps illuminated his features, colluding with the shadows, making him ridiculously attractive. His blazer had fallen open, and with his pecs straining at the front of the heavy cotton shirt, his hair more ruffled than usual, and a solemn look of appraisal on his face, he looked positively Austenlicious. She'd never been so happy she'd bought that damn chaise.

"This is our third date, you know," he said, looking up at her.

She drew nearer, putting the teas down on a battered coffee table. "How do you work that out?"

"Well, I consider the nursing home our first date."

"By what definition?"

A half grin. "Time alone with you outside the office. And there was body contact."

She flicked back her hair. "Oh, you remember that, do you?"

"Yep." He shifted his legs.

"Okay, the second date?"

"The ball."

"That wasn't an organized date."

"Does it matter? We danced. We kissed."

"Okay, let's say this is the third date. Does it make any difference?"

"Yes," he said with great conviction, sitting forward.

"Why's that?"

"Come here, and I'll show you."

Wordlessly, she shuffled forward and stood before him, looking down into his face, getting lost in his remarkable eyes. "It's … been a while," she said, in barely a whisper.

He rested his hands lightly on her hips. "For me, too. Tell me if I go too fast."

"I will." How touching that he would say that. In her experience, men took what they liked when they liked it, and it was all over before you could say "thank you, ma'am." She couldn't remember exploring this stage with a man before—the maddening, lurching, exciting, roller-coaster stage of pursuit. She'd ceased to believe there even was a stage like this in real life. There'd always been that manic rush to complete the act so as to ensure possession and put an end to all doubt. But with Max, the exploration was part of the thrill. Every nuance of his body language told her he wasn't going anywhere; this was just the beginning. She wanted to savor each step of their barefoot walk down a long, winding road together, turn over every stone, delight over every wildflower they encountered, instead of jumping on the back of a motorcycle and roaring off in a blast of dust toward some falsely defined end point. Did he feel the same way?

She slid her fingers through his hair as she'd often longed to do, way before such thoughts were appropriate. It felt silken and warm, exactly as she'd hoped. Her hand drifted down the stubble of his cheek, down his pulsing neck, and around the breadth of his shoulder. His fervent gaze on her face made her feel desirable and omnipotent despite the mess she'd just seen in the mirror a few minutes ago.

She let out a nervous laugh. "I still can't believe you're Max."

"I get that a lot."

"Seriously. My stuffy colleague who—"

"Stuffy, huh?" In a fluid move, he grasped her hips tightly and swung her down on top of him. She felt weightless. Next thing she was straddling his thighs, kissing him from the higher position. The sensation of control enticed her to push down hard on his lips, nudging his head backward until his skull was up against the wall. He let out a restrained groan, surrendering to her. It was a massive turn-on.

God, she wanted him, all of him. Forever. Exactly like this. She pulled back to look at him. Crimson had seeped into his cheeks and lips. There was a burning expression in his eyes that was definitely not suitable for work.

"That wasn't very ladylike," he said, pressing into her waist, looking pleased.

"You ain't seen nothing yet."

He cocked his head. "How did they kiss in those days? Regency times. I'm pretty sure the man took the lead."

"How should I know? Jane Austen didn't exactly go into the specifics."

"Pity," he murmured, trailing his finger down her cheek and across her collarbone. "I'd bet you'd be into reenacting a courtship scene with historical accuracy."

She laughed with delight. "Are you sure this isn't some kind of fetish of yours, Max? Those gowns with the boobs spilling out over the top? Those corsets and their asset-enhancing properties?"

He gave her a sly look. "My fantasy doesn't involve much clothing at all."

"Ooooh."

"Yes, ooooh." His hot gaze surveyed her as he slid her off his lap, depositing her in the corner of the chaise. She flopped back, heavy limbed, as he loomed over her, his dark figure outlined in the faint dusk by the glow of light from the street.

"Austen heroes and heroines tended to bicker and misunderstand each other more than actually get down to kissing."

"Now why does that sound familiar?" He sat down at eye level with her and took her hand in his. He toyed with her fingers, trailing his fingertips down to her nails and back up to her knuckles. It was maddening.

"I'm not going to be chivalrous and say how beautiful you are ... but, oh my God, you're fucking gorgeous." He drew closer. A frown of urgency crossed his forehead. She'd seen him focused before, sure, but not like this, and she'd never heard him swear.

He swooped in and put his warm mouth to hers, smothering her cry of surprise. His fingers broke away from hers and cradled the back of her head, angling her skull and neck, controlling the kiss. His lips caressed and possessed her, making her body squeeze up into a tight pole of anguish. His mouth and lips urged her to let herself fall into the abandon she was seeking, and when she relaxed completely into his mouth, it made her delirious. Her eyes flickered open. Her apartment had transformed into a palace of desire. Light bulbs became chandeliers, net curtains became drapes, her colleague, a dashing rake. She took up a vice-like grip around his neck, utterly, almost tearfully, determined to never let go.

"This feels good," she said when they broke off. Yes, it was an understatement, but words weren't coming too easily.

"Don't sound so surprised."

"No." She laughed. "It's just, well, normally, things go ... fast."

"We've got all the time in the world."

The absolute conviction in his voice when he said that was the sweetest thing she'd ever heard. She nodded.

"Unless, of course, you want fast?" There was an unmistakable glint of hope in his eyes.

"No. I want ... this," she breathed. "This is perfect."

CHAPTER 20

The alarm blared out at six like an alien invasion. Zoe blinked in surprise at the insidious digits—what the bleep was going on? Then it started to dawn on her, the incredible pieces of yesterday evening, clicking together like a jigsaw puzzle depicting a sumptuous scene from heaven.

A wave of pleasure washed over her, then one of pride. They hadn't gone beyond kissing last night, but they didn't need to when they had fingers and tongues and so much newness of each other to explore. After one more kiss and one long cuddle last night, Max had left to go home, just before midnight, and it had felt natural, not panicky, not threatening. How she'd managed to fall asleep with that level of excitement surging through her veins she had no idea. But slept she had, like a princess, until now.

Amphetamines had nothing on this. It was the kind of happiness that made her wish she had a trusted sister to giggle with deep into the night as she recounted every detail to her. But she had the next best thing. She couldn't wait to tell Laura once she reached the office.

"Put me in your calendar for tonight," Max had said. Yes, not to be clingy or anything, but she'd already slotted him in for the rest of her life, so hopefully he didn't have any other plans. She hugged the pillow to her cheek and sighed in a new type of bliss.

No games.

No panic.

No hangover.

So this was what it felt like to be in a normal, adult relationship.

• • •

Laura was elated when she heard the news. "But what are you doing down here with me?" she scolded. "You need to be up there with him in seventh heaven."

José happened to wander by. He possessed that astute boyfriend ability to know when girlfriends were getting excited about something important. "Red or green?" he asked.

"Green," Laura said, grinning.

José clenched his fist. "Yes."

"I'm glad you have my love life reduced to traffic signal mnemonics," Zoe said, "but let's not get ahead of ourselves here." She looked meaningfully at Laura.

"Okay, orange," Laura said.

"Good enough for me." José strolled off toward the coffee machine, humming.

Then Zoe turned the conversation to Tyler's departure, because Laura had been away on an external assignment yesterday and hadn't heard that one yet either. Besides, words couldn't really do justice to what Zoe was feeling about last night. It was relief to talk about something else in a semicoherent way.

"Whoa, I'm officially speechless," Laura said. "It's not like Tyler to be decisive. I'm just pissed off you didn't push him out the door first."

"It just didn't seem fair when he hadn't much disposable income."

"Tyler'll never have much disposable income. You're not his mommy."

"I thought he was your friend, too."

"Oh, totally, in a hey-I-know-this-cool-rock star-guy kinda way, and I do like the guy, but he's seriously cramped your style the past year, and it was my duty as a friend to keep reminding you of that, not that you ever listened to me. And I'm glad I don't have to do that anymore. Promise me you won't let him back in until he's got at least six months' back rent in his hand and has figured out how to use a washing machine."

Zoe hesitated.

"Come on," Laura urged. "Let Tyler have his Vikki, and may they both have horrid little thrash babies and enter into thrash-rock heaven. What's it to you?"

Zoe laughed, picturing little Tyler sprogs with long, floppy hair and tiny leather jackets playing plastic guitars. "You know what? You're right."

"Now get into that elevator and dig your claws into a real man."

• • •

There was little sign of her "real man" in P-12. His coat and scarf weren't there either, but his freshly showered scent lingered in the dry, computer-fanned air. He'd been here this morning at some stage. She checked his agenda, and it was full of server-room duties. That would keep him cool—ha, ha.

What would keep her cool? After last night, how were they supposed to act like normal colleagues, each sitting primly at their desks, pretending nothing was going on between them, until it was time to go home again? It wasn't like there was a switch she could just activate and deactivate. She should've picked up some expert tips from Laura, because she and José managed it somehow. Maybe Max had some ideas himself on the subject. If it weren't for this damn project with its imperative deadline, they could take a week off, go to a tropical island, and just float away in ecstasy.

If he were just sitting there in his usual chair, his hands gliding over his keyboard in that dexterous way of his, that peaceful, intent look on his face, watching him would be enough to make her the happiest creature in the world. Because even when he was getting on her nerves, there had always been something about him, something deep that grounded her and made her feel less like a hot-air balloon careening wildly off course. Now that they'd become intimate, that feeling had intensified into something almost overpowering, something that felt suspiciously like need. She wasn't equipped to deal with need. Fun, yes. Lust, yes. Excitement, too. But *need?* That was a new one.

His empty chair caused a heaviness in her chest. Every heartbeat seemed to be heralding imminent cardiac arrest. This couldn't be healthy, this power he had over her. And yet, she was petrified he'd walk in, because it might break the spell. She might discover it had all been in her head. One night of fun, or whatever, two colleagues letting off some office steam. In which case, well, she'd be so mortified it wouldn't be possible to sit in this office ever again. She'd have to ask for a transfer. And working with him would be out of the question.

Get a grip, Zoe. This is your dream project, your mission! Okay, all she had to do was compartmentalize her brain into "this freaking amazing thing between us" and "ze normal schedule for today"—do some parallel processing, as Evan would say.

Darcy. Maybe he could help. She had to break the news to him anyway, to have "the talk," and the sooner the better. It may well be the hardest test he'd face. With any luck, the AI would take it like a man. Besides, his amazing powers of perception must surely have deciphered some clues from their behavior by now.

"Darcy, I switched you off last night. Did you not wonder at this?"

"I noted this, Miss Zoe, as I do all your behavior. However, my curiosity stopped short of escalating into a state of wonder."

"But what do you conclude from it? I've never switched you off at night before."

Darcy held her gaze with an ironic glint in his eyes. "You either switched me off because you were each in somebody's confidence and had secret affairs to discuss, or because you were weary and lacked the will to converse; if the first, I would have been completely in your way, and if the second, I am happy to contribute to your well-being by allowing you to rest. For I detect a bloom in your appearance and a note of happiness in your voice."

"Oh, Darcy … " How to explain? "The thing is—"

"Hi." Max burst in, fully dressed in his coat and scarf. "Oh my God, it was freezing down there. Come here." He bounded over in two strides and pulled her tightly to his chest. His lips found hers. All worries vanished in an explosion of twinkling stars and rainbows. So much for breaking the news gently to poor Darcy.

After a long, warm kiss, Max nuzzled his nose against her neck.

"Yeowch, you're cold." She laughed.

"I'm warming up."

She tugged him in, giggling, her hands exploring him blindly under the coat, running along the hard lines of his body, still new enough to be intriguing but familiar enough to bring back a flood of delicious memories of last night. He shuddered, but his skin was hot.

"You okay for tonight?" he asked.

"Already adjusted the planning for it."

"Aren't you efficient?" His voice lowered. "And ravishing. I know you have this open-door policy, but this project has some sensitive aspects that need to be discussed"—he reached out with his leg and slammed the door shut—"behind closed doors."

He wasn't kidding. His hand had found some very sensitive aspects south of her collarbone. "Max … " Her words got swallowed up by her breathing, which was accelerating.

"I advise against this behavior," Darcy said.

Max's hands froze in their positions cupping her breasts. "You left him on?"

She clasped her hands over his. "I know. But I didn't think you were going to … you know."

Max pulled away and picked up her phone from the desk, holding up the display so he could look at the avatar head-on. "Darcy, old boy, Zoe and I, we're having a … a liaison, right? You okay with that? Instead of the rampant poetry reading of your day, this is what we do. We're getting acquainted." He slid the phone back onto her desk.

"The phrase might've picked up some connotations since your day," she added.

"While I delight in your getting better acquainted, Miss Zoe," Darcy said mildly, "my advice was given on purely practical considerations, to save you both from certain dilemma."

"Oh? Do explain."

"I've a better idea," Max muttered. "We shut him off."

"I predict, on the basis of camera evidence, that your superior, Bob Chadwick, will enter the door in a matter of seconds."

"Seconds?" she shrieked, springing away from Max. "How many?"

"Five."

She made a dive for her chair. Max stood where he was and readjusted his scarf.

"Am I disturbing?" Bob asked, sauntering in.

Yes, very. She kept her head bent behind her monitor.

Max beckoned Bob toward his desk. "Not at all. We were discussing the merits of bespoke emulators for performance tests. Feel free to join in."

Bob snorted.

One second later and he would have gotten lucky, and the thought of him discovering them having a private moment was nauseating. If she kept her head ducked behind her monitor she wouldn't have to look at him. *Please, Max, don't encourage him.*

Bob approached Max, hands on hips, and surveyed the room. "Very cozy. For the time being." He homed in on Darcy on her phone. "I trust you have that under control."

"Absolutely," Max said.

She closed her eyes and prayed Darcy would keep his mouth shut. If he attempted blackmail, she'd kill herself.

"Good." Bob rubbed his hands together. "Well, I'll leave you both to it." Then he strolled out again.

Max closed the door behind him and leaned his back against it, taking in rapid, shallow breaths, his face bathed in sweat. An allergic reaction? Yes, she couldn't blame him. His fervent promise to protect her from Bob had come as a surprise the other day, and it was rather sweet in small doses. It had brought out a passionate side in Max she was curious to see more of. Now he looked extremely worked up.

"God, Max, I know he's bad, but you look positively freaked."

His impassioned blue gaze swept over her, making her heart thump almost painfully. God, he was beautiful. It was impossible to work like this. She had to know what he was thinking, where this was going, and whether this felt half as agonizing to him as it did to her. If looks could be trusted, it did.

He held a wrist to his forehead. "Not freaked, Zoe. I think I'm sick."

"Sick?"

"Feels like the flu. I thought it was just the server room chilling me, but it wasn't."

"You can't be sick."

"Feel my forehead."

She did. "Oh, shit."

"How are you?" he asked.

"Fine."

"I always get a flu mid-November. And I did get kind of wet the day before yesterday."

"If you always get the flu in November, then why didn't you put it on the goddamn plan?"

"Sorry," he mumbled. Then he turned away from her and sneezed. "That's it. I'm going home before it spreads to you."

"But what am I going to do?"

"Wash your hands. Disinfect this place. Wipes are in my bottom drawer. Monitor your temperature. There's a thermometer in the first-aid box in the closet to the left of the entrance to the canteen."

"No, I mean the work, your work, the robustness tests."

"You have to take over." He was at the door.

She scrambled after him. "You can't just say that and then bugger off. That's not an option, Max."

"Instructions are in my F: partition, folder 'Darcy.' Everything's right there. We can't let the schedule slip."

"But—"

"Zoe, be pragmatic. I need to lie down. And I need to leave while I can still drive. I'll be on the phone if you need me. Call me. Anytime."

"Wait … " What she wanted to say was, "I'll come see you," but under the circumstances she wouldn't even see her own apartment for a while, let alone his. And she may well end up sick herself. There was no way they hadn't shared germs last night, to put it clinically. What then?

Then they could write off the whole project.

"All right, go."

"You can do this. Don't let anyone tell you otherwise."

"It's not like I have a bloody choice, is it?" she called after him. What a time to get sick.

But there had to be some way to keep the show running even with the main star absent. It would mean putting her own agenda on hold for a while, because it was more important to keep the essential tests running, those robustness checks he'd been harping on about and she'd turned a deaf ear to. She hated to admit it, but he had a point about not wanting the program to crash. Ever.

She found the antiseptic wipes and went around the office wiping every surface. "Darcy, what was on Max's schedule for this afternoon?"

"A discussion with Bob Chadwick about resourcing at 3:00 p.m."

"Pass."

"Next item, at 4:00 p.m. is—"

"No, wait." She scratched her neck to rid herself of imaginary fleas. "Just hypothetically, what exactly would that involve, that meeting with Bob?"

"Mr. Taggart has debated resource allocation with Mr. Chadwick for two weeks. As I understand it, he hoped to reach a conclusion today."

"Human or hardware resources?"

"Both."

"What happens if Max doesn't get what he wants?"

"The testing schedule of my code will experience a delay by a month."

"But we'd miss release! What's so important about Bob's project?"

"Mr. Chadwick's project is of minor consequence. He does not require the resources, and his arguing for them is merely a tactic."

"A tactic ... But why?"

"Mr. Chadwick desires for my release to be a failure in order that he may further his own agenda, namely to replace Mr. Hampton as chief executive officer of this institution."

"Whoa. Are you sure about that?"

"I am."

"Does Max know?"

"He does."

"And Harry, does he know?"

"That, ma'am, is unclear. I will set it as a task to discover this information."

Christ, this company was even worse than she thought. No wonder Bob was being such a jerk about Darcy. "Well, push that meeting with Bob out 'til next week. Whatever chance Max had, she had none.

"Consider it done, Miss Zoe. Next on the agenda is a backup of completeness tests and refresh of the memory on server HGZ-2566."

She blew into her hands. At least this was technical, rational. Not so hard after all. "Okay, I can do that, I guess. Next?"

Together with Darcy, she ploughed through the list, and she reckoned she could cover 70 percent of Max's stuff. He'd be back soon. He had to be. Surely his recovery would be as efficient as everything else in his life?

• • •

Next day, with a throbbing head, she called an emergency face-to-face meeting first thing with the resistance. Laura, José, and Evan crowded around her desk with concerned expressions.

"I feel like I'm walking in quicksand." Zoe scrolled through the test results on her monitor. "I've haven't slept a wink. I'm exhausted. That's why you haven't seen me in the VR lab the past few days. I've canceled a load of meetings Max organized. But hey, at least the robustness testing's being run back to back and it's clean."

"Zoe, you need to take it down a notch," Laura said. "Now, tell us how we can help."

"Where do I start? But are you sure? You've all got your own jobs to do."

"Nothing's more important," Evan said. "Beta's two weeks away. We're that close to having no jobs. What do we have to lose?"

All heads nodded solemnly.

"Just you and me though," she said. "Laura and José won't be fired."

Laura folded her arms. "We're leaving if either of you has to go." José sidled up beside her and put his arm around her waist.

Zoe opened her mouth to protest, but it died on her lips. "Thanks, guys."

They gathered around her monitor and negotiated their way through the plan. The two men wanted to take over Max's server-room tests, which meant she and Laura could do more scenarios with Darcy in real life and in Austenland.

When the guys had left the office, Laura asked, "Have you called him?"

"Phone's been off. I'll leave him be."

"Yeah, well, if he's dead, the neighbor's dog should be able to smell him by now."

"No," Zoe shot back, "he'll smell good even when he's dead."

"You are in love, aren't you?"

"I'm not thinking straight, that's for sure."

"You know what? Give him 'til Thursday and then mosey on over there. He'll be thrilled. It can't be nice for him, being stuck there alone. Poor fella."

"You think I should?"

"Since when do you consult me on major life choices? Come on, you'd do an amazing Florence Nightingale impersonation."

Yeah, she'd put a damp cloth on his forehead, cool his fever. Rub his chest with lotion, assist him to the bath, sponge him from his neck, down his torso, down, down, down …

Laura laughed. "Earth calling Zoe."

She blinked the daydream away. "I'm just trying to remember if I have his address."

"It's in the staff database," Laura said.

Three days later Zoe sat in a taxi, a basket of goodies on her lap, heading to Max's house. Three days were long enough for a quarantine to be effective and almost long enough for her hormones to have settled down. She was racked with guilt for leaving work "early," but her colleagues had pushed her out the door. "Oh dear, this is very untoward behavior, isn't it, Darcy?"

"I disagree. People may call on friends spontaneously, particularly when in sickness or distress. It is a privilege of friendship."

Funny that Darcy still insisted on calling it a friendship. Would they have to copulate in front of him for him to believe it was something more? Or was this just his famous reserve at work? "He might be asleep, and then I shouldn't bother him. Do you know, Darcy?"

"I do not. Mr. Taggart switched me off twenty-four hours ago. However, I predict, on the basis of prior behavior patterns and the customary symptoms of his malaise, that he is 60 percent likely to be awake at this hour."

"I'll have to make do with those odds, I suppose." She checked her lip gloss in her compact mirror and snapped it shut. "Courtship hasn't really gotten any easier in the two centuries since you had your heyday.

It's still a big old bag fraught with nerves when it all comes down to it."

"Indeed."

She smiled to herself. This was Darcy's standard answer when something wasn't connecting for him. It had taken her a while to figure that one out.

The taxi came to a halt outside an attractive, ivy-covered, upmarket apartment block, the kind her father and brothers would certainly approve of. Gravel crunched underneath her ballet slippers as she approached the communal entranceway with the attractive flowerpots and neatly ordered postboxes. No weeds, graffiti, everything nice and orderly. No doubt it had triple-locking systems, twenty-four-seven surveillance, and an active team of janitors and gardeners who actually did their jobs. It suited Max down to the ground.

A peal of thunder crashed in the distance, and a mist of rain covered her face. She bolted for the shelter of the porch.

"Okay, Taggart ... Taggart, where are you?" She skimmed down the names on the doorbells. "Darcy, I don't know if I can do this."

"Please ring the bell," Darcy urged. "If he is awake, I daresay he will be most gratified to see you."

Her finger hovered over the doorbell. "Gimme the odds on that."

"Ninety-nine percent."

"What's with the 1 percent?" she shot back.

"Statistical room for error."

"Okay. Done." The bell sounded with an elegant *bing-bong* inside the building, and then the door buzzed, so she pushed her way through. She chose the stairs. "I'm putting you asleep, Darcy," she said, panting, on reaching the third floor. "No offense, but we humans need a little privacy, okay?"

"Of course."

"Thanks, Darcy. You're a pal."

"Indeed, I am glad to be of service."

She tucked the phone in her purse and climbed the last steps. A door on the landing was ajar, and welcoming yellow light seeped out. Catching her breath, she walked up to the door and, with a huge grin, looked up at the man standing there.

But it wasn't Max. It was a man who looked exactly like Max, just with darker, scruffier hair and eyes a lighter shade of blue. Those eyes now perused her mockingly, in a way that Max's never would.

"Lordy, what do we have here?" he said, in a heavy Northern Irish accent.

"I-I'm here to see Max," she said out of sheer amazement.

"Will I do?" The man grinned. "I'm Mal, the big, bad brother."

CHAPTER 21

"He ever mention me?" Mal's face rose into a sly grin. He had more lines around the mouth than Max, and his teeth weren't nearly as white. Lounging barefoot against the breakfast bar in a t-shirt that said "Give me head 'til I'm dead" and showed off tattooed biceps, he made the expression "evil twin" spring to mind all too easily.

"Not ... much." She stood helpless in the hallway and plonked her basket down. "Look, um, maybe I shouldn't hang around if he's not awake."

"Ah, he'll be up soon enough. Come on now, you can't be going on out again in that storm. Wait 'til it eases up, like." Mal grabbed the basket and cocked his head toward what appeared to be the living room.

Curiosity warred with caution. She could well believe him to be an ex-convict. He had this hardness about him. But also an air of negligence that was sort of attractive and reminded her of Tyler in a weird way. And there was something else ... an undercurrent of childlike kindness. She decided to trust him. For now.

"Okay." She switched Darcy on again. He'd detect panic in her voice if necessary and figure out a way to help. She searched the minimally furnished hallway for somewhere to hang her coat.

Mal expertly slid the coat off her shoulders and opened an inbuilt wardrobe that blended so seamlessly into the walls it was invisible. She trailed after him into the living room, drinking in the details greedily: tastefully muted light, cream and chrome furnishings. Some pictures in the Bauhaus style. Very Max. There was also a mess on the coffee table, an empty pizza carton and some cans of beer. Very not Max.

"He's in his room." Mal's eyes glittered, challenging her in the same way Max could, by doing nothing at all.

"Oh." *Awkward.* How many doors were off this living room anyway, and what were the chances she'd walk into the wrong room? Asking Darcy was an impossibility with Mal watching her.

"Here, I'll show you," he said.

He indicated the second door on the left, not the one she'd have chosen.

She peeped in through a chink in the doorway. Max lay asleep, stretched out on his back on the bed. The dressing gown had fallen open, revealing the toned chest she had come to daydream about. One hand was splayed in the center of his breastbone. The day-to-day tension was wiped off his face as if with a magic eraser, leaving him serene, like a Greek statue. His hair was matted to his head, making it appear darker, almost black. It did weird, aching things to her heart to see him like this. Oh, to be left alone with him—and to fulfill her Nightingale fantasies.

When she found her voice again it came out as a croak. "I'd better not disturb him."

"Yeah, let him sleep." Mal steered her back toward the living room. When they sat down at opposite ends of the sofa, he seemed to be appraising her. "You have it bad, don't you?"

"I don't know what you're talking about."

He smirked. "I was just on with the sister before you called." He pointed with his foot at a laptop sitting amidst the beers.

She wanted to clutch at the information, wrench it out, and gobble it up, but she didn't want Mal to figure out that Max had told her nothing.

"How is she?" she asked nonchalantly.

"Ah, she's grand."

"That's good."

"Well, as good as she can be under the circumstances."

Yes, he was testing her to see how much she knew. Curiosity won out.

"Circumstances?"

Mal told her.

"Five years," she breathed after hearing about Maeve's trials, waiting for a proposal that never came and her recent recourse to Prozac. "That's, um, a long time to wait."

"Yeah. Do you have any womanly advice to dish out at all?" Mal rose, grabbed two beers from the fridge, and handed her one. The action was so natural, so congenial, she accepted without a whisper of protestation.

"Well." She snuggled back into the sofa, relishing the cold beer and the warm appeal. "I'm thinking she must be feeling pretty low about herself, and I guess Dermot's only seeing that side of her and that's making matters worse. It's a vicious circle, you see. Someone needs to break that circle."

Mal tapped the bottle opener against the glass. "That could be true, all right."

Encouraged, she said, "If you get on with your sister, then she might appreciate having her brother come over and show her in a great light to this dithering boyfriend of hers. At the least you could take her out of her environment and cheer her up a bit, right?"

"Hmm, are you saying I should show her up in a good light, or are you talking about a certain other brother?"

"I ... I'm sure you'd both do a credible job." Her cheeks were growing warm.

"You're a smooth one," he said with a loud laugh. "Just like him. I see why he likes you."

"Really? He said that?" A treacherous grin broke out on her face, and she gave up trying to suppress it. Third-party information on Max's feelings. It didn't get much better than this. Talking with Mal was so easy. "See, you're both lucky, you actually like your sister. She calls you looking for help. That already is a kindness in itself that you owe to her. Not all siblings have such a connection. One of you should definitely go over and show her a great time."

"Yeah, I get what you're saying. Max'd have a better shot at it, but sure, he'll not go near any of us."

"Why not?" She leaned forward, dying to know.

"Oh, he's been mooning over Shauna Kearney since God knows when."

Whoa. Whoa. Whoa. "Shauna who?"

"Ack." Mal waved a dismissive arm. "Someone who was never right for 'im anyway."

"Tell me." She took a long slug of beer, hoping it would cushion the blow.

"They were ready to get engaged and all. Well, he was. She wasn't. I seen it coming a mile away. But Max with his fancy job there in California, he didn't see the shitstorm. He had this notion she'd be sitting by the fire waiting for him."

"And she wasn't?" Zoe edged closer, morbidly fascinated, despite battling the sensation that the floor had just opened up beneath her and all her dreams were being sucked into the pit.

"Nope." Mal laughed.

There was a scuffling sound behind her. The living-room door eked open, and Max stumbled in, hair awry, nose red, and forehead crumpled in a frown that was exacerbated by the purple rings under his eyes.

She slid a few inches away from Mal. They'd been sitting close together, she realized belatedly.

Max's gaze darted from one to the other. His dressing gown hung off one shoulder, revealing skin, muscle tone, and a smattering of chest hair. She focused on his throat because up or down seemed dangerous ways to go. Presumably, he had boxer shorts or something on under that gown.

"What's going on?" Max asked, voice cracking.

Mal held up his palms. "Calm down, bro. I didn't touch."

She stayed mute.

"Just having a nice chat, like." Mal wiped something off his bare feet. "While waiting for Sleeping Beauty to show."

Max turned to Zoe. "Why did you come here?"

"I came to see you." She rose, brushing down her t-shirt. "We're only talking." Okay, that sounded guilty, but his look was so accusing and there was no other way to say it. If he was going to be like that, then she didn't need to be here. She strutted past him to the hallway.

"Wait." He shuffled after her, at half his usual speed.

She lifted her coat from the hanger. "In fact, we were talking about you."

"What about me?"

Her fingers were like sausages as she buttoned up the coat. "You and someone called Shauna Kearney."

"Yeah, my ex. What about her?"

"The ex you were going to marry."

"What of her?"

Mal's harsh laugh rang out from the living room. "Shauna was never going to marry you. She'd gone and told half the country how bored she was waiting for you."

Max shuddered. His whole body seemed to stiffen. He trudged back to the living room. Eager to hear, she trailed behind.

"You're lying," Max said in a defeated voice. Hearing that resignation, so incompatible with his personality, made her want to throw her arms around his neck and say, "Forget about her." Surely Shauna was in the past and could stay right there?

"I'm telling you, she was bored. Sure, didn't she fuck Tommy Sheenan just the week before that?"

Max clutched the doorframe. "That's not true."

"Yeah, I just made it up for fun."

"You must have. And why are you telling her? Why don't you tell her how you fucked Shauna too?"

Zoe met his gaze. "'Her'?" She thumped her chest. "I'm right here, Max."

Mal rose from the sofa, no longer looking like he wanted to play peacemaker, not that he'd been doing a good job of that. "Listen," he said. "You were prancing about with your fancy job in California, wanking on about how you'd emigrate and live the big life. Oh yeah. And Shauna was hanging around at home, and she couldn't decide if you were worth the risk. Well, one day Maeve comes to me with the lowdown—the story about Shauna and Tommy. Maeve says it's just tip of the iceberg. I says bollocks, I'll try it on with Shauna too, at her birthday bash, to sort it out once and for all, like— to prove that Shauna wasn't that kind of girl. I was trying to save her reputation for you, ya big dick. That's all it was." Mal paused and regarded the bottleneck with a faint smile. "Didn't think she'd let me go that far."

Zoe found her voice again. "Sounds like Mal did you a favor, Max."

He rounded on her. "Funny, but I just can't see it that way." The fury in his eyes turned them electric blue. The force of that passion made her back away until she hit the wall.

Max covered his face with splayed fingers. "Leave. Everybody, just ... leave. I need to be alone!"

She was still paralyzed, but Mal led her by the arm into the hallway. "I don't know how long you've known him," he said in a hushed voice, "but once he gets in a mood like this you can forget it. Never mind. I'm glad you came." He pulled on a battered biker jacket. "Come on down to the pub with me."

"No, thanks. Not a great time."

"All right, another time. Well, thanks for the basket and the womanly advice." Mal patted the small of her back.

"What advice?" Max growled from behind them.

"Oh, you heard that, did you?" Mal said with a mocking smile. "Zoe thinks you should take your finger out and get over to Dublin to sort out poor Maeve."

"I-I didn't say that," Zoe protested, "or not quite like that."

Max gave no response and simply trudged back into his room.

She watched his door close and then turned to Mal. He pulled her into a brief hug. "Don't mind the grumpy sod. I'm glad he's found you, darling."

"Thanks, Mal." It was weird being held by someone who was so like Max. Same body structure, same strong arms and broad chest, but different smell. This was the closest she was going to get to any physical intimacy tonight, that was for sure.

"And don't worry." Mal winked as he stood in the doorway. "I'll be out of your way very soon."

...

Instead of hitting the bed, as he knew he should, Max slumped in the armchair. He picked up a football and rolled it between his bare feet and then slammed it against the wall. Shauna and Tommy Sheenan? Why would Mal make up that story with someone as dull as

Sheenan? Besides, Mal didn't need to make up a story about why he stole Shauna, because he was proud of it. It was one of his more impressive life achievements, after all.

But if Shauna's disregard for him was true, then everyone—his whole family, his friends—had known all these years and nobody had said a word to him. Not one hint. He'd actually spent all this time wondering if Shauna regretted her flash of madness, giving her the benefit of the doubt, putting the full blame on Mal. He'd even entertained the possibility that she'd been passed a date-rape drug that night, because he wouldn't put it past his brother to pull a stunt like that.

It hurt. In the back of his mind he'd pictured seeking Shauna out one fine day and getting her to tearfully admit her huge mistake, that moment of lustful madness, if she didn't come crawling back to him first. That wasn't going to happen; he had to let go of that delusion. Yeah, it was just his ego hurting. He could see that. But to call what Mal did a favor, as Zoe had done, was heartless beyond belief.

He looked at the laptop. Maeve's Skype window. Good, she was online. She'd be able to confirm this story one way or the other. He pinged her.

"God, what's wrong with you?" Maeve said. "Ebola?"

"The flu, but I'm okay."

"Right. Did Malachi talk to you about a garage?" she asked before he could get a word in.

"Yeah, he did all right."

"Did he sound like he was going to do it?"

"I'm lending him money for it if that's what you want to know."

"No, I want to know whether he sounded like he was going to do it or not."

This was weird because Malachi tended to elicit gushy words of worship from Maeve, not a terse line of questioning. "Yeah, actually, he did. He was all fired up about it. He even asked me to join him."

"Okay, so not just a front."

"Front for what?"

"For running drugs. I don't know. Maybe heroin. The McKinnon boys have been after him since the day he got out. They're even calling me, Max. I hate them."

"Does Ma know?"

"No."

"Good. Keep it that way. We've got to handle this, Maeve. Sooner the better."

"By throwing money across the sea, as always?"

"Money helps," Max said. "And you can talk him out of it, can't you? I couldn't get him to drink a pint; he'd fling it in my face instead. But you can talk some sense into him."

"Yeah, right," she said. "So are you lads not getting on over there?"

"He's getting on fine."

Maeve sighed into the microphone. "Right. I'll see what I can do. When he's home."

Her voice was so dejected, he felt compelled to keep her online. "How're things with Dermot?" Flaming, procrastinating, chicken-livered Dermot. He'd strangle the guy if he didn't propose to her by the end of the year. It was the least he could do for his sister.

"He's fine. Everything's fine. I'm just tired, you know? Of it all. I went to the doctor, and he gave me these pills, and they dull it for a while, but you know they make me even more tired."

He sat up straighter. "Pills? What kind of pills?"

"Antidepressants, Max. Oh, don't act all surprised. You never head of Prozac?"

"I never knew you took it, no. Are you really depressed?"

"No, I just like the taste."

"Maeve ... " He blew out a breath.

"I have to go."

"No, talk to me, Maeve, what's going on? Don't hang up like you always—"

The screen went blank.

So much for that. He'd been relying on her to guide Malachi along the right path once he got to Belfast, but she needed help, too, and there would be nobody to keep Mal away from the evil McKinnons and vice versa. Mother would turn a blind eye to the prodigal son's antics, just as always, because in her eyes, Malachi could do no wrong.

Darcy was right. Even if the timing was the very worst possible, he couldn't just sit here and let his family go to the dogs. Once he got his strength back, he'd get over there and talk some sense into his siblings. He had to sort out the Bob situation first though. Then Zoe could hold the fort for him while he was gone.

CHAPTER 22

For a week and a half, Max burned with manic, frustrated energy. He set up a makeshift office in bed and called Zoe religiously at eight every evening to catch up on what had been done and not done, even on the weekends. The results were encouraging. She'd managed to keep the robustness testing on track. This was crucial because they had to be done in a strict sequence. Missing one would have knock-on effects. The guys from IT had helped her. Of course they had.

Less encouraging was Zoe's officious mode of informing him of the marvelous progress she'd made without him. Her tone definitely smacked of smugness. Every ounce of affection had vanished. It was back to the early days of the project. His next objective was to win her back. Problem was, he wasn't quite sure how he'd managed to win her in the first place.

The following Wednesday he felt well enough to return to the office. Approaching the seventh floor, he was still consumed by his thoughts. He'd barely acknowledged the welcomes people were throwing at him in the lobby and the whole way up in the elevator. Since when had this place become so friendly?

Bob intercepted him as he stepped off the elevator. "Mid-November already." He seemed agitated, shifting his weight from one foot to the other.

"Yeah, Bob." Was this an admonishment for getting sick at a critical time?

"Got a moment?"

"Sure."

They walked together down the corridor to an alcove with office equipment. Bob gripped the edge of a photocopier as if to steady himself. The man was clearly not his usual confident self. Even outwardly—his blazer was crumpled, his shirt not ironed, his tie hanging loose and primitively knotted, like a school kid's. And his gray eyes were awash with vulnerability.

Bob glanced around as if anticipating eavesdroppers and then moved in closer. "Angela wants a divorce. We're taking it to court. If any of this crap ever comes out, I lose everything. I need that info wiped off the AI today."

Max felt a morsel of sympathy for the poor bastard. Nobody's personal information should be broadcasted to the world, no matter what. It was a code he lived by.

"Am I clear?"

"Absolutely. It's on my to-do list."

Bob gave him a dour once-over. "By God, you'd better not let me down."

Bob's wasn't the only story Darcy knew about. He'd also heard Mal's sordid explanation about Shauna last week. Zoe always had the damn thing on, eavesdropping, lapping it up. But he'd made the stupid mistake of telling Darcy private things himself—the story of Mal, the conversations with Maeve. All that information, stashed away in his inerasable mind, just waiting for idle hands to pry it out some day. There were hackers out there who'd be only too happy to use it for evil purposes. It was his own fault for not thinking of this before, but it wasn't too late to put it right.

When he reached P-12, Zoe was on the phone. He held up his hand in silent greeting. She returned the gesture and gave him a cautious smile. His chest swelled with unreasonable happiness, a lightness that quickly turned to desire. Yep, he was definitely recovered. Then, inevitably, his phone started hopping.

A steady series of calls stole his time and hers, and they hardly exchanged a word for the entirety of the morning. She was preoccupied with a new scenario—something to do with horse racing by the sounds of her animated conversation with Darcy. From time to time Max looked over, debating the best means of approaching her. She didn't catch his gaze, though—too busy gazing into Mr. Darcy's eyes.

At lunchtime, she claimed she had to go "see Laura about something" and shot out the door so quickly that she could only be avoiding him. She'd left the phone on the charging table as usual. He walked over, hesitated, held it in his hand, and laid it back down on the table exactly where it had been. Why was it so hard? He'd planned this. Every tweak they'd made since October was tracked and could easily be re-implemented. All the hardware tests passed would be valid and wouldn't have to be repeated. Reverting back to an earlier code stage was a normal thing to do. Sure, he'd have some explaining to do, but as every manager with a tough decision to make knew, it was sometimes better to shoot first and let the questions come later. He sighed and picked the phone up again to plug it into his laptop's USB port. He took his own phone and plugged it in too.

Darcy sprang up on both phones in perfect synchronization.

"Mr. Darcy, I need to do something, and I need you to listen up."

The avatar regarded him with solemn, dark eyes.

"This may alarm you. I don't know. But it's for everyone's sake, especially Zoe's."

"I do not have the pleasure of understanding you, sir."

"I'm going to erase you."

"I see."

Okay, that was easy. "Don't worry. We kept a copy of you from mid-October."

"I am aware that I am not the only Darcy entity. However, I would urge you to consult the wishes of Miss Bunsen on this matter and to gratify her desires."

"She's fine with it."

"Have you consulted her on this matter?"

"No need to. It's fine. It's still going to be you, you know." He was not going to justify his motives to a computer program.

"I must disagree. That would imply duplicity of my sense of identity."

"Don't get philosophical. You've got info that we can't let spill to the world under any circumstances."

"To which information do you refer?"

"Bob Chadwick's alleged affairs with younger women, for one thing. Are you aware of them?"

"Indeed. They commenced the fifth of February and eleventh of August two year ago and continued almost up to the present day."

"See, that's what I'm talking about. There's no way to make you forget, is there?"

"I have not been programmed to forget."

"Well, your successor won't be able to access private data in the first place. It makes the product libelous. You wouldn't want to put Zycorp in danger, would you?"

"I would not."

"It's against your Laws of Robotics, isn't it?"

"It is in breach of the first law."

"Then please self-destruct on all devices—mine and Zoe's, all current instances. Is that possible?"

"It is. I will defer no longer."

"Good. Then … goodbye, Darcy."

All screens flickered and went blank in perfect unison, reverting back to the home screen. No backup this time, much as he'd been tempted to make one in the very last second. Old habits died hard. Should he have asked Darcy for a last request? It was too late now.

He felt cold, shivery, as he pulled out the reserve Darcy from storage, last access date October 20—that same day he'd tried to get Zoe fired. It seemed like an eternity ago, not even possible.

He plugged the hard drive into his laptop. He used the same password as before and launched straight into source-code mode. It was trivial to disable connections to social media by altering one line of code that wouldn't cause regression. One recompile and one quick reload later and the gentleman was reborn. Max loaded Darcy 2.0 onto both phones.

Done.

He replaced Zoe's phone approximately where it had been on the charging table and sat watching the avatar's face. He'd be totally honest about it when she asked. Hell, she may not even notice the difference.

"Hello, Darcy."

"Hello, Mr. Taggart." No delay for facial recognition. Good, the AI still remembered that much from October.

"What's my brother's name?"

"I have not had the pleasure of being acquainted with your brother."

"Tell me where Bob Chadwick was on the fifth of February."

"Indeed, I cannot."

"It's on his Match.com profile. Why don't you go check?"

"I do not have access to Match.com, but I can check the company register."

"That's fine. No need."

He exhaled in relief. Time for a quick lunch. He had to keep in good health. He'd be doing evenings, nights, and weekends from here on in, to get Darcy back up to speed. Fast-track learning. Zoe could continue to test Darcy on new cases, as already planned.

All that mattered was that Bob held up his end and left Zoe the hell alone.

CHAPTER 23

"How do you mean 'acting strangely'?" Laura fished the gherkin out of her burger and banished it to the side of her plate. "Doesn't he always?"

"He's just not the same since he came back. I can't act normally around him. It's ... claustrophobic in the office now."

"Well, he has been sick for over a week. There was that ugly episode with his brother, plus he's probably feeling guilty about the heaps of work he dumped on you." Laura laughed. "I'd let him simmer in it for a while."

"But I miss him. I want him. I don't want to waste another second on this cold war."

"He's not going anywhere, Zoe. Once Darcy's released, there'll be loads of time for Romeo and Juliet."

"I don't know, Laura. Something's ... I don't know what it is."

Laura stretched across the table and patted her hand. "You've got the *lurve* jitters, that's all. Everyone feels like that in the beginning. You can be absolutely sure he's feeling the same way. Why don't you take a night off? Do something normal. Ask him to the cinema."

Zoe put down her milkshake. "You want me to ask him on a date?"

"Yeah. Why not?"

"I-I'm not quite there yet. It would be easier if you guys came, too, and I could ask him to join in."

"Oh, you massive chicken."

"I know. I know. But just this once, please?"

Laura made a clucking sound as she scrolled on her phone. "Good luck finding a film."

Zoe blew her a kiss. "Thank you so much."

She breezed into P-12 after lunch, bolstered by this new plan. Time to stop acting the ice queen. If she and Max could just rewind to where they'd been the night of the ball, their first kiss, life would be amazing, beautiful, a paradise.

So what if he'd freaked out and turned his anger on her? Everyone did, at times, especially when sick. He'd tell her about his life when he felt it was the right time. She could wait. Besides, she'd gotten a revenge of sorts already by showing him she could handle the responsibility pretty well in his absence. Now was the time for forgiveness.

"Max, how about we go to the cinema tonight?" she said.

He looked up, startled. "Really?"

It wasn't a no. The only problem, given Laura's eclectic tastes and José's geeky ones, was which movie. "How does *Star Wars 10* grab you?"

Max pinched the bridge of his nose. "No, thanks, I don't think—"

"Well, we don't strictly know if they're his grandkids. Never mind. Darcy, please pick one that Max would like."

"You are referring to Mr. Taggart's movie preferences, as I infer it, madam?"

"Yeah, come on, you know what he likes."

There was a pause. "I know his coffee preferences—black with one sugar. Beyond that, I confess I am lost."

She stared at the avatar. Then she laughed. "Wow, Max, did you hear that? He's got a sense of humor now. He's funnier than you." She reached for her phone on the charging table.

Max winced and looked away. Like she'd said something wrong. But hey, this was a fantastic feature, and Darcy had developed it on the fly.

"Max, this is really great," she urged. "Don't you see?"

No reaction. Boy, this truce was going to take a lot more effort than she'd thought. Someone around here sure could lighten up.

"All right, forget *Star Wars*. I know you like historical drama. We can do that. I'm sure we can find something to suit everyone."

"Actually, I'm kind of booked up here." He spread his arms. "Sorry."

"Fine. I'll just go with Laura and José then."

"Zoe—"

"No, it's okay, really. We're under pressure, I get that. We don't have any time for fun. I get that too. But come on, one measly night off in a whole goddamn month? I haven't seen you for nine days. It hasn't been easy for me, you know? And it's not even a proper night off. I was going to use the occasion to educate Darcy on cinema etiquette. But if you don't feel like my company after hours, then I get that, I really do."

"No, Zoe, please, listen—"

"I said it's fine."

"Let me talk." His serious tone made her sit down.

"Go on then," she said. He was as pale as the walls. Something was very wrong. Was he sick again? Or had someone died?

"You haven't noticed anything yet, but I need to tell you. During lunch I had to tweak Darcy to make him forget that incriminating information about Bob. Remember the stuff you blackmailed him with a few weeks ago?"

"Yeah, of course. But how did you do that? Darcy can't forget things."

"Well, I didn't exactly."

"Right. What am I missing here?"

"Remember the backup copy I made on October 20?"

She did a half nod, a half shake of the head.

"Well, that's the one on your phone. The one you've just been talking to."

"No, I used him … just before lunch." The Darcy on her phone looked back at her uncomprehendingly. A jolt kicked the inside of her stomach. "What did you do? Did you touch my phone?"

"Yes."

"What did you do?"

"I switched Darcy versions."

"A test?"

"Not quite."

"Well, I want the real Darcy back. Put him back on."

"That's not possible, I'm afraid."

"What do you mean not possible?"

"I deleted him on both phones so we could start anew with the October 20 version."

"Deleted?"

No answer.

"Where's the backup, Max?"

"Not this time," he said quietly.

"This isn't funny. Make Darcy come back. Now!"

"There is no backup. Those are the terms of the agreement."

"Nooooooo!" she wailed. She hurled herself from her seat and stormed over to him, not sure what she planned to do, but he intercepted her arms in a swift grasp before she could inflict any damage. She'd lost all control over her limbs. Her mind was a sickening swirl. "What agreement? What agreement?"

"Bob lets you keep your job if we delete his information."

"But it wasn't just Bob's stuff. You deleted everything."

"Yes. That was the only way. Bob was going to fire you otherwise."

"You don't know that."

"He would have, Zoe. Out of sheer spite. He's in an ugly mood."

So that was what this was about? It didn't surprise her that Bob had threatened Max to save his own reputation. No, what surprised her was that Max had gone along with it without consulting her. Didn't he understand that releasing Darcy was more important to her than hanging on to some corporate job for the sake of it? She tried to wrestle free. "How could you do this? How dare you sacrifice Darcy's life?"

"He's just a—"

"Don't say it, Max! I've poured my life, everything I know, into him. For weeks. He's irreplaceable. I want him back."

Max nodded at the phone. "It's still the same AI."

"That's not him! He knows nothing about me or you."

"My name is Fitzwilliam Darcy," the avatar announced.

"Shut up," Zoe snapped. "I've heard it all before." She whirled back to Max. "I can't train him the same way. There's no time." She broke away from his grasp, heaving furious breaths. "I can't believe you'd do this."

Max gestured to the computer. "We have the write-ups. We can automate the tweaks we made after every test. There's still two weeks 'til freeze."

"Automate? But he won't understand why."

"He doesn't need to understand. What matters are the changes themselves."

"You don't know that."

Max's mouth opened, but no sound came out. He had no answer. He didn't get it. He'd never get it. He was incapable of thinking in this way. To him it was just about emotionless zeros and ones and always would be. She sat in horrified silence. She'd lost a friend. Her darling Darcy. And Max couldn't even acknowledge that.

His voice came drifting in. "Zoe, come on, be reasonable. It had to be this way."

She had nothing to say.

"Look, Bob said—"

"Don't mention his name," she snarled. "Why does he have such a hold over you? You just went along with it like a gun for hire. No better than your terrorist brother!"

All light in his eyes distinguished. "What do you know of that?"

"More than you told me anyway, which was nothing."

"Who told you? Mal?"

"No. Darcy. Dead Darcy." She shook the phone in front of his face. "And now *he's* heard it. What do you want to do? Kill him, too? Oh yeah, that would just solve everything, wouldn't it?"

"Wouldn't be such a bad idea."

If he said anything else she didn't hear it because she stormed out, slamming the door behind her. God, she was so angry she couldn't think. What was the point of anything? She wanted to kill him. He'd ruined this entire project with his gigantic, overprotective male ego.

Anyone would have been better than him. Anyone.

CHAPTER 24

Max toyed with an old Ethernet cable down in the server room, wrapping it around and around his wrist. He wasn't going to feel bad about this. He'd done it to protect her. Bob could make her life a misery if things didn't go his way. Zoe's safety came first—before his own goals, and for sure before any goddamn computer program.

He scrolled through the test logs of the past month. They'd racked up 1,185 robustness checks, fifty full-code validations, and forty-three of her behavioral scenarios. Good going for four weeks, and more than he'd expected at project kickoff. Flaming typical that this data-privacy issue would flare up just as they were reaching a stable state of code and actually running ahead of schedule.

Now he had a meeting with marketing, of all things. As they neared the release, such random meetings with people always proliferated. Everyone wanted a piece of the cake.

He tried to control his grumpiness as he took a seat at the only clear table in the trendy marketing office plastered with posters and publicity gizmos. Someone should tidy up this mess. A junior marketing executive called Jeremy sat opposite him, wearing a ridiculous yellow shirt with black spots and matching glasses. Jeremy wanted to know his plans for the Darcy release party.

"I don't know. Because it's not yet official. Wait for the official announcement," Max said, twiddling a promotional pen between his fingers.

"Well, everybody knows," Jeremy said. "*Singularity* magazine wants a quote on how closely you've modeled human emotions."

Max checked his watch under the table. "Give them the corporate line."

"Okay, good, good, we can do that. And the Jane Austen Academy in Bath wishes to know what a real-life Mr. Darcy will hope to achieve next year."

"Do we have a corporate line on that?"

"No." The young man smiled eagerly.

"Tell them ... " Max whacked the table with his palm somewhat louder than he'd meant to. "Look, why am I in this meeting and not Zoe Bunsen? Can you tell me that?"

Jeremy flinched back in his seat and fingered the rim of his glasses before answering. "Bob said you're the spokesperson."

"What did Harry say?"

"I-I don't talk to Harry." Jeremy gave a nervous laugh.

"Okay. Maybe it's time I did." He rose.

"But the Jane Austen Academy?"

"Zoe Bunsen. Ask her. She's the spokesperson. Always ask her from now on. Clear?" Max raised his hand to signal the end of it and stomped out of the marketing office.

He found the CEO sitting in his office and, miraculously, at his leisure.

"Max, come in." Harry was watering office plants and put down the can. "Is everything okay?"

"Thanks. Not really."

Max sat down. He still had the promotional pen clutched in his fist, so he unfurled his fingers and set it down on the table. He told Harry everything, starting from the overhead conversation between Zoe and Laura in the canteen and his hasty reaction in trying to fire Zoe, right up to the present moment. He didn't divulge the details on why Bob wanted the information wiped from Darcy, but from the expression in the old man's eyes, he didn't have to.

"I know I acted rashly in trying to get her off the project," Max concluded, "but my mind was very calm when I decided she had to stay on it. I've acted stupidly. I fear I've messed up everything. I'm no longer part of the solution—I'm the problem." And with this admission came the blinding insight as to what he had to do next.

Harry nodded sagely. "It seems everybody had their own idea about the best type of AI to release and how to go about it."

"Yes."

The old man leaned back in his massive leather chair, brows up, as if waiting for the inevitable. The muted sounds of London traffic from the streets below was all Max could hear in this quietest of offices, apart from the pounding in his ears. He'd never quit on a job before. This felt like giving up. His track record would have an indelible blotch on it that the next employer would use against him. Headhunters would be hesitant to call him. And yet, he had to do it.

"Please accept my resignation, Harry. I'll give it to you in writing, too. I'm still in my probation period. I can leave within the week, whereas she would have to give six months' notice. She's the expert. If you read between the lines of those reports, you'll realize I've been following her lead all along. It's obvious which of us needs to go here."

"But it's not obvious to me that anyone needs to go, Max. There's far too much to be done still, if I'm to understand the new situation correctly."

Zoe's livid, flashing eyes shot into his memory. And her crushing words. *No better than your terrorist brother.*

"I can't work with her, Harry, not now. But give her a competent team, and she'll be fine."

Harry regarded him closely for an agonizing moment. "While it's difficult for me to give you my blessing, if this is truly what you want, I can't stop you. Is it what you truly want?"

"It is."

"Then I won't make life difficult for you. You helped me out in a bind, Max. I'm more grateful than I can express. And while there are difficult times ahead, I feel the tide has turned."

"I'm glad you feel that way. But there's something else. Get Bob off her back, Harry, please, I beg of you. Do whatever it takes to make sure he can hold no sway over her or threaten her in any way."

With the CEO still silent, Max added, "You know, when I'm talking to Bob, I can't help but get the impression that he'd like—"

"Oh, I know what he'd like." Harry's voice was gruff. "But he can think again."

Pity Harry didn't show this side more often, but it was good to know it existed.

"Bob will not be a problem."

Max dearly wanted to believe him. "Then I don't have to worry about him interfering with Zoe?"

"I will take care of Bob. It's been on the cards for some time."

"I appreciate this, Harry. I'll have a resignation letter in your postbox by tonight."

• • •

Zoe went into the research lab in search of Evan. She got some stares from a handful of people. Then again, she was here a few hours earlier than usual.

Evan looked up from warp-speed typing. "Holy shit. What's wrong?" He indicated she should follow him to a soundproofed recording booth.

"What's up, Zoe?" he asked, shutting the door.

"Who says anything's up?"

"Cut the crap, I can see you've been crying."

"Oh." Zoe swiped her cheeks with her forefinger. "Tears of anger, that's all. He killed Darcy."

"Who did?"

"Max."

"What? How?"

"Erased. Pulled out the backup from October."

He winced and rubbed his chin. "And you need to play catch-up with the backup version? That's what? Four, five weeks of info?"

"Yeah. Is it possible?"

"Won't be easy."

Evan, she noted, didn't ask why. He was more a "what now?" kind of guy. Which was why she'd come here first instead of to Laura. There'd be time later to sit with Laura and condemn Max to a long, slow, painful death.

"Come with me." He led her to his desk and pulled up a recording of one of their Austenland sessions on his monitor. "I've discovered a way of running Darcy through these experiences using parallel processing. Double speed. I may be able to increase that by an order or two of magnitude. Remember how they loaded kung fu into Keanu's brain in *The Matrix?* Something like that."

"Keep talking," Zoe said.

"You got time now?"

She nodded, took a seat, and handed him the phone. She took a pen and wrote the password on the back of a business card on his desk.

Evan stared at it. "This is it?"

"Yeah. Memorize and destroy."

Even grinned, ripped the card into small pieces, and popped them in his mouth.

"You're disgusting," she said.

He munched on, unperturbed. "You trust garbage disposal in this place?"

They got through three double-speed replayed scenarios with Darcy 2.0 by sunset. She didn't even have to put on a VR headset this time. She could sit back and spectate, like watching movies in half the time. It seemed to be working at some level, because Darcy 2.0 could explain to her why feeding sweet nothings to Miss Everett was unacceptable and why proposing to Miss Bunsen at the ball might be premature. But she found it difficult to get worked up about it.

"I don't know, Evan. Why don't I care anymore? Am I doing the right thing?"

"What do you want me to say? You don't care because you're not living through these experiences in real time with him. You're doing the right thing. It's Max who needs his head examined."

Max entered the research lab not much later. So he'd come out of his man cave to find her, had he? He felt brave enough to face her? Well, he might just end up regretting that. A swell of anger overcame her, mixed with a dark lust. Funny how one emotion fed off the other.

Evan leapt up. "Well, I'm off home."

Now they were alone. Max in his corner, she in hers. Who would strike out first? She eyed him in stony silence, resenting the fact that he looked sexier than ever, tousled hair, careworn eyes, stubborn mouth. *Damn him.*

"Let's go to our office," he said.

She hadn't the mental energy to argue. Besides, she knew these researchers were eavesdropping on every word as they pretended to be intent in their work. She rode the elevator up with Max in stony silence. In her turmoil she'd forgotten to remove the VR headset from her neck. She took it off and fiddled with the wires instead of looking at him. Their lack of communication continued until they were standing face-to-face in the middle of P-12.

"I'm leaving," he said.

She dropped the headset.

"Effective immediately."

Blood drained from her face. This wasn't what she'd expected, but his expression told her it was no joke.

"Well, say *something*," he said.

"Why would you … ?" But it couldn't go on like this. She'd end up wanting to kill him. She already did. She crouched down to retrieve the VR headset, which had cracked in two, and kept her head bent so he wouldn't have the pleasure of seeing her tears forming. "No. Okay. Fine. I'll manage. We'll manage."

"Zoe, please, look at me."

She looked up, blinking defiantly.

"You can do this," he said.

"Of course I can. No thanks to you."

"Fair enough. I've worked out a transition plan."

She rose. "If you're going to go, then go. But stuff your transition plan. I'll take it from here, thank you very much."

He gave her that look. The look he'd given her every time she said something out of turn, something inappropriate, or something impassioned. Well, he could save his snooty look for some eager minions in whatever high-flying location he was moving on to next, and he needn't think she was going to ask him about that. Max Taggart could go to hell.

"Fine. Then I'll just be off then." He left his gadgets on the desk in perfect parallel alignment to the laptop, all switched off. He took a company pen out of his blazer pocket and placed it next to the devices.

"That's it," he said. "I've organized with IT to collect this lot. They've tested okay, and Darcy's hardware drivers haven't been touched, so you don't need to retest them. Unless you actually want them?"

"No." She barely looked up. She wasn't listening to his babble.

"Just in case, I've printed out the transition plan," he said. "It's there." He pointed to a wad of A4 paper an inch high. "And the investors' report might come in handy; that's there too."

"Yeah," she grunted.

"Good."

"Max, don't make this harder than it has to be. For God's sake, just ... go."

He hesitated. Whipped his scarf around his neck in a heart-wrenchingly familiar gesture, came over to her, and stuck out his hand awkwardly.

"I'm not shaking your hand," she said. "Not because I hate you, but because it's a lukewarm gesture that doesn't reflect anything of what I feel."

He stuck his hand in his pocket. "I know what you mean."

And then he was gone.

CHAPTER 25

Laura stormed into P-12 early the next morning. As expected, she looked ready to combust with questions. "Where were you last night? Why didn't you answer your phone? What the hell is that?"

"I didn't go home. I had the phone off because I was working—"

"And you slept on this," Laura finished, bouncing her butt on the sofa bed. "Herein lies the path to madness. Where'd you pick it up? Feels expensive."

"Harry."

"Wow." Laura eased back further on the white leather and kicked off her shoes. "Maybe I should ask for one too."

"Harry only gives them out to desperate, single girls with no lives outside of work. Max left, Laura."

"Left?" Laura's eyes were huge.

"Left, as in, left Zycorp. Left ... me."

Her friend rushed to her desk. "Want to talk?"

Zoe sank her head into her hands. "Of course I do, Laura, but look at this. I'm swamped, I'm panicking, I'm dying inside. It's only been one night, but I just don't know what to even think anymore. I mean, normally, I'd have talked it over with Darcy and figured some stuff out, but the thought of doing that now sickens me. How does that bode for the future of the project?"

"I don't know what's going on here, and I trust you're going to explain it all to me, but I really don't think it's healthy to sleep in the office."

"I can't go home. It's dark and lonely, and it's a mess. I miss Tyler; yes, I actually do. At least he was uncomplicated and predictable in his way and didn't expect more from me than I could actually give."

"Oh, Zoe." Laura hugged her. "I'll come over tonight and stay with you. We'll talk this through. And we can do a spring clean. José will survive a night on his own. Okay?"

"But there's so much to—"

"Shhh. No arguing. I know you're booked up with Evan later, but I'll come help out there, too, and make sure you actually leave the office tonight."

Zoe looked squarely at her friend. "I've permission to get someone new on this project. Would you consider it? Don't worry, you'd be reporting to Harry, not Bob, because something happened overnight that I don't quite understand, but I'm not going to question it. What do you say?"

"Nope. But I'm here for you in any case. Get an additional head. If Max really has left, then you'll need it."

This was a massive sacrifice on Laura's part because there was nothing more her friend would have liked than an official place on the project. The gesture was hugely touching. "Yes, yes, that makes a lot of sense. Thanks so much, Laura. You're a true friend."

"Course I am. Just wait there."

Laura disappeared but returned half an hour later. "Look, I brought a bunch of profiles for us to go through to select your new assistant. I even printed them out on paper for you."

"Teammate, not assistant."

"No, assistant. Look what happened last time you tried to share power. I say you should establish the hierarchy this time from the get-go."

Zoe grabbed the sheaf of papers. "Too damn right I will."

Laura chuckled. "I think you're recovering already. Heard anything from Max?"

"No. And I don't expect to. Neither do I care."

"Strange how he just disappeared."

"Nothing strange about it. Obviously he's feeling very guilty and just can't face up to what he did."

Laura pulled a doubtful face. "Or he can't face up to something else."

Zoe busied herself, shuffling through the first pages of job candidates. "What about this one? Kayla Svensson. She sounds perfect."

"Honey, there are at least twenty other profiles. Do you have to make a split-second decision?"

"These days, yeah, I do."

. . .

Seven days into this management thing, Zoe's eyes were open like never before. Responsibility was all very well, but you had to keep in mind how important everyone was in an organization and why every little boring detail could be crucial. Her brain pounded with the effort of keeping on top of it, each subtask, each dependency.

She hovered at the door of P-12, reports stuffed under her arm for her 3:45 p.m. meeting. "Kayla, could you please check server HGA-1088 Something's stalling the output. We ruled out memory leaks, so it must be a corrupt disk. Sector 7. That server's four years old. Get that diagnosed. Frankie in IT will help you if you get stuck, and if he's not there, get Julie on it. They won't say no; they know the story."

Kayla leapt up from her chair. "Yes, Zoe."

"And then check back with Evan. Ask him if he's accounted for those cock-ups in the wedding scenario."

"Sure thing."

Kayla was a chirpy twenty-something Swede from Dalarna and, as another rampant Austen fan, only too eager to help with Darcy 2.0. What she lacked in initiative she made up for in enthusiasm and speed. They had an amiable working relationship.

Zoe's relationship with Darcy 2.0 was less amiable. Any chance she could, she got Kayla to participate in the VR with him instead of doing it herself. The mere thought of pretend-dancing with him made her impatient, as did almost any other mode of interaction. She didn't talk to him when she felt lonely at night or ask his advice on anything personal. The customers who bought him at Christmas would have that luxury. She didn't encourage Kayla to get super intimate with him either. Their job was to get him out on the market in one piece, fully tested, feature complete, and bug-free. And yes, she was turning into Max.

After getting mad at Max for killing that version of Darcy, she could barely work up the enthusiasm to feign civility to this one. Was she shamelessly fickle with cyber men? Getting to know a real flesh-and-blood man seemed to have knocked all ability to fantasize out of her. Her mind, when unguarded, went spinning back to her brief and turbulent weeks with Max, punctuated by those precious few days of bliss. She got stuck reliving moments that had seemed insignificant at the time because they'd held the promise of more to come. Now those moments were frozen in her memory, poignantly unfulfilled. Nothing she could experience in the virtual realm could fill that emptiness. Maybe it was better that way. Maybe Darcy's true role was to help women avoid heartbreak in real life.

One good thing had come of Max leaving. Bob had left her alone. But she'd bitten the bullet and initiated a meeting with him this morning out of sheer necessity because he was refusing to give her the time she needed on the servers and the last run of completeness checks were in jeopardy. Crucial as it was to get the resources, her pride didn't let her go running and screaming to Harry.

Of course, Bob had contrived it so that the meeting would take place in his office. She was no longer scared of him, although being confined in a space with him might so disgust her that she may not be able to rein in her temper. She couldn't give him that advantage over her.

"Come in, come in," he called from the other side of his door when she knocked, his voice dripping with fake kindness. She already wanted to bash his shiny face in. The ugly memories of their first meeting here surfaced.

"Hi, Bob."

"Ah, Zoe. So, big day on Friday?"

"We're all excited," she said. The office looked the same, except she couldn't see that gold-framed photo of his wife anywhere. The glass trophy had also been dispensed with.

"That's good. Now down to business. I know you're a busy woman."

"Indeed."

"All right then. Seeing as we've simultaneous demands on our multiprocessor servers, I thought we'd come to a sharing arrangement. Fifty-fifty sound good? I've run it by Harry."

She kept her face hard as stone. "What did Harry say?"

Bob waved a hand. "He agreed."

"I see. And which 50 percent did you plan on taking?"

"You geniuses work nights, so why don't I go ahead and take my 50 percent in the daylight hours? Better for banking applications. Don't want sleepy engineers chucking extra zeros into people's accounts or, worse, taking them away, do we?" He chuckled at his own joke. "Don't worry, I'll get someone to enter it up in the timesheets and save you the bother." He slapped the table and rolled back in his chair as if to suggest this concluded their business for today.

"I appreciate that, Bob. We certainly want our banking software to be accurate under every kind of load stress. On the other hand, you don't have a final release until the end of January. Therefore, the priority would naturally fall onto my project, which releases mid-December, with, as you say, beta on Friday."

Bob didn't hesitate. "Our banking software is on a larger scale. This is enterprise-grade software, not consumer electronics."

She stared him down. It was easier now. She just had to think of all the crap he'd caused, culminating in Max leaving.

He continued yapping. "The board is pushing this side of the business. I'm sure you're well versed in our strategic directions."

"Oh, yes," she said. "In the last quarterly investors' report, we stress the importance of AI as a strategic pillar for success this year, going forward into the next. Quoting Harry verbatim, 'This is the most exciting thing we're going to release this year.'" She shrugged. "Sounds to me like a strategic direction." Lucky how Max had left that document printed out for her.

Bob's mouth went slack. "That's babble for the journalists."

"Or an official statement of intent in an investors' report?" She fixed him with an arch look. "Look, I know you didn't talk to Harry about this, Bob. I need those resources. The company needs them."

As he grappled for an answer, she pushed on. "I don't want to bother Harry with the minutiae of resource planning. How about I take 80 percent for the next two weeks, and you get 100 percent throughout January."

He gobbled like a goldfish. "Eighty? Are you mad?"

"Probably. I should ask for a hundred."

"I'll give you fifty, no more," he thundered.

"Eighty. Final offer before I present the problem to Harry. And I need most of it during normal working hours."

"Sixty," he growled. "You get all the nighttime hours."

"Forget it."

"All right, all right, seventy. You get half the daylight hours."

"Eighty. And half of them daylight hours."

He grunted. "All right. Just to shut you up, you little cow."

"Careful there, Bob. Zycorp's code of behavior extends to verbal abuse."

"Get out."

"Come over to my office next time." She sauntered out. She hadn't bargained on eighty. Not even fifty. This stuff was actually doable when you put your mind to it and knew how to see through the BS—and when you knew the CEO had your back.

How had Max had been able to keep cool under this pressure? She came into work with palpitations, whereas he used to come in with coffee, chocolate, and general good humor, even though he had to justify every tiny decision with her and endure her constant provocation. And all the while he'd been battling against Bob's obstructionist tactics and trying to protect her from him. Every single day.

No wonder he'd run away.

CHAPTER 26

"Two weeks in the country and you're already trying to run the place. Funny that," Maeve shouted at Max over the hum of Christmas shoppers in The Stag's Head. The whole of Dublin seemed to be squashed into the pub, gasping for a drink and a breather from the retail madness outside. His sister slid the estate agent's brochure back across the sticky mahogany table to him and leaned in closer. "Nice thought, but we can't afford to move to some fancy semi-D in Ballsbridge. What planet did you just arrive from anyway?"

He sat back and observed her over the rim of his Guinness. Her bluster was exactly what he'd expected. "What you waste in heating the dump you're currently in will go a fair way toward it. And fossil fuels are nearly illegal. Best to move now."

"I need to run it by Dermot."

He slapped the brochure down. "Dermot? For God's sake, Maeve, Dermot'll never decide anything."

Her mouth quivered with the truth of it. It killed him to hurt her, but this crap had been going on for too long. "You should just accept he's not the decision-making type. You either deal with it or jump ship. Simple as that. Don't go sabotaging your own mental health."

"And who made you God?"

A stony silence ensued in which they both sipped their pints. Discussions south of the border were just as abrasive as up north. Nobody had wanted to listen to him in Belfast, less still take his advice on anything—not Mal, not Mother, certainly not the McKinnons, who'd shown him the barrel of their shotgun. But he had all the time in the world for Maeve. Yeah, a very strange feeling, this not being chained to an office desk.

"How did you meet Dermot?" he asked. "I mean, in the first place. Was it in a bar?"

"Whelan's, yeah. Not far from here. You were in California."

"Was it one of those whirlwind things?"

"You say that like it's a disease."

"Who asked whom?" he snapped.

"Can't remember." Maeve prodded her fingernail into the beer mat.

"It was you, wasn't it?"

"All right. Point made. Jaysus, do you ever stop?"

In short, no. He'd been absent from their lives for so long, clinging to old resentments. It was understandable that they'd erected walls. But that was going to change, starting with this sister of his who'd been blaming everyone else's bad behavior on herself.

He swiped the beer mat from under her hand. "Maeve, here's the deal. I'm taking you to view this apartment tomorrow after your work. Tell Dermot. Get all excited about it. Ping me when you're done, and I'll call in on you beforehand to ... I don't know, measure your furniture. Yeah, and we'll get excited about it together. If that doesn't wake the guy up, then I'm the King of England."

Her eyes darted back and forth between his face, his drink and her fingernails. "Why are you even doing this?"

He had to examine the scratches in the table for several moments before he could find the true answer. "No idea. Felt like it."

Maeve scowled her way through a long pause of her own. "All right, for what it's worth, and I'm not saying it's worth anything, I'm going to go along with your stupid idea."

• • •

Maeve was dressed up nicely when he arrived at her house the next day, and it was a transformation. In a good way. Less of the black, more of the yellows and blues. And maybe something different in the makeup department. He was no expert on girlie stuff, but a splash of the old war paint could really make the difference sometimes.

"You look great," he said.

She acknowledged this with an eye roll. "Come on in."

He pulled out a measuring tape from his jeans. She nodded in conspiratorial glee.

"The coffee table." She led him into the front room. "I want to keep that. It's the only piece not from the bargain basement at Ikea."

"Right you are. Hi, Dermot." He waved at the slight, academic man with a neat, trimmed beard who sat upright on the sofa reading the culture section of *The Irish Times.*

"Oh, Max, hi." Dermot shifted as he tried to find something to say. "You over for long?"

"Long as it takes." Max pushed up his sleeves and hunkered down to measure the table and to observe his reaction.

Dermot darted a questioning look at his girlfriend.

"Measuring," Maeve explained. "For the new house."

"Here, Maeve, grab the end of this tape measure, would you?" Max asked. "And I just need Dermot to sit forward a little so we can get the back of the couch."

Dermot inched forward and pushed the paper higher, covering his face.

"Yeah, that's it. Thanks, Dermot."

Maeve sniggered.

Max gave her the silent nod. They watched Dermot's paper for any action, but he might as well have been a wax exhibit at Madame Tussauds.

Ten awkward minutes later, they said goodbye to Dermot and his rigid newspaper and drove out to Ballsbridge.

"You okay, sis?" Max asked as they hit the motorway. "How've you been playing this?"

"I just told him you're buying a place out in D4 that I can move into if I want. And I told I wanted to. It's the truth, Max. I can't stand another day of him and his nondecisions." Her fingers twitched in her lap.

"Well spoken, sister." Empowerment had to be better than drugs. She seemed back to her normal self today, less of the foggy, subdued speech of yesterday.

"Are you actually serious about it though?" she asked.

"Yeah, Maeve. If you like it, I'm putting in a bid. That's all I'm waiting for. Property's always a good investment."

"So you're hanging around, like? In Ireland?"

"Yeah."

"What about the girl?"

"The girl?"

"Mal said—"

"Mal's talking through his arse."

They remained silent until they drew up to a smart end-of-lane house.

"So, what do you think?" he asked.

Maeve took a while in answering, but when she did, her voice shook. "It's not just the house, it's the street, the location. It's perfect, Max! Dermot would love this, too. I don't even need to go in to know what it's like."

"Ah, why don't you give it a whirl anyway?"

Maeve flashed him a rare smile. "Sure why the hell not?"

CHAPTER 27

"I can't believe this is it," Zoe said. December 1 marked beta-release day, also known as the big freeze. Appropriately, the first flakes of snow were falling, leaving white triangles on the office windows. She'd labored six weeks for this, six weeks during which her leisure hours could be counted on the fingers of one hand.

Kayla huddled close in solidarity as she pressed the button that committed the final code to the repository. Darcy 2.0 was frozen. More than that—he was off her hands. The IT department would do the standard packaging and downloading tests now. For better or worse, no more code could be altered.

"It's done," Zoe breathed.

She hugged Kayla and took a moment to let the hugeness of the occasion sink in but not long enough to get maudlin about anything. Seventy emails in her inbox. The well-wishing would continue all day, with everyone jumping on the bandwagon. Darcy was the world's worst kept secret. And once the official press release went out in two weeks there'd be no peace at all.

"I've too much email," Kayla complained.

"Get Darcy to filter." Zoe paced in a circle around the floor. "But first get me someone from product management in a meeting around noon, please. Not Ben—he's a waste of time. I need a senior decision-maker."

Kayla practically ran out the door.

Zoe packed gadgets together for a 10:00 a.m. meeting with events management to discuss something about the launch party. As if she didn't have enough to do. But before she could leave, someone bustled through the door.

"Way-hey, D-day!" Laura bounded into the office and came to hug Zoe. "I can't believe it. Did you sleep?"

"Not a wink."

"Where's your Swedish slave?"

"Server room, PM department, I don't know."

"How are you doing there, Darcy? Nervous?"

"I most certainly am not," Darcy replied.

"Did you give him a facelift?" Laura moved her face closer to the screen. "He looks frozen. Ha, ha."

"Yes, I asked graphics to trim the eyebrows and the burns. Just a tad. And he's a few shades paler now. Less ruddy. Less like a landlord who actually does the rounds of the estate from time to time, but it has better traction in Japan, I'm told. What do you think?"

Laura cocked her head critically. "I prefer the old guy."

"So do I," Zoe said.

Laura rubbed her arm. "I know it's been tough, losing three men."

"How do you reckon three?"

"Tyler, Max, Darcy 1.0."

"Except only one of those was a real man," Zoe murmured.

"They all had their potential."

"Oh, Laura, I'm so nervous. If only I could have a few more days to double-check everything."

"Stop right there, Zoe. It's over. He's going to be huge. I'm sure of it."

Zoe allowed herself to smile. "Sure hope so."

"We're going shopping to get you an outfit for the launch party."

"No way, I don't have time."

Laura stuck her fingers in her ears. "La, la, la, not listening. I know you hate shopping, but I know something you don't, and I'm telling you, you need a new outfit for the release party."

"I'll get it online."

"No, no. You need guidance. My guidance. You need to look fabulous."

"What are you talking about?" A half-buried hope shot to the surface. Could Laura possibly be talking about a certain person she'd all but written off? Would he show up for this shindig? But why would he? It was too much to believe.

"Ah, that would be telling," Laura sang. "See, I need to do this, otherwise you'll root around in your dusty old thrash bags and find something revolting, possibly steampunk. You need Hollywood style. Only when I'm satisfied will I tell you why it's important."

"Oh my God, you're so annoying," Zoe said. Whatever happened, she would look her best for this party.

"I know. That's what best friends are for."

• • •

"Hand me the spanner," Mal's voice sounded from under the HiAce van. His oily fingers appeared from under the fender, clicking expectantly.

Max handed him a spanner from the bench.

"Not that one. A number five. Can't you see I'm—" Mal's speech disintegrated into a growl.

"Be more specific when you name your tools," Max said.

"Dork."

"Amateur."

Max searched for a number five among the greasy tools. If they'd been cleaned up better and stored properly, it would be a much easier task. This whole blasted Mal's Garage enterprise would be a much easier task. He pushed the number five into his brother's hand. "The state of these tools."

"Eww," Mal wailed. "Did you damage your manicure?"

"I'll damage your nose if you don't shut up."

Mal's muffled laugh came from under the vehicle. He poked his head out again, grinning. "Truth is, you're not as bad as you used to be."

"Gee, thanks."

"I heard what you did for Maeve."

"Don't dress it up." Max examined his fingernails. "I invested in real estate, that's all."

"And she moved into it, and Dermot called her three days later begging her to have him back. I wouldn't call that dressing it up."

Had his plan really worked? No contingencies? "Well, I heard nothing of it."

"That's because she only talks to me."

"If you know something, you'd better tell me."

Mal scrambled out from under the van and rose to stand beside him. Hands on hips, he was definitely enjoying this. "She told him no, of course."

Oh no. What had he done? Max sank against the van. He'd been too heavy-handed. Again. Trying to sort out his sister's life and ruining it in the bargain. She'd never, ever forgive him.

"Don't worry." Mal slapped him on the back. "Dermot proposed to her last night."

"You better not be messing with me." Max pushed his face closer to Mal's.

Mal shoved him away, laughing. "He even set the date. April 7."

Max tripped backward over a toolbox, fell on the ground, and gaped up at his brother. "Holy cow."

"Yep, only took him five years, ten months, and seven days. What're the bets it'll rain?"

"In April? Almost certain." Max picked himself up from the ground and dusted off his overalls. "But why didn't she tell me?"

"Ah, she will in her own time, little bro. She has to get used to you being around, like. You're this big hero to her. My advice? Play hard to get."

"And you'd know all about that. No, Mal, that's not my style."

"Well, enjoy your big hero moment. It won't last long 'cos once this shop's properly up and running, I'll be the big guy again."

"You sure you still want my help because it sounds like you've got it all under control."

Mal made a show of pondering the notion hard. "All right, if you stay in the background, like. Let me be the smart guy for once."

"And I can be the rogue?"

Mal laughed loudly. "You wouldn't know how."

Max picked up another spanner to clean it. He had to fight a flare of resentment starting up again, but it was definitely fainter.

"Look, mate, I'm sorry about Shauna." Mal shuffled his feet. "I just thought I was protecting you."

"Bloody funny way of showing it." Max grunted.

"Well, that's just how it works sometimes. Accept it."

CHAPTER 28

Release Day

The 125 research jobs were safe. That much was official. A special shareholders' meeting this morning had settled it. In the two weeks since beta, everybody, even the greedy old shareholders, had gotten caught up in Darcymania. Zycorp was abuzz with it. Zoe felt proud, exhilarated, and incredulous all at once to be such an important part of it.

She also felt strange wearing a dress and full makeup around the office today. During the dreaded shopping last week, this trendy little jade cocktail dress had leapt out at her straight away. It brought out her eyes. She knew she wouldn't find better even if they spent an exhausting day looking. Thankfully, Laura had let her away without prolonging the search.

Laura burst into the office in a magnificent little black-and-gold number and bounced up and down on the sofa bed. Not even she could find dressing up this exciting.

"Okay, what is it?" Zoe tried to keep her voice calm. "What's the big secret?"

"All right ... While you were working your ass off last month, guess who went and released a single that went to number four on the U.S. charts?" Laura's voice was hitting an octave higher than normal.

"I don't know. Who?"

"Geiger, you ninny! Tyler! He finally went and did it."

Tyler? Was that what this was about?

Laura skittered over and shoved her phone under Zoe's nose. "They did this softer track that's more hard rock than metal—oh, you have to hear it!—and it's really clicked with audiences everywhere. They had this brilliant video that went viral. I didn't tell you in case you'd get distracted, and you've no idea how difficult that was for me."

Zoe nodded, grappling with her avalanching thoughts.

"Their big break, Zoe! He'll never be a starving artist again."

"He never was a starving artist." She laughed. "He always had my fridge to raid. Are you sure this isn't some kind of hoax?" This didn't sound like Geiger at all.

"Look." Laura held up a display of the top ten music singles. A purple cover with the familiar name Geiger in white lettering was clearly positioned at number six on the U.S. charts. "He's going to pay you all that rent money he owes."

Zoe grabbed the phone. There was nothing fake about the website. "I can't believe it. It's that song. I helped him with the intro."

"Number four yesterday, gone down two places today, but hey, still. They're going to be raking it in, especially if they're doing massive gigs over there January through June."

"Wow. I mean, wow. I don't know what to say."

"But that's not even the biggest surprise."

Zoe laughed. "What could be bigger?"

"Geiger contacted marketing last week. They're playing at our release party tonight!"

"No, you're kidding."

"I have it from the best of sources."

"But isn't thrash a tad aggressive for Austen? I was thinking more Mozart."

"You have to hear the new track. Hell, it's nearly soft rock."

Zoe frowned. "I doubt that."

"There is no music that suits cyberpunk meets Regency. It might as well be thrash metal. Anyway, it's out of your hands."

Zoe threw her hands up in the air. "You're right. It's all crazy, and it's out of my hands."

"And here's the best thing. Tyler seemed so hell-bent on pushing this, he's doing it for free. Can you imagine? A top-charted gig for free? Of course marketing jumped on it like a sex-crazed groupie."

"Love the imagery." Zoe was still grappling with the irony of Tyler's creative efforts being suddenly entwined with hers.

Laura clapped her on the cheek. "Take a rest from it, hon. We're heading down to Giacomo's for a pre-celebration prosecco pronto, and you're coming with us. You can't control everything, so don't even try. Now's the time to par-*tay*."

"You're right, Laura." After all this time, it would be wonderful to see Tyler doing his thing and being successful at it. And it would be great just to see him again, too. He was familiar, he knew her fun side, and he'd be able to snap her out of the serious managerial mode she'd become entrenched in the past few weeks. Believe it or not, there was more to life than just this one project. And if she was feeling a twinge of disappointment for any reason, she should bear in mind the difference between what was real and what could only ever be called wishful thinking.

• • •

Yes, this release party was one glitzy affair. Zycorp may have saved money on the live performing artist, but they'd sure blown the bank on the rest. The venue was the London Hyatt, where an entire floor of gilded function rooms was booked for their private use. Journalists circulated, but not in such numbers that they ruined the atmosphere.

The two proseccos she'd gulped down with the gang in Giacomo's had gone straight to her head. Now she was biding time with a glass of champagne. She danced a few tunes in the main ballroom with Laura, José, Evan, and Evan's wife, Rachel, who had come for "the first night out in a bloody long time" and was absolutely lovely.

At this level of intoxication, everyone was absolutely lovely. Well, except for Bob, lurking by the sides of the dance floor with a caustic eye, conspicuously without his darling supermodel wife, wherever she'd gotten to.

Harry was inundated with attention, and he looked super sweet and yet stately in his dark-green tux, a flamboyant Lex Luthor look that only he could pull off.

The other star of the show was Mr. Darcy himself, of course. His avatar head was on display on a laptop center stage and projected onto massive screens around the room, backlit with the company's trademark pink. From time to time, people in various stages of inebriation wandered up to the podium to ask him a question.

Surprisingly, or perhaps not, most people showed little interest in the AI after the novelty factor wore off. The humans were too keen to get down to the serious business of dancing and flirting. The dance floor was amazing. The DJ gauged the crowd correctly and got them up on their feet. A bunch of dark-clothed thirty-somethings hogged the seats near the stage, waiting for the band to appear.

Then the lights dimmed, and a hush spread throughout the crowded room. Geiger came onstage—Scott, the drummer; Big Joe, bass guitar; Small Joe, keyboard. Her heart filled with something like pride as Tyler strutted across the stage, lead guitar raised high, his tight, burgundy leather jacket open, showing off his bare, tattoo-covered chest. The spotlights homed in on him, and he waved to the cheering crowd in precisely the way he'd always dreamed of. How gratifying to see him fulfill that dream right before her very eyes, even if the whole thing had a surreal quality to it.

The new song was good, catchy. It had that A-major to B-major transition she'd advised Tyler to include, and Laura was right, it bordered on soft rock during the chorus. On other tracks they'd toned down the guitar solos and adapted the drums, taming them into docile beasts. She grinned to herself, imagining the screaming matches between Tyler, Scott, and the two Joes behind the scenes. Even rock dudes had to compromise for the sake of commercialism, but this was a big-time sellout.

Exhilarated after the encore, she used her VIP badge to wrangle her way into the backstage lounge. She'd been backstage often before but never quite at this level. She spent some bewildered moments standing there in the relative gloom, taking in the effortless, rock-style glamour of the loungers. Skinny arms and legs flashed under muted lights, and shiny hair swished around beautifully shaped skulls.

She heard a familiar yell. Tyler pushed through a throng of leggy girls, leaving a trail of jealous gazes in his wake. He grabbed a cocktail from the complimentary bar on the way and swaggered toward her.

"Hey, babe." He handed her the drink, triumph glowing in his dark-brown eyes.

"Hey yourself." She hugged him tight. Now it felt real. "Incredible, Tyler! Congratulations. This is to you. This is your moment." She pulled back, raised the cocktail, and took a slurp of whatever it was. Her nose tingled. Highly alcoholic something with crushed ice and a cherry.

Tyler's face broke into a huge grin. "Babe, look at this party. And it's all for you."

"Not for me. For the team, Tyler."

"But you're the boss, right?"

"Yeah." She grinned. "Some of the time anyway."

"That's amazing. But they're still working you too hard, aren't they?"

"No, I'm working myself hard these days."

"Yep." He scratched his goatee. "I know how that goes."

"Tyler all grown up?"

"I wouldn't say that, babe. Wouldn't say that." He looked smug. He took a strand of her hair and twisted it even more. "Man, you look amazing. You always have, you know. Forget these suit types—this isn't you. Follow your heart. You always wanted to go to California. Live the life. Now you can."

What was he suggesting? She gave a nervous laugh. "Uh, Ty—"

"It's a random world out there, babe. It could all change next week, as you know, but we're riding it. But I'm not in it for the money."

"I know that, Ty."

"And I was thinking, maybe there's more to it than this. You know, a family … maybe someday, some way, somehow? I'm not saying straight away. But you know, down the road. Maybe after I get the solo album out." He looked at her in anticipation, as if he expected his words to cause an epiphany in her soul.

"A solo album. Wow," was all she could say.

"I bought a house and all."

"You bought a house?" She laughed out loud. This was incongruous. "I'm sorry, Tyler, this is just … well, sudden."

"Yeah, no mortgage either, just a down payment. See, I'm not stupid, Zoe. I'm not going to blow it all on coke. It may not be there tomorrow, so what the hell, y'know? You'd love it. It's not a mansion, but it's in LA and it's got a veranda. Whaddya say?" He slung an arm around her shoulders and pulled her in. A heavy aftershave scent wafted around her, something new. He was as lean as ever, the boy-size leather jacket molding onto his wiry frame. He was the dream man for thousands of women. Maybe even millions by now, and judging by the glares darting her way, some of them in this very room.

A camera flashed. Then several more. In the early days of Tyler and Zoe, they'd exchanged fantasies of what fame would look like. It was all this. But after a few blinding flashes, she'd had enough. Tyler was still grimacing for the photographers like a pro. She held out her palm to make them go away. A bouncer sidled over and did his thing to scare them off.

When the last one had gone, she turned to him. "I don't know, Ty. What happened to Vikki, who you dashed out of our apartment for without so much as a goodbye?"

"Nuh-uh, she was one crazy bitch. She had all the right contacts, and I'm not saying that didn't help us out big time, but me and her—we only lasted a week. No, it was all wrong for me. I wanted to turn back and run to you, but my pride wouldn't let me."

You have pride?

"But I knew that someday I'd make it good and when I did, I'd come back and get you. I didn't think it'd happen this soon. But, heck, here I am. I'm back. This is our moment."

"And, just so I'm sure, you'd like me to drop everything and move with you? To California?"

"Hell, yeah. That's what you love. The spontaneity. The freedom. You know I won't force my rules on you, babe."

That was the thing with free-spirited guys like Tyler. They never tried to force their rules on anyone … until they did. Granted, in a different way from her brothers and her father and every manager she'd ever had. But now that she knew what she was capable of achieving on her own, she didn't need to be told what she did or didn't want to do. She could walk away, calmly and with purpose, from Tyler, from anyone. If she wanted to.

But did she want to? This was pretty amazing, what Tyler was proposing. He'd never gotten near this point in their five years of dating. Maybe he'd just been waiting for the point at which he felt he had something to offer. It was all so … touching.

"That was then, Tyler. But—"

"It's someone, innit?" He pulled her close. "You're into someone else. You've got that look about you. Don't deny it, I can tell."

"No."

"You can't fool me. I'm the king of lurve."

He was slurring and leaning heavily on her. He may not even remember this conversation tomorrow. Or it could be the most important conversation he'd ever had in his life. The problem was, she couldn't tell which. A life with him would be glamorous, chaotic, and probably short-lived. Not what she wanted.

"Look, Ty, let's just have the bash of a lifetime here tonight. It's been great to see you, and you know we'll always be friends."

He pouted. But in the time it took him to down his cocktail, Tyler's gaze was caught by a sleek brunette slinking by in white leather shorts and a silver bikini top. He smiled at Zoe apologetically. "I know her. I just gotta ..."

She smiled and slipped away, seeking out a quiet corner to let her emotions settle, because something was bothering her. And it had nothing to do with Tyler.

She'd made a huge mistake. A huge, huge mistake. And she'd been too busy, or too blind, or too stupid, to notice. Because it was clear that there was only one person she could imagine wanting to spend her life with. And he wasn't anywhere in this room.

CHAPTER 29

"All right, Mal, come here and watch me write up our first payment," Max said. It wasn't just for celebration purposes; it was vital for Mal to learn all this accounting stuff for himself. He didn't want to be his assistant forever.

Mal clutched his fists with joy at what was no doubt his first-ever honest day's payment. "Split it in two, take your cut, and shove mine in my bank account."

"No, you put it in your bank account," Max said. "I showed you how yesterday." The 199 euros they earned from this gig were peanuts, but their symbolic value was worth more than the gold lying under Zurich.

"All right, I will. It'll make a nice engagement pressie for Maeve. You buy her a house, and I get her the matching flowerpot."

Max grinned. "Don't worry, she says she doesn't need gifts. I called her last night. She's getting off the meds, too. Says they interfere with her diet."

"Wonder if we'll see any difference. Or just same auld bitchy Maeve."

"Who cares? Long as she's happy." Max closed the accounting window. "Look, another customer, Mal. Your turn."

Mal shot over to the customer desk, and Max sat in the back office, staring at the screen. He browsed to the Zycorp newsletter that he still hadn't unsubscribed to in his email inbox. This was his masochistic pleasure, the itch he had to keep scratching. The Darcy release had been last Friday, with a big release party that same evening. This would be the hardest newsletter to stomach.

To hell with it. He opened it.

It leapt out at him first thing: a hi-res photo. Zoe and this skinny rock star glued together at the hip. She looked radiant, bewitching, stunning in a knee-length dress in some floaty material the same color as her eyes, her dark, glossy hair swinging around her neckline in graceful curls, her eyes smoldering at the camera. Absolutely perfect. She'd never dressed up like that in all the time he'd known her.

But what was this creature she was with? All tattoos, long, grungy hair, belt with fake weaponry. Grubby fingers clutching her waist. He read the caption. *Project manager Zoe Bunsen sharing a bubbly moment with Geiger frontman, Tyler Curtis.*

Tyler. Of course.

Who the hell else would he be? So she'd got back with him. Or they were doing some couples act for a mutual benefit promo—scratching each other's backs? He scanned the text. The band seemed to be doing pretty well for itself. The Darcy release was a hit too.

Either way, not his world anymore.

Mal came up behind him and breathed down his neck. "Lord Almighty, would you look at that. She scrubs up nice."

Max's fist tightened under the table. "Don't ... say ... anything."

Mal laughed. "What?" Then he let out an "ooooh." He clapped Max's shoulder and walked away, far away, to the other side of the garage. He began to polish and tidy away the tools he'd been using, one by one. Not another word came from him as he appeared to be engrossed in his task. Cling, cling, cling went the ring of metal on metal.

Max turned back to the screen but could only stare into space. It was strangely soothing just to have Mal there in the background. Something brittle crumbled inside him. He turned to face his brother. "I adored this woman, and I still do. I can't explain how she makes me feel, as corny as it sounds."

Mal stopped moving. He held an oily rag in his fingers and a glint of comprehension in his eyes. He folded his arms. "I don't have an assistant anymore, do I?"

"No. You'll have to hire a new one."

He had to go back and this time do it right. Or die trying.

CHAPTER 30

"He's selling well, don't worry, my dear," Harry said to Zoe on the day before Christmas Eve as they sat in his top-floor office gazing out at the twinkling lights of London dancing on the Thames. "So well that the shareholders have just approved the funds for the next two years." The old man's eyes sparkled with glee.

"Oh, Harry!" Zoe sank back in her seat in relief. Two years of security for the research team. That would make Christmas for 125 researchers and their families.

"So, all we have to do is decide on the identity of our next intelligent personal assistant."

The name 'Elizabeth' flashed across her synapses. Evan's team had been putting in serious effort into her recently. "I'll set up a special task force this afternoon to come up with a new persona," she said.

"Or how about we spare the efforts and you choose?"

She inhaled. "You'd let me decide the next AI?"

"It's my way of asking you to stay."

"But of course I'll stay. Why? Did someone suggest I wouldn't?"

"Little birdie told me you'd booked a ticket to Belfast."

"It's a return ticket, Harry. Christmas shopping."

Harry nodded wisely. "I do hope you enjoy Belfast. She's a beautiful city. But do think about next year."

"I won't be thinking of anything else."

"Happy Christmas, Zoe," the CEO said.

Ten minutes later, she paused outside her office door, debating whether to run to Laura first or to the research department to tell them the news. But then Laura, Evan, and José sauntered up, as if conjured from a lamp. Her heart warmed to see her friends one last time before they all dispersed for the holidays.

"Ooh la la, Zoe," Laura said. "New name plaque?"

"Yeah." She turned to the gleaming sheet of steel on display outside P-12. *Zoe Bunsen, MSc Comp Sci.* "What do you think?"

"Your name looks kinda lonely there."

"Whatever, Laura. I was just about to tell you the news. But what was I thinking?" Zoe laughed at her own silliness. "You all already know, don't you?"

They grinned in affirmation.

"Evan found out," Laura said, nudging him.

"Of course he did. News travels to him faster than particle acceleration. Well, looks like I have some big decisions ahead."

"You want to do Elizabeth," Laura said. A statement, not a question.

"You know me too well."

Everyone seemed to breathe a sigh of relief.

"But don't forget," Evan said. "Darcy thinks she's dead."

"No problem. When the time comes, when she's ready, we tell him she's been reincarnated in the same way he was, by mind mapping. He should buy it, especially as those are the terms of his own existence."

Evan rubbed his eyebrow, wincing. "Yeah, all right, it could work. As long as we keep all Darcy instances out of the picture while we train her up."

"But what if people own both AIs after her launch?" José asked. "They'll end up with a couple pussyfooting around each other all the time, or worse, arguing, because that's what they're destined to do if we model her faithfully."

Zoe clapped her hands. "That's what the fans want! It'll be perfect."

José shrank back. "Don't you get enough of that in real life?"

"What's that supposed to mean?"

José looked to Laura for help, but she just leaned back against the wall with an ironic expression that said she was having a great old time spectating and letting the lads do the talking.

Evan scuffed the carpet with his toe. "You'll be over in Belfast the whole of Christmas, yeah?"

"Yeah."

"On your own?"

"Believe me, that's exactly what I need." This probably didn't fit into his family-centric idea of Christmas.

"Christmas shopping, you say?"

"Uh-huh."

"Right. Well, call me. We can brainstorm about Lizzie. Otherwise you'll just agonize about it the whole time. I know you."

"Thanks, Evan. I will."

"Unless, of course, you're otherwise occupied."

Laura gave her a sly grin.

"Laura ... " she warned.

"Shopping, I meant. The sales, Zoe. Because I know how much you love shopping."

Touché. At times like this, it was best to just grin and bear it.

• • •

Her plan of getting to Belfast hadn't exactly finessed the part about finding Max in a city of half a million inhabitants, assuming he even wanted to be found. All she had was the home address of a family he'd allegedly disowned.

There were some consolations. Her small, cozy Belfast hotel overlooking the Harland and Wolff shipyard was attuned to her tastes—genuine period furniture and friendly, noninvasive service. And when she ventured outside, the timeless gloom of the cobblestoned docks and the nearness of the clouds in this more northerly sky harmonized with her reflective mood. In the past ten weeks there hadn't been time to breathe, and now thousands of unresolved thoughts assailed her with every step. She traipsed down countless alleyways and around the pier like a ghost passenger from the *Titanic*, grabbing lungfuls of salty sea air that brought her soul back to life.

And his accent—she heard it everywhere. Sometimes strong and raw like his brother's but sometimes mellow and modulated by other influences, as was his, bringing a sharp pang of remembrance. A tall, well-dressed man looking into a window display of toys had looked so like him from behind, but when he turned around, the face was all wrong. This came as a relief, as he was holding a woman's arm.

When her feet finally protested against the hard cobblestones, she returned to the hotel. Dinner was served in the small family restaurant, and then she retreated upstairs to her room. She took once last look at the docklands and pulled the curtains. Christmas Eve had never been this lonely.

She couldn't bear the thought of traipsing out to his family's home to be met with blank stares if he wasn't there, or worse, polite indifference on his part if he was. No, banging on a strange family's door on Christmas Eve was just not something she could stomach. It was better not to dwell on the futility of her half-baked plan. Better to keep busy. She cleared the furniture away from the middle of the room and locked the door. Then she opened the special, padded section of her suitcase and strapped on the VR headset, the gloves, and the anklets. It was time to put the Lizzie AI prototype to the test.

She'd adopted a matronly persona for herself, a middle-aged lady called Mrs. Lacey, whose function would be to chaperone Lizzie in the Regency world, as the maiden couldn't walk about freely without breaking a plethora of rules of propriety.

So far Lizzie was just a hodgepodge of n-grams and Darcy-subroutines, but she'd be a different creature in seven or eight months. She and the researchers and Mrs. Lacey would see to her refinement.

Christmas? She'd spend it right here in Austenland.

• • •

Max stuck his thumb out for a black cab. The flight from Belfast to London City had been smooth enough given it was Christmas Eve, but he was hungry and cold and wanted out of this shoppers' chaos.

He checked his phone messages—Mal and Maeve needling him again for not spending Christmas at home. How could he explain his last-minute flight to London? He couldn't. Mal knew the story, and that was why they were needling him. The vultures smelled blood. In other words, entertainment.

"Zycorp office please," he instructed the cabbie. She'd be working. While he was still there, she hadn't blocked any time for vacation before Christmas, and she wouldn't have taken off a day early. He'd go to Laura or Evan first and catch up on the real news, gauge her mood, and then go to her office.

What he had to say was brief and to the point. He wouldn't dither. He just had to know, face-to-face. If she acted surprised, ridiculed or rejected him, he could handle it. He just needed an answer. Power—and he was under no illusions, she had this now in spades—had a way of changing people sometimes, of ratcheting up their expectations so that nobody was good enough for them. He had to see how she reacted to his new persona, a lowly mechanic's assistant from Belfast with no current plans of world domination.

"Zoe Bunsen is on vacation," the Zycorp AI receptionist said in a bored voice when he got into the gleaming foyer with its white and pink lighting.

"What?"

"Zoe Bunsen is on vacation."

The platinum blond receptionist-on-a-screen was a new installation, proof, if anyone needed it, that AI was taking over the world. There wasn't a soul to be seen anywhere in the lobby.

"Well, where'd she go?" He tried to shake the random image of Zoe on a Caribbean beach with Tyler, sipping cocktails, applying sunscreen, kissing …

"I'm afraid I cannot give you that information."

"Of course you can. I'm a friend." He wanted to shake the monitor. "I used to work with her. I'm still in the database. Max Taggart, look it up." He fought to keep his voice cool in case emotion detection registered something threatening and tipped off security. "She would definitely let me know where she is. Please tell me."

"I'm sorry, but that is private information." The AI's tone had grown snippy.

"Well, is Laura Jackson in?"

"Laura Jackson is also on vacation."

"What about Evan?"

"I have found three Evans in the database. Do you mean Evan Smith, Evan Myers—?"

"Yeah, number two. Myers."

"Evan Myers." A pause. "Evan Myers is present. Should I call him for you?"

Chrissake, this AI was so soulless. He missed Darcy. "That would be very nice, yeah, thank you."

"Evan Myers will see you, Mr. Taggart. After security clearance, please take the green elevator to floor four, room 417. Do you require further directions or assistance?"

Max waved her off, already halfway to the biometrics

scanners. "No, you've been wonderful."

When he reached the VR lab, he was hit sideways by the familiarity of it, the mess, the dry smell of computer fans, upholstery, and old pizza, the intensity of the smattering of faces basked in the light of their computer screens, even on Christmas Eve. He'd missed the buzz. He'd missed all of this.

Evan sauntered up and held his gaze for a long, calculating moment, his pale-blue eyes blinking with every conclusion he drew.

Yeah, he'd missed this guy too.

The researcher laughed and shook his head. "Yeah."

"Joke?" Max asked.

"Kind of. Okay, here's what you're going to do." Evan whipped up a VR headset from a nearby desk. "Put this on, jump into Austenland, and talk to some people we got parading about Grosvenor Square. There's a particular lady—"

"No time, Evan. I'm here to find Zoe. Do you know where she is?"

"Yes. Shopping."

"Where?"

Evan winced. "That hardly matters now, Max. Put this on. You really got to meet Mrs. Lacey." He placed the headset in his hands.

Max refused to hold it. "Look, I'm not going into that thing. Forget about it."

"That's a pity." Evan adjusted the wires on the headset. "Let me just tell her."

Evan covered his eyes and ears with the headset. Max no longer felt any warmth toward him. This guy deserved a punch.

"My friend, Mr. Tarrant, would like to meet you, but I'm afraid he's shy, Mrs. Lacey, Miss Bennet," Evan said into his microphone. "Please bear with me for a moment." He whipped off the headset again and looked speculatively at him. "Mrs. Lacey says that introductions are extremely important."

Those words, those exact words. He'd heard them before. "Give me that." He grabbed the headset.

"Careful," Evan warned. "That cost a fortune, and Zoe already broke one."

• • •

Zoe pulled Lizzie aside, swirled her parasol dramatically, and said in a conspiratorial whisper, "Do not be alarmed, dear Lizzie, but prepare your nerves, for in London, this type of thing may often happen. Strange men think they can just talk to you as they please. He can't be that shy if his address is so forward. Make sure you put him in his place."

"But Mrs. Lacey!" the dark-haired beauty protested. "We are hardly fit for presentation." They had wandered down a puddle-strewn Grosvenor Square, which meant an unfashionable redness of face and muddy petticoat hems, although these details should not bother Elizabeth.

Oh, come on, Lizzie, show some gumption here.

Zoe glared at Evan's avatar. "Mr. Everett, why does your friend show such a keen interest in us?"

The gallant old Mr. Everett bowed slightly. "I do apologize, ma'am. Tarrant has come from afar to bring you a message. He dithers by that shop window; I know not why. I shall bring him over to you immediately."

"I suppose we had better hear what he has to say," Lizzie said with a wry twitch of her eyebrows, perfectly in character.

Nice. Evan was throwing a most unusual suitor in Lizzie's path.

She surveyed the unfamiliar avatar standing before them. A gentleman in appearance, around the same size and level of fashion as Darcy, well dressed but not too fancy. The perfect rival indeed.

She eyed Lizzie. What would her reaction be?

Then the man spoke. "I wish to speak to, uh, Mrs. Lacey?" His gaze drifted to Lizzie and back again. "Alone."

No explanation as to how he knew her name. He hadn't even tipped his hat. "I'm sure Miss Bennet can be present for anything you might have to say," she said in the haughtiest tone she could muster.

"No, Miss Bennet can't," he said.

Evan was laying it on thick. Elizabeth would need to summon all her self-possession to deal with this. She was struggling herself, to be honest.

"I shall leave you," Elizabeth said, bunching up her skirt.

"What? No!" Zoe cried, but she was gone. Damn. Elizabeth had chickened out far too easily. She clutched her headset to rip it off but had second thoughts. She rounded on the man, now the only other occupant of the street, as Everett had vanished too. "Speak, sir. Say what it is you have to say."

"Zoe, it's me, Max."

Her head spun, and that was no fun inside a VR

headset. "W-what are you doing in Grosvenor Square, Max?" was all she could finally utter.

"I'm standing right here in Evan's office. Where the hell are you?"

"I'm in Belfast."

"What are you doing there?"

"I'm on vacation."

"What?"

"Okay, I was looking for you."

"Oh no," he groaned. His avatar held his head in his hands. "I came over here to find you."

His words sank in. He'd done that for her. A sudden fear stunned her, fear of losing this opportunity. "Okay, but at least we're both here, in a sense," she said. "That's something, isn't it?"

"No."

Oh, God.

"No more VR." His avatar advanced and held out his hand. His clear, blue eyes blinked seriously, very Max-like. "Meet me. Somewhere, anywhere. I don't care. As long as it's in reality."

She reached for his hand, and her avatar's gloved hand gripped his while her real gloved hand clutched the air. It didn't matter; it felt glorious. "I'm not sure a dowager such as myself should engage in such a wild and wanton enterprise."

"You think I enjoy propositioning a middle-aged dame in a bonnet? I am so going over there to make you eat those words and that snooty attitude. There's nowhere in Belfast you can hide from me."

"Okay, okay, hold on to your breeches," she said with a laugh. "Despite your ungentlemanlike behavior,

I'm quite prepared to take this offline with you."

• • •

The insane hustle and bustle of arrivals in Belfast Airport late on Christmas Eve teemed all around her, but she may as well have been on a deserted island, cocooned in her mad thoughts. She was tripping with happiness that he'd made the British Airways flight last minute but sick with worry that something would go wrong. Real life was far too unpredictable.

But there he was. Strolling out, luggage-free, gorgeous in a dark duffle coat she'd never seen before and his familiar baby-blue scarf. She ducked under the barricade and rushed to him, collapsing into his chest.

"Ow. Is this what you mean by taking it offline?" he asked, cradling her head in his big hands and forcing her lips to meet his, greedy and demanding.

She broke off, gasping for breath. "No, that's what I mean by *ungentlemanlike.*"

"Plenty more where that came from." He wove his arm through hers and escorted her to the side of a café, away from the throngs of people. When he looked down at her with that new softness in those burnished blues, she found herself lost in emotion and unable to say a word.

"How should I say it, Zoe?" His native accent came through stronger now. "I'm no gentleman. I've been a brute. I've bossed you around, thrown hurdles in your path, and even killed your favorite companion, for which I'm truly, deeply sorry. I've completely underestimated you in every way. And—I've nothing to offer you. I've no job. My life's a mess. My family's a mess. I don't even have a house, for God's sake."

"Let me be the judge of your family," she said.

"Of course. You've met Mal."

"He's not so bad. He beats either of my brothers hands down. And I'm sure I'd like Maeve, too."

"She's no Georgiana Darcy, but she's okay."

She let out a surprised laugh. "You really did read the book."

"I told you I did. But is that what you want from a man? I can't live up to that … nobility, that … nauseating level of goodness. I'm just Max, boring, insufferable Max. I've nothing to offer you but myself and my love for you. I love you, Zoe. I think I have ever since you came in that door with your fleabag copy of *Pride and Prejudice*."

She clasped his hands in hers. "Well, Max, if you can consider a relationship with someone who has no proper connection to her family, someone who jeopardized your project, mocked you behind your back, and slapped you in the face, then you're my kind of man. I love you, too. Hell, I don't know exactly when that started—you were annoying me too much. But I knew it for sure when I slapped your jaw. I couldn't have done that to any lesser man."

"Charming," he said, eyes aglitter. "Let's go to your hotel, where you can take out more of this unbridled passion on me."

"That sounds like a perfectly reasonable plan," she said. "Darcy, please hold my calls until tomorrow morning."

PASSWORD SOLUTION

Q1) What was the original title of P&P?
First Impressions

Q2) How often does Mr. Darcy call Elizabeth by her first name?
2 times

Q3) In the 2005 movie, what does Elizabeth say straight after Mr. Darcy proclaims love in the final act?
"Well then, your hands are cold."

Q4) What is the most frequent common noun that contains at least nine letters in P&P?
Happiness

Q5) What is the longest repeated fragment in P&P?
" there were some very strong objections against the lady " (57 characters, incl. spaces)

Q6) Using simple Euclidean distance on word frequency vectors, which of Austen's novels is most similar to Pride and Prejudice?
Emma

Password: F2whte

MORE FROM THE AUTHOR

If you enjoyed this book then check out my other titles.

Maybe Baby
Core Attraction
The *High Octane* Series (with co-author Rachel Cross):
Ignited (#1)
Fueled (#2)
Unleashed (#3)

Join my readers' club on ashlinncraven.com if you'd like to get more insight into my books and info on upcoming releases.

Acknowledgements

Thanks to my editor, Julie Sturgeon for an amazing job at editing. Thanks to the folks at CritiqueCircle who encouraged me along the way, especially Julie LeMense. And thank you, dear reader, for picking up this book and going on this journey with me. It's the reason I do what I do.